Sea Species

SEA SPECIES

In the Southern Arizona desert a group of idealistic scientists, refugees from the Biosphere 2 project, have constructed an isolated community called Kihhim (Tohono O'Odham for the Village). Away from the prying eyes of the press, the public and government regulation, they built a society along the principles of Biosphere 2.

At the foot of Baboquivari Peak, the Tohono O'Odham legendary birthplace of the People, they are a space colony, yet on the Earth. To maintain an independent and almost closed ecosystem, genetically manipulated plants grown in their greenhouses have enhanced productivity.

When the body of Marty Hinson, a prominent environmentalist, is found on their property, they come under the very scrutiny they sought to avoid. Accusations are lodged, and they are investigated by the United States as isolationists with potentially harmful technology. Religious zealots and terrorist Ralph Whitney attack them for their biological technology and genetic abilities.

Kihhim flees the United States, leaving behind their leaders John Vance and Katherine Levey, imprisoned as subversives. They construct a giant catamaran of supertankers establishing Kahchk Kihhim (Tohono O'Odham for Sea Village), a floating nation. Security Supervisor, Leticia Gardner extorts recognition and protection from the United States by threatening the existence of humanity.

This marine civilization uses genetic engineering to adapt themselves to life at sea. The shield of protection established by the United States is breached, and prominent figures of both Kahchk Kihhim and the United States are killed.

The ensuing investigation reveals backing for the attack by a major world power, embroiling Kahchk Kihhim in global politics. The extent of their genetic engineering is revealed, and the major powers in the world realize the potential resource and the threat to humankind these people represent.

Kahchk Kihhim understands that once their extortion threat is nullified, they will be subjugated or destroyed. Under the leadership of Katherine Levey, they race ahead on a program to grow a new underwater habitat utilizing genetic engineering. The citizens of Ocealla, their new home, consist of humans, modified humans, modified dolphins, and a completely new genetic construct.

SEA SPECIES

EVOLUTION RIVER SERIES

Volume 1

The Future History of Human Evolution

By

R. L. Clayton

Edition 2: July 2013

Edition 3: October 2017

ISBN 9781948015042

I had two reasons to rewrite Sea Species. I have learned a lot about writing since I published my first book. This was my opportunity to correct much of the errata.

As I finished Dead Reckoning, the third book in my Dead series of thrillers, I decided to tie it into Sea Species. I had to make some changes. Minor though they are, The Evolution River series now is an extension of The Dead series. The fourth book in that series Risen from the Dead will follow the rise of a character in The Envoy and The Genesis. The two series now take us from today eons into the future. What fun this has been!

This book contains an excerpt from the forthcoming book The Envoy by R. L. Clayton. This excerpt has been set for this edition only and may not reflect the final content of the forthcoming edition

"<u>Sea Species</u> has an absorbing story line which takes today's scientifically <u>possible</u> across the line to the evolutionary <u>unthinkable</u>. A compelling read, I hated to put it down! It's an incomparable blend of Sci-fi and contemporary mystery/suspense. Spell binding!"
COL S.C. Volgyi, USA (Retired)

"Fascinating! A departure into evolution that returns man to the sea. The author displays enough scientific knowledge to be convincing. Thought provoking."

R.E. Strange, Retired CEO, Commercial Cold Storage, Inc

"Sea Species by R. L. Clayton is a fast-paced technology driven, reality based thriller that will keep you turning the pages to see what happens next! This interesting look at one possible pathway for potential human evolution; gives readers a glimpse into a radical adaption of not only mankind but other flora and fauna to create a synergistic relationship with the ever-changing environment. Using the aid of recent technical advances that are the building blocks of life, scientist could create entirely new species."
Katharine Nelson, Author and Arizona Community Connections Magazine, Publisher

ACKNOWLEDGEMENTS

I wish to thank my goad and guru Teri Vonn, without whose continued support and help this novel would have returned to being a dream in an archived file. Keep pushing me, Teri. We have a lot of work ahead.

I also owe some of my success to my wife, Linda. Without the prod of her doubt that this book would ever get done, it wouldn't have. See, I told you so!

Thanks to Steve Linebaugh (artist_stevel@tx.rr.com) for the cover art. Good job and great patience with me! More to do.

Katharine Nelson, thank for showing me I wasn't done when I thought I was. We're better now.

To contact R. L. Clayton and to find out about his upcoming books; please visit www.evolutionriver.com or www.rlclaytonbooks.com

Cover design by Steve Linebaugh. For more information about the artist, please visit him at artist_stevel@tx.rr.com

FORWARD

Webster's Encyclopedic Unabridged Dictionary of the English Language defines Biological Evolution as the continuous genetic adaption of organisms or species to the environment by the integrating agencies of selection, hybridization, inbreeding, and mutation.

All species on Earth are evolving. Humans have reached a unique turning point where the ability to genetically adapt the world's flora and fauna can be controlled through genetic engineering. We will soon be able to re-engineer aspects of our world including ourselves to co-exist and thrive in whatever environment exists, or we create.

For better or worse, we are manipulating the DNA of hundreds of plants and animals with quiet disregard to the fragile connections between all living things. We ignore the delicate balance that has existed for millions of years. Our world is on the brink of a major evolutionary advancement, which will leapfrog over the generational changes of natural selection as we manipulate ourselves, our environment, and other species in mere months or years rather than in centuries or millennia.

The current physical characteristics used to define species will no longer apply as we direct the power of life to grow any form we deem necessary.

Wielders of this God-like ability will hold the key to the next evolutionary steps for all life as we know it.

Humanity is on the brink of an evolutionary journey that will take us beyond the limitations of happenstance and into an enlightened existence. This will forever change our relationship with the living world. Synergy with nature is the lock that this genetic key opens, and mankind's over-whelming dominance is no longer an option if our world's interlinking species are to survive!

In evolutionary progression, species are supplanted by those more able to survive. Extinction is a natural event. The question is how far are we willing to go?

Katharine Nelson, Author and Arizona Community Connections Magazine, Publisher

Prologue

The angry buzz roared in his head, overpowering the ringing in his ears from the fall. A distant flash of lightning pushed the dark away for an instant, lighting the cold black eyes of the rattler as its tongue flicked out trying to smell him. Marty was frozen, the snake coiled inches from his face. Jagged rocks gouged him in several places. Glacially, he tried to spread his weight out and ease the pain.

Marty had been halfway to the fence surrounding the compound in the valley when a lightning bolt struck within yards. The thunder shook the ground from under him, the rock he'd been balanced on shifted. He stifled a yell as he fell, reaching down and twisting to land on the backpack, trying to protect himself from the jagged rocks. The ploy hadn't worked. His head smacked a rock with a dull splat and he blacked out.

The wind-driven rain stung him awake as more earthshaking thunder rattled him. When he tried to rise, his wrist collapsed in pain. After an agonizing eternity, the storm passed, and he started crawling to the fence in hopes of setting off an alarm to get help. The dry rattle had yanked his attention from himself to the vision of death facing him.

Since early morning, the puffy clouds over Baboquivari peak exploded upward as he observed the small compound called Kihhim (O'Odham for 'The village'). There had been little activity in the valley below and no traffic on the road leading into a tunnel cut into the low hill facing him. It was obviously an entrance to the underground facility. Tall glass walls enclosing the terraced hillside were filled with plants, clearly greenhouses. Perhaps they were growing drugs inside.

Other than the greenhouses, there were only a few small buildings. What kind of place was this? People living underground, giant greenhouses, a security fence surrounding everything, a single road in with a guard shack. It was completely isolated.

Kihhim had gone to great lengths to remain invisible to the public. Marty needed to find something to bring unwanted attention to Kihhim, and nothing was visible from outside, so he decided to go in.

The Arizona monsoon storm was both a blessing and a curse. The tempest would give him cover as he scaled the fence, but he also might be caught in the open by it. Lightning was always a danger. With his night-vision glasses, he had worked his way down the hill toward the boundary. The tight-fitting black suit over his slender build made him invisible, another shadow moving among the rocks and cacti.

Under the expanse of grass and weedy bushes following the fence was a thirty-yard wide strip of broken football-sized rocks. He ignored the small voice that told him to go back.

A last lightning bolt struck, and he flinched. In slow motion, he saw the snake's cottony mouth open and the fangs unfold. The points moved toward his face, and he jerked aside, but felt the sharp stab in his neck. As he lay in shock, the burning spread like scalding liquid.

His brain grew sluggish from the pain; he couldn't think, couldn't move, and dragging in each breath became an effort. Numbness crept through him as he sank down. A distant rumble of thunder brought him back.

Kihhim, a place he would normally applaud as environmentally green, became a target because he'd sold his soul to the devil. Marty was going to die, and attention would indeed fall on Kihhim. But he wouldn't reap any benefit. He closed his eyes, and through the leaping fires of pain, the numbing darkness came to meet him. He welcomed its soft embrace.

PART 1
DISCOVERY AND EXPOSURE

G.M.O. (Genetically Modified Organisms) regulation is deficient in the United States. Some products aren't covered, and the system is incomprehensible.

WILLIAM Y. BROWN Washington, Sept. 16, 2012 The writer, a senior fellow at the Brookings Institution, was a science adviser to Interior Secretary Bruce Babbitt in the Clinton administration.

Chapter One

Leticia Gardner stepped out of the guardhouse into the clear dawn. She was medium height with dark hair that glistened and a complexion like fine tan suede. With full lips, a small, lightly freckled nose, and intense eyes, she was attractive. The seams of her shirt strained against her shoulders, but the narrow waist and slender hips bespoke of someone extremely fit. Her movements radiated confidence.

The storm last night cooled the desert, but today the sun would cook that moisture out, making the day hot and humid. This was the first storm of the rainy season and brought the countryside alive, turning yesterday's brown into today's green. It happened so quickly here. She hadn't gotten used to the desert yet, but the clear blue skies and clean air seemed a slice of heaven. Almost daily storms would follow for the next month.

Leticia had come to Kihhim from Virginia where she had been an FBI agent specializing in communications and surveillance. Originally from a small parish in Louisiana, her family had been in law enforcement, her dad the sheriff and her mom the dispatcher. As an only child, they thrilled at her acceptance into the FBI.

Leticia moved up rapidly within the organization until her ethics got in the way of an investigation.

Leticia's refusal to bend the truth resulted in a downward spiral intended to force her out, making room for team players. She had been assigned to the Tucson, Arizona office. Not a bad location, and with all the drug and people smuggling, it was very busy. But her assignment was split between shuffling papers across a desk and field work on the remote reservations in the scorching heat.

During one of her lunch breaks at the downtown sandwich deli, she'd become acquainted with Katharine Levey, a tall, attractive blonde woman, who was an attorney. They met whenever both were in town, and Leticia commiserated about her dissatisfaction with her career.

Katharine lived at a small community southwest of Tucson in the process of installing a security system. They needed a consultant to oversee the project. After the ass-chewing Leticia had gotten this morning over nothing, she agreed to look at the site and consider the job.

The visit and tour were enough to convince her to take the contract. Though the pay wasn't great, it came with an apartment and meals.

After the first month of equipment installation, Kihhim offered another contract to design and install the communication system. By then, she and Katharine had become fast friends, and Kihhim had grown on her. The serenity of the remote site and the closeness of the residents reminded her of home. She was becoming a resident, spiritually as well as physically. Leticia didn't miss the politics of the outside world at all.

Leticia looked to the west as the rising sun lit Baboquivari peak. She and Katharine walked the undisturbed desert to the fence line, sometimes beyond to the foothills. They needed an early start this time of year because the temperature would be above 100 before noon. She turned and entered the underground parking garage. As grounds security and communications supervisor, she checked out the systems and reviewed the tapes from last night, a two-hour task.

***

In addition to her duties as attorney for Kihhim, Katharine Levey was second in charge under John Vance. Completing her college-prep education at Kihhim, she entered the University of Arizona. The undergrad degree came easily (Magna cum laude).

Used to the small community life of Kihhim, university life could be overwhelming. To protect herself, she formed an aloof style that seemed to match her Lauren Bacall looks. She had picked up Bacall's self-assured manner from watching the old movies.

Katharine attended Harvard Law School and accepted a position with an east coast law firm, throwing herself into it putting her social life on hold. Katharine returned to Kihhim when her father became seriously ill. After his death, she stayed, becoming the attorney representing Kihhim.

She saw the message light blinking as she entered her apartment. "Play," she said

"Hi, Katharine," came Leticia's voice. "I'll meet you in the garage at 07:30 so we can beat the heat," said Leticia. "Bring extra water."

***

Leticia and Katharine stepped out of the dark tunnel into brilliant sunlight. It was hot already, but they were determined to at least make the west fence. As they turned in that direction, both noticed the spiraling black specks in the sky.

"Looks like the buzzards have breakfast," said Leticia.

"Some hapless rabbit parts left over from coyote dinner last night, probably." The peaceful walk to the fence proved a delight, but the morning cool was rapidly becoming uncomfortable by the rising heat and humidity as they approached the fence.

The heaped black bundle was obviously not a rabbit or any other wild creature. Leticia called John. "Katharine and I are at the west end and it looks like we have a body just outside the fence. I wanted to call you first before calling the sheriff."

"Can you tell anything about it?" asked John.

"Not from here. We will stay on this side of the fence so we don't contaminate the scene. With the storm last night, there may not be much evidence to gather, but I'll stay until the sheriff arrives. Hopefully, Harry's on duty."

***

John Vance put the phone down and sighed. Perhaps this was an illegal crosser who'd gotten lost in the desert, not an uncommon occurrence in this part of the country. Both drug and people smugglers considered this a prime corridor, and the factions warred over control with the crossers as the victims.

Years ago, John had been manager at the Biosphere 2 project. He was fascinated with the idea of building a space colony on Earth.

It would be sealed and self-sufficient. Only energy and information would pass from outside to inside. This enclosed habitat represented a miniature world. Everything would have to be in balance. The knowledge gained would be used for man's expansion into space and eventually the Solar System. It was a magic dream that excited the imagination.

John Vance, Abraham Levey, Rich Lewis, Jamie Wong, and Donald Brown had been members of the Biosphere 2 team. They all dreamed together. Eight Biospherians entered their world for the two-year study with a lot of fanfare. The project ended amid the salacious derision of the press, other scientists not included, and the public.

The friends decided not to return to the mundane work of industry. They found this site, pooled their resources, and built Kihhim, incorporating the knowledge and engineering that had applied to Biosphere 2.

Like the Biosphere 2 project, they constructed it for minimum footprint upon the Earth. They named it Kihhim because it was their village bordering the Tohno O'Odham nation and their escape from the politics and viciousness of the world. Here, they continued and expanded projects began with Biosphere 2. Kihhim took outside contracts for work without oversight or condemnation by remaining under the radar.

Being self-sufficient, Kihhim generated its own electricity from photovoltaic cells and wind power. Water was recirculated and reused throughout the system. Food and oxygen were produced in their greenhouses, but they didn't seal Kihhim from the outside world as the Biosphere 2 had been.

To maximize the plant production, they used Jamie Wong's genetic technology. Companies contracting for environmental and genetic research with them were bound by a strict confidentiality contract not disclosing any information about or reference to Kihhim. Their community grew as more people wanted to escape the high pressure and sometimes violent outside world.

The residents operated the schools, medical facilities, and agriculture facilities. It was a thriving little community. Occasionally, John admitted to himself that he'd become embittered toward the outside world, building this refuge as an escape. It could only remain so as long as Kihhim remained out of sight. This situation with the dead body could threaten that anonymity and would have to be handled carefully.

***

Deputy Harry Kisto radioed to the Pima County Sheriff dispatcher he would need a forensics team at Kihhim. He had been careful to preserve the site, but visually the signs were those of a snakebite victim.

Obviously, this man wasn't an illegal crosser. The black skintight suit and night-vision goggles spoke of someone on a surveillance mission. Who was he and why was he here?

"I'm glad you came out," said Katharine. "You know Kihhim well."

Harry, six feet tall with straight black hair, was a member of the Tohono O'odham nation, raised on the reservation. "I've missed this place. Maybe my son can go to school here like me. You still have scholarships available for the Res, don't you?"

"We have three students now, two from Sells and one from Quijotoa. As with you, they stay here and go home on weekends."

"I cannot express how much the education I got here means to me. After finishing at the U of A, I thought of getting into law, but my heart belonged on the Res. I can do the most good in law enforcement. Without Kihhim, I'd be in jail for smuggling drugs, or dead."

"We enjoyed having you, Harry." Katharine nodded toward the body. "What's going to happen now?"

"The forensics team will be here in about an hour. They'll wrap the scene. We'll take him out, ID the body, and notify next of kin. I don't see that there will be much impact on you."

Something in the back of Leticia's mind said it wouldn't be so simple. The who and why would be a problem.

Chapter Two

Television reporter Dayton King and a cameraman from a local television station arrived at Kihhim to cover the discovery of a body outside the fence. Normally this would not warrant a news team. Illegal border crossers were found weekly, having succumbed to the desert. But the description of him and his equipment given over the scanner had raised flags.

As Dayton waited at the gate for his guide, he looked at the area. To the west, Baboquivari Peak rose into the sky, a massive knob of granite. Inside the fence, tall glass structures covered the side of a hill. The road through the gate entered the hill through a mine-tunnel like hole.

The desert in the valley below the hill seemed untouched, totally natural. Quail calling from the brushy wash broke the silence. What an idyllic place, he thought.

A petite brunette with shoulder-length hair approached from the tunnel. Glancing at her, his eyes widened. She reminded him of someone he had loved and lost years ago. But he had painted those features on many women in hopes. This time it wasn't his imagination! Carol Goldman, his ex-fiancée was coming toward him. With hammering heart, he realized this would not be a routine assignment.

Her mouth opened as she recognized him. She recovered and moved into business mode. Dayton did the same. They could talk later. He accepted her invitation to enter the grounds, the easiest access to the grisly discovery.

When the body was tentatively identified as that of Marty Hinson, President of Environmental Sanity, he sensed there was a lot more here–especially about Kihhim. The cameraman shot the scene as Dayton did the voiceover.

"What was environmentalist Marty Hinson doing here?" he asked looking into the camera. "What does this small community hold that drew the interest of Environmental Sanity?"

The coverage of the body was sent back to the station. They told him to find out more about Kihhim.

Over sandwiches and tea, he and Carol watched the clip on the noon news in the reception area. The room took Dayton's breath away. A partially darkened glass roof three stories above lit the huge atrium. The sound of flowing water filled the air. A ramp spiraled around the circular room with doorways at different levels.

Plants filled it from top to bottom, some hanging, others in beds. The room was a riot of colored flowers and brilliant green. The waterfall cascaded into a central pool with a soft background rush.

Sunbeams sparkled around the room and framed the pool in a rainbow.

"Do you have any idea why Marty Hinson was here?" asked Dayton.

"None," responded Carol. "We're the epitome of environmentally friendly."

"Nobody knows about Kihhim. The station would like me to find out more."

"I'll have to check with John Vance about that," said Carol. "We've made an effort to stay out of the public eye."

"Successfully I would say. I found very little information about Kihhim."

There was an awkward silence.

"Carol, how did you end up here?"

"After the rape trial, I changed. For a while I wanted nothing to do with men, actually with anybody. I would go home at night and stare at the television, not hearing it or seeing it until I would fall asleep in my chair. I felt it was my fault. Then I got angry at the world. I pushed you away." She gave him a weak smile.

He reached for her hand. "I know. I tried to adjust, tried to help you but my career was at a critical point." He sighed, "I just couldn't handle it all."

"It wasn't only you. I needed help. But I didn't know it. I attended the trial, of course. It was brutal having to recount the rape." She was silent.

Dayton felt a pang of guilt. "I'm sorry I brought it up."

"No, it's okay. I've learned to deal with it." She looked at Dayton, then around the atrium. "It was my attorney, Katharine Levey, who recognized my need for help. She took me under her wing and brought me to Kihhim. John and the others here embraced me, acting as my family. That's how I got here."

"What do you do here?" asked Dayton.

"I'm a counselor."

With the sound of voices, two people came in. The woman in a loose fitting robe was tall and slender. Her blue eyes and dark blonde hair made her quite striking. Carol put a hand on Dayton's arm. "I'd like to introduce you to Katharine Levey and John Vance."

Dayton rose and shook Katharine's hand.

"We saw your report earlier. Nice job," she commented.

He turned toward John, an older man, with graying hair and a slim build. "Dayton King," he said, holding out his hand.

"John Vance, Mr. King."

"My station wants me to get more information about Kihhim," said Dayton. "Carol informs me you would be the one to grant that."

John looked at him coolly. "We'll have to see."

Carol spoke up, "It's almost time for the News at Four. Let's see if there's any more about Mr. Hinson."

The large monitor came on, the theme music intruding into the peaceful roar. The local Tucson news anchor looked into the camera. "Earlier today, we brought you a story of a body discovered close to a small isolated community called Kihhim near Baboquivari Peak."

The scene changed showing Dayton standing in front of an eight-foot fence. Over his shoulder the camera zoomed in and focused on the black ragged heap barely visible in the grass and jagged rocks.

The scene switched back to the studio. "Later in the day the sheriff's department identified the body as Environmental Sanity President Marty Hinson. The cause of death is still unknown, but the sheriff's department is treating it as an accident, pending autopsy results. We reached Environmental Sanity for comment."

The scene changed. "Lisa Colmbs at Environmental Sanity headquarters. "We're speaking with acting president Bill Broaderick."

The suntanned bearded face of Broaderick looked into the camera. "Marty was a very loyal and loved member of our community. He spent a large part of his life on behalf of the environment. He will be greatly missed."

"Do you have any idea why he was at Kihhim?" asked the reporter.

"Kihhim has been killing Gould's turkeys, an endangered species. Marty was gathering evidence. Maybe they found out," said Bill bitterly, staring into the camera.

"Are you saying Kihhim had something to do with his death?" She held the mic out for his response.

"Until I hear different, I believe Kihhim was somehow responsible for Marty's death," Bill said.

"Did you know about Marty's activities there?" asked the reporter.

"He and I spoke about how to get the Department of Game and Fish investigation moving. We both believed if we could present evidence, investigators could no longer ignore these violations. That is what Marty was doing."

"Was he trying to break into Kihhim?" asked the reporter.

"He didn't tell me," said Bill. "Marty was an environmentalist. This could not have been an accident," said Bill. "We are organizing a vigil at Kihhim to honor Marty."

"There you have it," said the reporter. "Live from Environmental Sanity headquarters, this is Lisa Colmbs. Back to you, Dave."

Dayton looked at the shocked faces around him. John's phone rang.

"Vance," he answered.

"John, this is Shana at the gate. A few people are picketing us."

John turned to Dayton. "Perhaps you should consider staying the night."

Hinson had been discovered just this morning. How had they gotten here so fast, wondered Dayton. This story was growing.

Chapter Three

Broaderick smiled to himself as he turned off the television. The story was a complete lie. Last week a surprising call had come in from Ron Emerald, a local developer. Bill and Marty had opposed Emerald Development many times as he built his Planned Communities across the Southern Arizona desert.

"Marty, Bill, I'll cut to the chase. We've been on opposite sides for a long time. I applaud what you are trying to do, and I'd like to support you and Environmental Sanity."

Bill looked at Marty. What was going on here, he wondered. Some of their most bitter battles had been against Emerald.

"There are several large tracts of land I planned to develop in the Rincon mountain foothills, and I'm willing to donate those to you for caretaking. I would expect you to seek protected status, and I'll aid you in this."

Bill and Marty's mouths dropped open.

Emerald continued, "I would also like to have you consult on another of my projects. This project is a site just off the Tohono O'Odham reservation north of Sasabe near Baboquivari Peak.

"The fee will reflect the value you bring to the project, and let's be honest, your retirement plan from Environmental Sanity sucks."

Bill's first impulse had been to tell Ron Emerald to go to hell. Marty interrupted, "Why do you need our help?"

"I've approached Kihhim with several very fair offers to buy their property. They've shot me down every time. This village is an almost self-sustaining underground development, one you guys would approve. I want to use it as a model for future eco-friendly projects."

"Mr. Emerald," said Bill, "you've always been a slash and burn developer. What are you trying to pull?"

"Emerald Developments believes that the wave of the future is not just eco-friendly, but a minimal footprint. Kihhim is ahead of the world in this."

"Won't they let you visit? Have you offered to contract their help?" asked Marty.

"They allow no visitors. The zoning application says they're doing medical research, but why would a lab be so remote? I need that property, and I'm willing to fund Environmental Sanity and pay you guys for your help in getting it."

"We'll consider it," said Marty as he hung up.

"Our retirement plan does suck," said Bill.

***

"Kihhim's location is in the habitat section where we released the Gould's turkeys eight years ago," said Marty pointing at the Google Maps on the monitor.

Bill looked. "That endangered species has recovered well since the release."

Marty scanned the county records. "Kihhim owns 200 acres of land listed as agriculture and residential community with some medical laboratories. Two hundred residents is the cap." He rubbed his chin. "I'm wondering the same thing Emerald is. Why would anyone put medical laboratories out there? It's so remote."

Bill shrugged. "The satellite map shows a fenced area of about 100 acres with only the greenhouses and a few small shacks. Environmentally, it's really clean. Normally, we'd approve of a development like this." He looked at Marty. "Why are they so secretive? What are they doing there?"

"Records are non-existent," said Bill, staring at the monitor. "Secrecy seems to be a priority. With attention, they may want to sell. The satellite photos show nothing that would justify the attention of authorities. I'm going to have to go inside to find at least enough to lodge an accusation," said Marty.

That was then, and this is now, mused Broaderick. The attention he and Marty had sought to focus on Kihhim happened at the expense of Marty's life. It was time to step up the ante. He called in his secretary.

"April, we need protesters at the Kihhim site today. Get it organized." Next he dialed the sheriff's office.

Chapter Four

John didn't think he'd been asleep at all when the tone jarred him. "Hello," he said into the darkness with a thick voice and thicker head.

"This is Ricardo at the gate. Bureau of Tobacco, Alcohol, Firearms and Explosives agents here with a warrant to search for weapons. What should I do?"

The fog in his brain evaporated. "I'll be right there," he said. "What time is it?"

"Four-thirty."

As the leader of Kihhim, John's job was to worry, but the last years had brought only small worries, problems he could solve. John Vance was sixty-four, with sandy gray hair and lightly lined face that hardly told his age. He was a handsome man and patriarch to everyone at Kihhim.

This would be the greatest test he had faced since he had left the Biosphere 2. Knots of doubt and fear began to burn in his stomach.

He called Katharine Levey. To her sleepy hello, he said, "Your tip was right: it's started. We need to get the cameramen ready." He next called Carol Goldman and Leticia Gardner asking them to meet in the communications room. Leticia was already there–not surprising. He had to buy time.

John exited the tunnel into the pre-dawn desert air. The eastern sky glowed against the star-studded blackness and the guard shack lights were a red ember, but the gate glinted in the harsh headlights of several vehicles. Behind the vehicles were the tents of the make-shift protesters camp. The news report of Marty Hinson's death had brought them out.

Bulky figures crouched alongside the vehicles–men in body armor with helmets. John walked directly to the gate, nodding at Ricardo. "I'm John Vance, the Director of Kihhim. Who is in charge?" he asked.

A figure, face in the shadow of his helmet, stepped forward holding papers in his hand. The man was tall–six foot four–and at least 250 pounds. There was no gut on him, the body armor struggled to protect his large frame. The letters BATFE glinted in reflective letters on his Kevlar helmet. An MP-5 sub-machine gun hung loosely over his shoulder.

"I'm Special Agent David Moldovan, Bureau of Alcohol, Tobacco, Firearms and Explosives. I have a warrant to search these premises for illegal firearms," scratched a gravelly voice. "Open the gate now."

"We are a small community, not hurting anyone. We have no illegal firearms and just want to be left alone."

"Open this gate now or I'm going to break it down," came the gruff threat.

"May I see the warrant please," asked John holding out his hand. David Moldovan glanced over his shoulder at his troops. Only their eyes moved, shifting nervously. He passed the papers through the gate.

"May I take these over to the light to see them more clearly?" John asked.

This was David Moldovan's first time in charge of an operation and he was acutely aware of his men's appraising stares. "Open this gate now!" The roar of his voice hung in the still air. Heads popped from tents and sleeping bags in the camp of Environmental Sanity protesters behind them.

"If this warrant is as you say, it gives you the right to search. We will not resist. I only wish to look at it to see the specifics and who signed it. Please give me a few minutes so we can avoid any mistakes." Without waiting for a response, he turned his back on the open-mouthed Moldovan. At the guard shack, John held the papers under the red light to read them.

From the tunnel a hundred yards away, ten shadows emerged into the predawn light. It was difficult to see them as they walked toward the gathering at the gate. John turned back to the armed agents.

Moldovan barked an order, and a menacing click-clack rang into the stillness as his men chambered rounds and aimed at the approaching group. Spotlights shot from the vehicles and froze the figures resembling deer caught in the headlights. The red dots of laser sights danced over them like a swarm of insects.

John raised his hands over his head and moved toward the gate. "Don't shoot! Don't shoot! We're unarmed! We're unarmed!" he screamed. He stopped in front of Moldovan, looking down the barrel of the MP-5. It yawned like a tunnel.

Time stood still as he looked from the gun into Moldovan's stony face. No one moved in the tableau of frozen figures. The ringing of the phone in the guard shack pierced the silence.

"John, it's Katharine," Ricardo's voice called out.

"May I answer that?" asked John.

Moldovan nodded. With his hands raised, John turned and walked to the shack.

"John, the restraining order is here," said Katharine. "I'm coming down there with it now."

"Things are tense but not out of control. Hurry." John returned to the hulking figure of Moldovan.

"Have all of those people throw down whatever they are carrying and put their hands over their heads," ordered Moldovan, his eyes never leaving John.

"They're only carrying cameras. May one of them approach?" asked John.

Moldovan nodded. Another gun trained on John as he waved one of the figures to come to the gate. Moldovan's gun was steady as the man neared with the camera clearly visible over his head. Slowly and deliberately, he placed it in Moldovan's hand.

"What are you going to do with that?" he asked.

John faced him squarely. "We want no mistakes. Your warrant allows you to search. By having each of your men accompanied by one of ours with a camera recording the search, there will be no questions. They will not interfere, they will not touch anything."

Moldovan's mouth dropped open and then closed with a snap. "You will not! Get all of your people lined up over by the shack. Now open this gate or we'll use the cutters!" he bellowed.

Chapter Five

The tall blonde woman, hair flying wildly about her head, sprinted down the hall to the communications room. Dear God, let it be here, Katharine Levey prayed. With growing alarm, last night she had watched the news conference. Bill Broaderick's blame of Kihhim for Marty's death shocked Katharine.

No one at Kihhim was aware that Environmental Sanity even knew of them, much less was investigating them for anything. As soon as the news report ended, she called Judge Roy Emerson, a friend of her father's. He answered immediately.

"Your Honor, this is Katharine Levey,"

"How are you?" he responded warmly. "Sorry I haven't called in a while, but things are extremely busy. I always had a fond place in my heart for you." He paused. "Is this a social call, I hope?" the judge asked.

"I'm afraid not," said Katharine, hesitantly. "I'm now living out at Kihhim and representing them. As you may know, we had trouble. First was the discovery of the body of environmentalist Marty Hinson." She took a deep breath.

"I've learned we're being investigated for firearms violations. It's groundless, but it started me thinking about our status. In addition to being an independent community, we have biological laboratories where we do contract research. Our lab work is very sensitive and needs to be protected from contamination," she said. "It is critical we keep those labs sterile."

"What kind of contamination?" asked the judge.

"Clean-room procedures. Some of our work deals with pathogens. I know we could not refuse a search, and we want to comply. We do not want to endanger anyone or the work going on here."

"Pathogens," commented the judge, "as in dangerous?"

"They could be. That's why it is critical we protect everybody."

"Of course, you're right," said the judge.

"We would take the search personnel through our procedures. That would protect them and our work. Some of the projects represent years of development."

"All areas would need to be inspected," said the judge.

"Yes, sir and we won't resist. All we're asking for is consideration for our procedures to protect everybody," Katharine restated.

"Fax me an argument and I will issue a court order ensuring protection," he said.

"You will have it within minutes," she said. "Thanks for all of your help. I'll buy you a dinner after this is over."

"You're welcome," said the Judge. "I'm looking forward to that dinner," he answered, a smile in his voice.

"Thanks again, Your Honor."

Katharine silently thanked the sister of one of their residents who worked with the sheriff's office. She was cautious to stay within the law on disclosure, but Broaderick gave a deposition after the discovery of Marty Hinson's body at Kihhim.

While he was being deposed, the BATFE arrived to participate in the interview. Though the statements were sealed, it didn't take much intuition to see that an investigation was sure. Not sealed were orders for overtime officers at the site. In today's world, the government could not ignore any potential threat and acted quickly.

Katharine burst into the communications office and two worried faces looked up. "Any faxes for me?" Leticia pointed to a lone sheet atop the desk. Without a word, she picked it up, glanced at it, and ran.

***

John Vance and Special Agent Moldovan turned at the yell from an approaching woman, her hands up, a paper fluttering in her fingers. The agent's gun wavered between John and her. She read his nametag.

"Agent Moldovan, I'm Katharine Levey, legal representative for Kihhim. I have a court order," she held it out to him, "directing you to maintain the integrity of our labs and property during your search.

If anything happens, the cameras hold a record that proper procedure was followed. Lacking that, any problems will be directly your responsibility."

He glanced at the top, then at the signature. With eyes reflecting growing fury, he glared at Katharine and then John.

The burley agent turned and barked to his crouching men. Slowly, they rose–guns still ready. John opened the gate. They entered cautiously, eyes glued to the group in front of them, guns trained.

On his tablet, Moldovan brought up a plan of Kihhim obtained from county records. He directed each of his men to different areas, admonishing them, with a sneer, "To carefully follow any procedures needed to protect each site." As each left, a cameramen fell into step behind, the camera trained on the agent.

Chapter Six

Newsman Dayton King awoke, lost for a few seconds until he remembered where he was. The tone sounded again. "Hello," he mumbled.

"Dayton, this is Carol. Something has happened. Come to the communications office, now!" His mind did not understand. "Hurry," she said. The room was silent as she hung up.

Last night when he finally broke away, he was exhausted, only dimly remembering Carol escorting him to his room. Wiping sleep from his eyes, he wondered, now what?

Within minutes, he arrived still tucking in his shirt. Carol Goldman and Leticia Gardner were looking at the monitors. "Look at this," Carol said, pointing. The screen showed the front gate in the greenish glow of light enhancement.

Helmeted figures with the letters BATFE pointed their rifles into Kihhim. As Dayton watched, John Vance moved toward them to speak with one.

Suddenly the agents chambered their rifles and aimed at several people walking toward the gate. John, hands over his head, yelled as he walked forward. Leticia reached over and flipped a switch. John's voice cried in alarm. "Don't shoot! Don't shoot! We're unarmed! We're unarmed!"

Carol whispered to Dayton, "When I called you, things were happening so fast I didn't think you could get your gear together in time to catch this. We can share our video."

"Making two copies now," Leticia said. She touched a switch and zoomed in on one of the figures holding something high in the air. Dayton saw that the object was a camera. Carol explained their plan to record every aspect of the search.

"But how did you know about the search?" asked Dayton.

Leticia ignored the question. "There's Katharine with the court order." Dayton saw her run to the gate yelling and waving a paper. Leticia spoke over her shoulder, "Don't worry; we're making copies of everything."

They watched as the gates opened and the agents entered. The agent in charge spoke to the men, handing them papers. Cameramen followed each agent. The agent in charge walked away, entering a van.

As Leticia touched another switch, voices filled the room. "The bastards have a court order saying we have to meet security restrictions to protect their labs and research areas," Moldovan sneered. "It's signed by Judge Emerson."

Leticia looked up at Dayton. "That's David Moldovan, the Special Agent in charge, speaking to their control center."

"How the hell did they get that so goddamn fast!" replied another voice.

Dayton's eyes grew, as he realized what he was hearing. "They also got a camera following each of my men recording everything they do. We'll shut that off in a goddamn hurry."

"Actually, it's probably a good thing," said the other voice. "Make sure your men comply with instructions, but search thoroughly. We don't want another Waco. I'll call this in."

A touch of another switch, revealed a garbled transmission. Leticia tapped the keyboard. In a few seconds, the voice from the van related the situation to someone else.

"I'll find out about this court order," came the reply.

Leticia looked at another screen full of squiggly horizontal lines. "Here's a different one." She hit a switch.

A different voice spoke. "Yeah, that's right. BATFEs showed up, but they have Kihhim people with each agent. They're searching now," he said.

"Will they find anything?"

"We have our man on the team. Of course they'll find something!"

"Can you reach him?"

"No. Too risky."

"If you don't get enough evidence to move them off that property, I ain't paying, and you're now in line for Marty's share, too. My whole development rests on that site. Keep me informed." The connection was broken.

Frozen in place, Leticia, Carol, and Dayton stared at the monitor. What was going on here? Leticia switched back to the BATFE team frequency and the agents reporting their positions and situations.

"This is Villalobos," a voice said. "I'm at the first greenhouse. They're insisting I go through some kind of decontamination procedure and wear a special suit before I enter. This place is huge. It'll take a month to check this out."

"Follow what they say," admonished Moldovan. "The office is checking on the order now. How long do you really think it will take to search the greenhouse?" he asked.

"First, I gotta take everything off, including my body armor. I'm not liking that much."

"Villalobos, I've spent the last two years trying to get you to wear it. Now you're bitching about taking it off! How long?"

"If we have to dig everything up, about a month." Voices rose in the background. "I'm getting some pretty hot argument about any digging," said Villalobos. "We might be able to use metal detectors."

"I'll check with the boss," said Moldovan.

"This is a real goat screw," said another voice.

"What's the problem, Hendrickson?" asked Moldovan.

"They won't let me into the labs. They say there's critical materials and the area's sterile. There's biohazard signs on the door."

"Don't go in there! Check the offices. I'll get help from headquarters," said Moldovan. "Do your search outside while I get an answer."

One-by-one the agents checked in with the progress of their search.

Leticia and Carol listened while Moldovan spoke to the U.S. Attorney General's office. He related the situation. "We'll get you additional help," came the reply. "The FBI has consultants–specialist teams, biohazard agencies, and the CDC in Atlanta."

Moldovan groaned. "This will drag out, won't it? Glad I won't be in charge when this goes south."

"Moldovan, it's not going south. We'll get the experts in and finish up in a day or two. Let the agents do their job until help arrives."

"Yeah," grunted Moldovan, "maybe they'll find something, but I doubt it. These people are not the everyday run-of-the-mill radicals. And they were ready, so we have a leak somewhere."

"Stay cool. We'll take care of things."

"Cool!" exclaimed Moldovan. "The temp will be way over 100 degrees. I'm already sweating."

Chapter Seven

The news anchor looked out from the TV monitor. "Last night, Dayton King filed this report from the isolated village of Kihhim." In the atrium, Carol, John, Katharine and Dayton watched the morning news. Dayton appeared on the screen, with the gate and guard shack lit in the background.

"Friends and associates of Marty Hinson have gathered outside of Kihhim for a vigil looking more like a protest by environmentalists." The camera zoomed in on a crowd spotlighted at the gate waving signs. One read 'KIHHIM, MURDERERS OF ANIMALS AND PEOPLE!' Another read 'NO KIHHIM!' Are the protestors on KIHHIM property right outside the gates?

Dayton continued, "Kihhim leader John Vance agreed to give a statement."

John's face filled the screen. His voice was soft, yet strong. "Our village of Kihhim has nothing but the deepest regret and sorrow about this tragic death. We do not understand why Mr. Hinson was here. As a small community of everyday working people, we cannot understand why the environmental movement is here. Kihhim is very mindful of the delicate desert in which we live. Again, we offer the most sincere condolences to Mr. Hinson's family and loved ones." John's lips pressed together.

"Thank you, Mr. Vance. From the small isolated community of Kihhim this is Dayton King." The scene cut back to the studio.

"We'll continue to cover this developing story."

John looked at the faces around him. The next chapter in this story, the search by the BATFE, yet unreported would be far more significant. This was beating him down. For the first time he could remember, he felt his age. Katharine took his hands, pulled him up and guided him from the reception room to his quarters.

"John, it will be all right. We'll get through this." Sitting beside him on the couch, she looked into his face.

He returned her stare. Katharine was the daughter of Abraham Levey, John's early mentor and once his dearest friend and cofounder of Kihhim. Katharine was the most practical and honest person he knew. If she said something was so, he believed it.

His mind settled into a comfort zone, giving over responsibility to her, at least for a while so he could rest.

"I'm afraid this will turn into a repeat of the Biosphere 2 project with the government and the press driving investigations until we are destroyed. After the bio and cyber-attacks on the U.S. people are afraid, see the worst and want any possible threat, real or not, squashed."

"John, we both know the BATFE search will find nothing."

"That doesn't mean we won't be charged and prosecuted," John snapped. "We may join the sorry heap of bodies laid upon grave of freedom."

"John, we've done good things here, and we will do more. You're afraid of publicity hurting us. We don't have control of that. It will come."

He started to object, Katharine cut him off.

"Let's make it work for us, present the accomplishments we've made. Perhaps we've been under the radar long enough. Let's not hide anymore. Covering up has destroyed presidents and kings."

Perhaps she was right. They certainly had nothing to lose.

"John, you need rest. I'll call you later." He lay down on the couch as she closed the door behind her. They had done good things.

***

Leticia turned off the television broadcast, shaking her head. This situation was going down faster than crap from a soaring vulture, with the same result if they didn't pull things together soon. Kihhim was a new life. People cared for each other.

What a refreshing change. Kihhim was a small enough community that people knew each other and supported each other. There were no strangers here. She liked that. Time to look in on the search progress, and then she needed rest. She had to protect Kihhim.

Chapter Eight

The news anchor looked into the camera. "In a breaking story exclusively from Channel 11 News reporter Dayton King, there's a disturbing new development from a small community near the Mexican border town of Sasabe." The picture changed to an outdoor scene of Dayton King. In the background, a road wound up an incline and entered the mouth of a large dark tunnel cut in the side of a low hill.

"In the predawn hours this morning Bureau of Alcohol Tobacco Firearms and Explosives agents descended on this small underground community with a warrant to search for illegal weapons." The scene switched to the recording made by the monitor atop the guard shack. Shadowy figures of uniformed BATFE agents in firing position, aimed their rifles at several people frozen in the glare of headlights.

Suddenly one ran toward the gate, his hands raised, shouting clearly, "Don't shoot! Don't shoot! We're unarmed! We're unarmed!"

Dayton continued speaking. "Luckily, cooler heads prevailed, and the agents entered to begin their search. No illegal weapons have yet been found, and the search goes on. We will continue to bring you updates as they occur. This is Dayton King live from Kihhim."

The news anchor again appeared. "All we know about Kihhim at this time is that it is a small community established twenty years ago. Built underground, they are located in the foothills east of Baboquivari Peak near the Mexican border. We'll bring you more information about this unique facility at a later date. Please stay tuned to Channel 11 for the best in news."

"Dayton," said John, "We haven't talked. We'd like to have you introduce us and Kihhim to the world. We want to give you a tour and relate some of our history."

Dayton looked at John. "I tried to find out about Kihhim online, but information is very sketchy. There is data about you though most of it is old. I gather you left your career with Biosphere 2 Ventures after they had serious internal political problems, and the money man pulled out."

"Do you know much about the Biosphere 2 Project?"

Dayton shook his head. "That was before I moved to Tucson."

"Let me give you some history from an insider's point of view," started John. "In 1984 a project began in the Southern Arizona desert near Tucson. It was an ambitious project, fueled by visions of creating independent ecosystems, understanding man's relationship with his environment." John smiled, recalling his feeling of awe.

He glanced at Dayton. "We dreamed of breaking free of Earth, building orbiting colonies in space, colonies on Mars, and then the solar system."

"Colonies in space and on Mars seems rather farfetched," commented Dayton.

John smiled. "We built the Biosphere 2, a three-acre completely sealed habitat north of Tucson. As a space colony on Earth, we designed it to include everything to support six people for two years. Nothing would pass into or out of the enclosure except energy and information. It had to be a complete ecosystem, no dumping."

"That sounds really difficult," said Dayton.

"Difficult? Oh yes. Did we make mistakes? Certainly, but we learned. Biosphere 2 was a gigantic laboratory." John nodded. "As part of the space program, we did genetic research to maintain species over the periods of months or even the years needed for trips to the planets and the stars. Zygotes, fertilized eggs, would be carried away from the Earth. Seeds weighed too much and took up too much room." He smiled. "This was an experiment to learn what long-term existence in space and voyages to other worlds required."

"A really ambitious project," exclaimed Dayton.

"It was. Though privately funded, it was not immune to political considerations, some of them internal. Eight Biospherians lived inside for two years, which exceeded the original design. Unforeseen oxidation occurred, throwing off the balance. Oxygen and food had to be added, which was the ammunition the critics needed. Even then, the Biospeherians emerged back onto Earth's surface painfully thin."

Bitterness crept into John's voice. "From the beginning, the Biosphere 2 Project was derided by some scientists as 'Not truly scientific,' but to us it seemed most of those critics were jealous about not being part of the project. Scientific or not, we developed tremendous amounts of knowledge vital to man's existence, on or off Earth."

"I did research on the Biosphere 2 venture," said Dayton. "As you say, it was not considered a true scientific project. That it was entirely privately funded I found most interesting. Millions were invested."

"We considered that a blessing. Government manages to screw up everything–too many ignorant bosses with image as their primary objective. We did have corporate politics.

"When the infighting started at the Biosphere 2 Project, it was divisive and public, with the press pouncing on each juicy tidbit. Our dream blew apart." He looked Dayton in the eye. "Many left, but a few did not give up the dream."

John smiled. "That's what brought us here. We were determined to work together to build a community with little adverse environmental impact. Publicity was nothing but grief to the Biosphere 2 Project, so we decided to live quietly and unknown to the rest of the world."

"My lack of research results shows you were successful," said Dayton. "Almost nothing exists in the public arena about Kihhim."

"Kihhim is much simpler than the Biosphere 2 Project since we are not completely sealed off from the world. We are a small community and still think of ourselves as an Earth colony, taking as little as possible, living in balance."

"And here you are, the target in a government investigation," murmured Dayton.

Chapter Nine

"Would you like to see what we've done? Some of it is amazing." He touched a monitor and a 3-D plan view opened on the screen. The glass top of the atrium was on one side above the ground level of the hill as were the greenhouses. The rest was buried underground. Like spokes of a wheel, tunnels radiused out into the hill with rooms on each side. The end of the tunnels intersected a circumferential tunnel surrounding the top level. More rooms were located around the circle.

"This top level is mostly residential space," said John. He moved the drawing down a level. "You can see we repeated the same pattern. Those rooms on the west side are the entrances into the top levels of our greenhouses where we grow our food."

"Wow," exclaimed Dayton "it's huge."

John nodded. "Just wait." He moved the image down another level. The radius construction repeated but the rectangular spaces for the greenhouses were larger.

"This is a mid-level access to the greenhouses with residences and processing spaces. We also have conference rooms on this level along with labs. We do plant research in these labs and create strains compatible with our greenhouses and our needs." He again touched the screen and the next view appeared.

The radius tunnel design repeated but the greenhouse spaces were much larger.

"This is another mid-level in the greenhouses with processing for the plants grown on these levels. We have more labs and residences here. We have little office space. Each residence has workstations." He moved the view down.

"This is the level we are on now. You can see the atrium and the cafeteria. On the west side is the access to the entrance tunnel and the ground floor of the greenhouses." The view went down another level.

"This is our bottom floor. Here we have the clean-room laboratories and the maintenance and treatment facilities for the utilities within Kihhim."

"Being underground, power consumption is small. Lighting conducted through gathering domes on the hillside during the day and LCD lighting at night. We recover methane from waste digesters for gas and use large solar panels for electric. Those panels help shade our greenhouses to prevent heat buildup in the summer. We are definitely off the grid."

"This is amazing," said Dayton. "Doesn't being underground get claustrophobic at times?"

John changed the view on the screen. "This is a typical residence." Space was utilitarian with the room designed for multiple functions. "The workstation and the bed fold up against the wall. This room is an office and bedroom at the same time. The kitchen is small as most people eat in the cafeteria except for snacks or drinks. We use 500 square feet like most homes use 1200. Notice the walls."

Dayton looked at a large plate glass window view of the desert area around Kihhim. "Is this room on the surface?"

"That's a real-time projection looking to the west. It can be changed to any view or artwork, whatever the resident wants." John continued showing Dayton different areas of Kihhim. "Carol can give you the live tour. We can offer you video for your report if you want to use it."

Chapter Ten

By noon, a crowd of nearly one hundred milled around at the gate, shouting, shoving, and especially sweltering. Many were just curious after seeing the news reports; others wanted an excuse to drink beer. The few sheriffs' deputies trying to control them were exhausted in the punishing heat. Sweat streaks soaked their backs and under their arms. Shade was at a premium. An aid station was set up in the parking garage for the deputies.

To the west above the mountains the first puffs of afternoon clouds appeared, growing rapidly, and hinting that larger dark brothers would be hatching. The weather service issued flash flood warnings for south central Pima County. A big storm was coming.

In the communications room, Leticia spoke to John, Carol, Katharine and the other group leaders on the intercom system. "The agents are searching now, and so far they are respecting the court order. The FBI will arrive in an hour with equipment and personnel to begin the search of the labs and greenhouses. I've arranged for more monitors to record those agents. On the official side, things are not going too badly."

Carol's voice broke in. "Dayton's report this morning was good for us, but the other networks and services want access. We need to hold a press conference. Do any of you see a problem sharing information and tapes with them?"

Leticia spoke immediately, "Exposure would reveal the extent of our network. In the end, it will make things harder. They're already wondering how we got that court order so fast. They suspect a leak. Electronic monitoring hasn't entered their little pea brains yet."

"Luckily, our telephone records show we called this morning and did it all in the short time they were at the gate," said Katharine. "But they will wake up to the fact we are ahead of them."

"There is something else we need to consider," Leticia pointed out. "We intercepted this yesterday." She reached over a flipped a switch. Bill Broaderick's earlier conversation chilled the room. "Seems like Bill has another agenda. Any idea who the other person is?" Nobody spoke.

***

"This is Dayton King with a special report live from Kihhim. FBI agents arrived to join the Bureau of Alcohol, Tobacco, Firearms and Explosives in the search for illegal weapons. Due to the nature of some of areas, specialists from the Department of Agriculture and the Center for Disease Control are here to assist them." A jungle scene filled the screen. In the center of the picture, four white specks looked like grains of rice in a lawn. As it zoomed in, they resolved into human figures in white coveralls. Two were easily identified as agents by the helmet and flak jacket with FBI in big letters. They looked like the Pillsbury doughboy going to war. One swept the ground with a metal detector.

Behind them were two other white-suited figures, one carrying a camera trained on the agents. Sweat streamed from all of them. Dayton's voice filled the background. "There has been no resistance from the residents of Kihhim. They are cooperating fully, even supplying guides to assist in the search. No illegal arms have been found, and one has to wonder if this is not a wild goose chase."

The scene switched back to Dayton standing with a white coated man. "This is Dr. Donald Brown, Supervisor for Agriculture at Kihhim." A short figure with a light complexion and black hair filled the screen. "Dr. Brown, we notice everyone in the greenhouses is wearing white coveralls. Can you explain?"

"Our greenhouses are controlled environments. We need to protect them from contaminants."

"Why is that?"

"Many of our plants are special hybrids having no resistance to outside diseases and pests. Contamination could destroy them."

"Why is that important?"

"We grow our food in these greenhouses. The federal agents have cooperated fully in helping us maintain the integrity of our facilities."

"Do you have any illegal firearms here?"

"No! I don't understand why the government is even looking at Kihhim!"

"This is Dayton King live at Kihhim. We'll have more in a later broadcast. Back to you."

The co-anchor at the station came back on. "Tonight at nine o'clock we will air a special in-depth report on Kihhim by Dayton King and the Channel 11 news crew. Please join us."

"In other news, three FBI agents were ambushed and killed in Duck Creek, Idaho. The agents were trying to arrest..."

Carol turned to Dayton. "That was terrific!" she said.

"Thanks," said Dayton. "Wait until they see the detailed report tonight. Kihhim is going to wow 'em."

Chapter Eleven

Darkness descended as if the sun was turned off. One minute the late afternoon sunshine baked everything below. The next, it was blotted out. Heavy ebony clouds boiled up over the mountains, roiling across the sky casting an ominous blackness over the valley. The desert grew still awaiting the tempest.

A clap of thunder sounded like a starting gun. The demonstrators at the gate awaked, scurrying to stow everything loose and find shelter. Another bolt struck closer and louder. The first gusts of wind chased plastic cups and paper around the vehicles. Another explosion rattled the ground. A few solitary figures dodged the sniper fire of flying debris as the storm's attack began.

A blinding flash and a deafening roar followed a loud sizzle. The large saguaro near the guard shack erupted into green shrapnel and turned into a torch, fire sputtering toward the sky. Another ground-shaking crack sounded and heads burrowed into shelters like foxholes.

The first few drops of rain struck like bullets, whapping loudly as they kicked up puffs of dust. Then a bucket in the sky turned over, and it was impossible to see anything through the sheets of water. The sandy ground could not absorb the rain fast enough, and within minutes, it became a shallow lake. Those inside the vehicles were deafened by the rattle of the deluge.

The tumult lasted less than an hour as the storm moved off to ravage more of the desert. Pale faces pressed against windows, noses flat. Hands wiped at the moisture shrouding the glass. The pond that surrounded them reflected the brightening sky, and only occasional splashes broke the image.

The emerging sun chased the clouds away, and a brilliant double rainbow framed the retreating black-bottomed thunderhead. In the valley to the east, a column of water connected the cloud to the earth. As it moved, the scoured desert glistened, fresh and newly alive.

Cautious heads appeared from the cars, vans, and motor homes. A roar of rushing water came from the normally dry wash that crossed the road a short distance away. Nobody would be using that road for at least an hour. Even then, it would need work to make it passable.

***

BATFE agent David Moldovan sat inside the field ops van when the storm struck. At times, he was sure the van would be rolled like a can on the highway behind a passing semi. The close lightning strikes knocked out his communications as he was forced to weather it out.

FBI Regional Agent in Charge William Black had arrived half an hour before the storm informing

Moldovan the FBI was now in charge. Black immediately asked for a status report. He took one look at the court order and shook his head. In addition to the six agents, they brought an agricultural specialist and a disease specialist from the Center for Disease Control. All disappeared into Kihhim before the storm, and there had been no word since.

Something else was going on here. The warrant said weapons, and Moldovan believed they wouldn't find any illegal weapons. These people did not act like terrorists or revolutionaries, but they were isolationists. They had no religious symbols, Christian, Muslim, or anything else. Moldovan had been on several operations where the groups were religious. He was not comfortable going after Christian groups. His own fundamentalist church could be considered radical.

Some of those greenhouse plants did not appear natural. If these people could do this with plants, they may well have been changing animals. They were exploiting nature, manipulating God's way for their own gain. International laws controlled the development of new species, and on the surface, it looked like they were abiding by those restrictions.

Chapter Twelve

FBI Special Agent Robert McWilliams was trim, six-foot-three and forty-two years old. Of African-American heritage, he was handsome, with dark hair, a square jaw, an icy stare, and used to getting what he wanted. He was still on the upward ladder within the bureau. This morning he received orders to take over this action from BATFE before they ended up with major egg on their faces or worse. Once the bureau received footage of the greenhouse searches, alarms went off. The United States and The European Union had initiated United Nation resolutions aimed to protect the environment against genetically engineered species. Kihhim did not appear on anybody's radar.

The Justice Department maintained special consultants as part of a team to investigate possible biological and chemical threats. The call this morning set the wheels in motion. Kihhim was not the 'run-of-the-mill' gun toting isolated militant group spoiling for a fight with the government.

McWilliams became increasingly frustrated with his agricultural specialist Dr. Brian Denton. The team arrived from Washington a few hours ago with instructions to relieve the BATFE agents and coordinate with the local FBI.

Dr. Denton and Dr. Donald Brown, Kihhim's Supervisor of Agriculture, knew each other from previous work. They chatted like an old boys club. When McWilliams pressed, Denton did not support the search needed, because "It would damage the crops and vegetation." Between his own so-called expert and the court order, he was restricted to two people and only metal detectors.

From the viewing window, the vast greenhouse opened out before him. Christ! Far below his agent waved the metal detector while a goddamn Kihhim cameraman followed. A short distance away, Denton acted like a kid in a toyshop. The balding Denton, far from slim, waddled beside Brown as they worked their way through the bottom layer. It would take a week to search each of the greenhouses at this rate.

It took thirty minutes just to get through the goddamn decontamination procedure. Something was out of line here–not firearms. Some of the vegetation appeared radically modified, like the living bamboo structure that supported everything. How had they done that?

At the slightest hint, he would get another warrant allowing him to go over this place with a fine-toothed comb. These people were a cult, with science and technology as their God. They certainly were not mainstream American. He truly hated people who did not show appreciation for the American way of life.

The look in his men's eyes when that bitch lawyer got the judge to back her up rankled. Once they found something, the Justice Department would grind them to dust and poverty. These little breakaway communities, no matter how sophisticated, could not be allowed to flaunt the authority of the government.

After the war and the attempt by California to secede, it was getting harder and harder to hold the nation together. Thank God, Congress saw the danger and passed laws preventing the spread of dangerous secessionist ideas.

McWilliams had the pleasure of shutting down the Voice of the West an underground paper. Their separatist anti-government rhetoric fueled several small insurrections. A recent one cost three agents their lives.

The press fought hard against the Sedition and Terrorism Act, but the First Amendment did not give anyone the right to yell "Fire" in a crowded theater. That is what these papers did. The unstable conditions in the country could be pushed either way, and in the end, national security issues had to prevail.

This legislation and the new definition of Hate Crimes allowed the federal government unprecedented power, but it would be a long haul before things were under control.

An expanded definition of illegal firearms and weapons of mass destruction had not resulted in a flood of arms turned in. They expected that, but computerization in the last decade now tracked all purchases. Even though there were millions out there, computers mapped strategic and systematic programs for seizure. A voice in McWilliams ear broke through his train of thought.

"Robert, this is Stephenson. I have Justice working on the court order to free up your search. Have you seen anything we can use to expand this search?"

"Not yet," McWilliams said. "There is something here, but it's not guns. We'll need time and a warrant for access to the books and lab records."

"That may take a while," said Stephenson. "Let's see if we can find anything on the big three, drugs, child abuse, terrorism. With those, we can get whatever we need. Rumor has it you will be on the six-o'clock news on Channel 11."

"Christ! The boss won't like that! What does it say?"

"Sorry, no time to preview."

"Okay, I will let you know if I find anything. We may have to make it happen."

Chapter Thirteen

"Listen to this," Leticia said to the small group gathered in the communications room. She pushed a button. "Stephenson, where the fuck did they get those tapes?" screamed McWilliams. "We have to stop this publicity. The footage on Kihhim is hindering our search. We have to shut this down. That asshole Dayton King hurt us on the news report. Get an injunction because this is an ongoing investigation. We need to confiscate all film and tapes as evidence and get these goddamn cameramen off our asses. We'll find something illegal then."

Stephenson tried to calm McWilliams. "I'll get a court order to back these civilians off to the highway for their own safety. The same with the press."

"I need more men," shouted McWilliams. "This place is huge. I want to move the inhabitants out—they're getting in the way. Get me an electronics expert."

Stephenson interrupted. "Robert, I'll do what we can. We're trying to get a federal judge to issue another warrant, but we need something to base it on. I'll call you."

The communication room was silent. Katharine spoke first. "All of this tape footage has to be sent out of here. Dayton, can you help?"

"Maybe, depends on what the station will do. Can you package everything for quick transfer?"

Leticia looked at Rich Lewis. The jeans and tee shirt-clad engineer was rail-thin with a shaved head and their mechanical, electronics, and computer specialist. "No problem." He started a program compressing files. Dayton picked up his cell phone, but Leticia held up her hand and shook her head, pointing to a phone on the table. Dayton dialed the station. The night receptionist answered.

"This is Dayton King. I need to speak to Charlie."

"I'll put you through to his office."

"News Director's office."

"This is Dayton. Let me speak to Charles."

In a few seconds, Charles Todd came on the line.

"Boy! You sure stirred things up. The other news agencies are clamoring to get information, and… Hold on, Jerri's ringing me and she only does that if there is a real problem."

The line went dead for a few minutes. Charles came back. "Okay. That was the owner. We're having a meeting with some FBI agents and attorneys in an hour. Know what that's about?"

"Yeah, I do, and it's not safe to talk on this line any more. I'll call you at our favorite luncheon counter in fifteen minutes. Can you get there?"

"You're sure being secretive. I'll leave now."

Fifteen minutes later, the pay phone at Eegee's Sandwich Shop rang. Charles picked it up. "Okay, what's so mysterious, and what in the hell is going on?"

"The feds will edit the Kihhim piece or pull it. All raw footage will be confiscated, what you have there and we have here. I need a safe download. Any ideas?"

"How the hell do you know this?" Silence met his question. After an uncharacteristic pause, Charles uttered his favorite words. "Okay. Okay, I'll give you a number to call, but give me ten minutes to set it up. Okay?" He read off the number.

"I have a feeling they may try to move us out of here tomorrow. If I can stay, I'll call you at ten-thirty on this same number." Dayton hung up and looked at the others. "I think we'll be all right."

"The download will ready in a few minutes," announced Rich. Beside him grew a stack of disks. "You can try to take copies out when you leave. I've also set this up to make continuous copies of the incoming feeds. We might get out a squirt transmission of them, too."

Dayton looked at the monitors showing each of the searching FBI and BATFE agents. He dialed the number Charles gave him. After several rings, there was a curt answer. "I know who this is. Begin your download in ten seconds." Dayton glanced at Rich, who nodded. After a tone, Rich pushed a button and the phone in Dayton's hand went dead.

"It's automatic from here," Rich said. "Your guy has a fast system, but we have a lot of bytes here. It will take at least an hour."

Leticia shushed them and flipped a switch. On the monitor, McWilliams was using his cell phone, and his voice was an exasperated hiss. Things were not rosy. "What were you able to do for me, Stephenson?"

"We're heading for a meeting now with the station owner. There should be no trouble getting the segment pulled. Their license comes up for renewal next month." He laughed.

"Instead of making a stink about confiscating the information out there, bottle it up. Let them record everything they want. Just make sure it never leaves the site. As long as they think they are doing good, it will cause fewer waves."

"Yeah, sure. Sounds good. I'll put a clamp on this place tighter than a duck's asshole, and that is watertight. Can you get me jamming equipment?"

"It's on the way, along with your electronics and communication expert and more people. We're sending you armored vehicles so you can form a proper blockade. They'll be there by noon tomorrow. It's stuff the locals are itching to use. But by God you better find something!"

"Okay, I need to spell my people. They've been going flat out. Call me after the meeting."

In the security office, they mutely looked at each other. "Rich, can we keep anything open?" John asked.

"We'll let them shut down the communications from here. We'll put a duplicate communication system in, distributed among the workstations in the residential area. They won't be able to see anything, and we'll continuously shift the locations. When it comes time to transmit, we'll squirt it out. We should be okay."

"Okay," said John, "start with the financial records, and then go to the lab records. Let's move accounts to our shell companies offshore."

Chapter Fourteen

By eight-thirty in the morning, additional agents arrived, and the civilian demonstrators were moved out to the highway. Two greenhouses and the labs remained.

McWilliams' supervisor sent a clear message. "Find something within the next twenty-four hours, or we pull out." In his heart, McWilliams didn't think they would get what they needed that fast.

The electronic and communication experts arrived and went immediately to Kihhim's communication center. When they entered with their cameramen shadows, only one person was in the office.

"Ms. Gardner, I am Special Agent in Charge, Robert McWilliams and this is Special Agent Liu of the FBI electronics branch," said McWilliams gesturing to a small man behind him. "The FBI is now in charge of this operation. Agent Liu will take care of your communications and computer information systems during our investigation."

"Am I to understand you will be holding us incommunicado and investigating our electronic records?" asked Leticia.

"Let's say we will monitor them," replied McWilliams. "We would appreciate your cooperation in this."

"I'm sure ya'll would. Let's find out," said Leticia, slipping into a Louisiana drawl. She called Katharine while Liu removed equipment from a satchel.

"Katharine, this is Leticia. Federal Bureau of Investigation Special Agent Robert McWilliams and another agent are here in the communications office settin' up ta listen in on all our communications, and they want our computer records. You might wanna come over," she said. There was a pause as she listened. "Maybe you oughta make that call from here so's there won't be any misunderstanding. See you in a few." She turned to McWilliams, giving him a syrupy smile.

"Agent Liu might oughta wait a few minutes before installin' his equipment. Our lawyer'll be here to call the judge who signed the warrant. We'd like clarification on the extent of the search allowed."

McWilliams grimaced and signaled to Liu to hold off. In a few minutes Katharine arrived with the warrant in her hand. "According to this, you are authorized to search for illegal weapons. Do you have a court order for wiretapping?" she asked.

"Not yet," answered McWilliams.

"Let's call Judge Bassit about this and see if the warrant covers electronics and computer search and wiretapping." She turned and dialed the judge's number, as though from memory. She had looked it up just before coming into the office. McWilliams did not appear happy.

The judge's secretary answered. "Carol, this is Katharine Levey at Kihhim. We have been served with a search warrant signed by the judge, and the field agents need to clarify the extent of search allowed under the warrant. Is he available?" She listened. "When do you expect him to be out of court?" A pause then, "Perhaps you should advise the agent in charge about continuing his investigation?" she said, handing the phone to McWilliams.

"This is FBI Special Agent in Charge Robert McWilliams." He listened. "Yes ma'am, I understand you are giving me your opinion," he said in a softer voice. "Please continue." He knew where the real power was. "Yes ma'am, what you say sounds solid. Thank you. Yes, please have the judge contact me as soon as possible. Thank you."

Handing the phone back to Leticia, he turned to Liu. "Hold off on the communications but start looking into the firearms transfer records. Ms. Gardner will accompany you to the armory." Leticia nodded and rose. They left with a cameraman following. One remained, camera trained on McWilliams. He looked around the room, glared at Katharine and the cameraman, then headed for the door.

"You have moved the demonstrators out, and no traffic is coming in, except yours," Katharine noted.

McWilliams responded. "Yes ma'am. It is for safety."

"Whose? Does this mean there are restrictions on our movements?" she asked.

"As long as we are conducting this search, we will restrict who comes in and goes out."

"And our communications?"

"We cannot do that yet, but you may experience trouble in your communications. We think it's the rise in sunspot activity," he said, smiling. Katharine smiled back. He gave her a sour look and headed for the door, cameraman following.

As the door closed, she reached for the phone and redialed Judge Bassit's number. "Hi. This is Katharine Levey again. Could you check the judge's calendar? I'd like to get in to see him tomorrow? Seven-thirty will be fine. I'll be there."

Chapter Fifteen

Dr. Brian Denton could not believe the things he was seeing. Since his arrival, he had been continuously amazed. The whole greenhouse was alive, like a single entity. Many of the differences were invisible to the untrained eye. The number of melons growing and the size of the leaves were out of proportion to normal cantaloupe. Living material made up the support structure and the nets.

Nothing like this existed anywhere else in the world, by far the most efficient agricultural system ever, at least by a factor of ten. In addition, the fruit load on each plant greatly exceeded a normal plant with the fruit in different stages of ripening. They produced continuously.

How had they made these changes? This was a quantum leap in agriculture! Denton turned to his guide, the questions all over his face. "How....?" He gestured toward the greenhouse, at a loss what to ask first.

"Please speak with Dr. Brown. I am not sure what he will tell you as we are submitting patent applications now."

Brian glanced at the ever-present cameraman, beginning to understand how much was at stake here. But this technology cannot be restricted to one group. This could feed the world! Patents be damned! He looked at the BATFE agent moving the metal detector along a vat, completely ignorant of what was right in front of his nose! He must talk to Dr. Brown! This could not be kept a secret! He turned back to the guide.

"Dr. Brown will speak with you after the inspection of this greenhouse." Brian turned back to the drudgery of the search, trying to formulate what he would say to Dale Donald? Brown.

***

Communicable Disease Center specialist Dr. Adriana Getzwiller looked through the glass into the sterile lab. Listed as a CDC field-consultant to domestic law enforcement, she'd received the call to come to Tucson yesterday. At fifty-two she kept in shape with regular exercise but lately, she'd been overwhelmed by her job and personal matters.

Never a fashionista, when she looked in the mirror this morning, she saw only the lines on her face and short straggly fading hair. The extra weight she'd put on these last few months didn't make this trip any easier.

Adriana's task was to supervise the FBI and BATFE agents in the search of the labs. The lab records told her no hazardous materials were within, but she had to be sure, and if the agents tramped around, they would contaminate everything.

Transparent walls enclosed the incubation areas— they would not need entry unless something specific was required. She observed a few blacked out incubation units. Arrangements were made to look into those.

What she'd seen so far had perked her up. Adriana knew they wouldn't find any firearms within these labs. As a high quality lab system, it would be very difficult to maintain sterility if firearms moved in and out. In fact, the quality surprised her.

No one at CDC in Atlanta knew of this lab or the work being done here. That was troubling. CDC tried to keep up with every facility capable of bioengineering as part of their watch against bio-terrorism.

This one didn't show up on anybody's list. When she asked for the staff personnel list, they refused, but the names of Dr. James Wong and Dr. Ruben Sanchez were on some lab sheets. These names she knew well. Among the most eminent in genetic research, neither had published nor been heard from in over two years.

One of the agents called to her, breaking her train of thought. Standing in front of a shrouded chamber, he asked if he could open it to search. She turned to their guide, eyebrows raised in question.

"I'm to assist you in the search of this chamber. Electronic devices are not allowed in here, so a visual search is necessary. This is an ultra-sterile chamber and entry will require an additional procedure. I must caution both of you about the confidentiality of what you find in this chamber. The cameraman will record your agreement to not reveal anything you see."

Adriana agreed not to disclose anything seen within. They looked at the agent.

"As long as no legal violations are present, I have to agree."

Though dim, several large glass vats with highly aerated liquid inside were visible. Adriana saw things moving around in the agitation through the murky liquid. The agent glanced at the vats and then looked at the cabinets and supports. Obviously there were not any firearms in here.

Adriana peered into one trying to make out what was inside. Suddenly one of the objects moved next to the glass. It looked like a human heart! She felt as if she were in a bad B grade science fiction movie. Another object resolved itself into a kidney. My God! These vats contained human organs! They were alive! What were these people doing?

She turned to their guide who nodded at the back of the agent looking into a cabinet. The agent turned and pointed at the door, signaling he was satisfied. The cameraman recorded everything, including her start at realizing what she's seen in the vats.

The air lock cycle took forever, but at last it opened, and they stepped out. Adriana tore off her hood, and started to speak, then noticed Dr. Sanchez, finger to his lips. He motioned her into a small office. The agent left on break, and a cameraman followed Adriana as they entered. She tried to speak, but nothing came out.

Dr. Sanchez was a small Hispanic with black hair and a large mustache. "Yes. What you saw were human organs, grown, not harvested. We have techniques to grow organs and then imprint them with the DNA code for the patient. Patients receiving organs from us have a 100% acceptance, because their body recognizes them as the patient's own organ."

Adriana was overwhelmed. They had achieved a huge leap in medical care. There was not even a hint anyone was close to being able to do this. "Why didn't you publish?" she asked. "Why haven't you offered this to the world?"

"We are applying for patents now, and they will be approved, but we do not believe they will hold up. When patents are in the national interest, they can be taken. We believe we'll lose our rights," he said, shrugging .

"Also troubling is the eventual outcome of being able to replace organs and extending life, maybe for decades."

"But you must offer this! You cannot keep this to your selves!"

"We are looking at long term effects now. Our oldest implant is only 1-1/2 years old."

"How did you fund this without anyone knowing? How did you get approval for human testing?"

"Dr. Getzwiller, you have agreed to confidentiality. Even so, we will not reveal any more to you than necessary. It is enough that you know that as grown materials, not harvested, there was nothing illegal under the terms of the warrant. You are not to say anything of this to anyone. What we do with this for now must remain secret. Do you understand?" Ruben said looking sternly at her.

Adriana opened her mouth to protest again but knew it would be meaningless. She nodded. His admonition ringing in her ears, they left the office.

The search in the lab area drew to a close. It had gone much faster than expected, and they would be finished by the end of the day, which was good. She had to do some serious thinking about what she'd seen.

Chapter Sixteen

Brian Denton was shown into Dr. Brown's office. The cameraman stayed outside. The room was institutional without adornments or awards. Brian turned to shake hands.

"Please sit," Don Brown said gesturing to a chair. "We need to talk about our greenhouses and what you've seen. First, I need to re-emphasize the confidentiality agreement you signed. In it you agreed to not disclose anything you've observed during your time here."

"Of course I remember that, but what you have done here is a quantum leap in agricultural advancement. This could go a long way in feeding the world. You cannot keep this a secret!"

Don Brown held up a hand. "Without arguing morals, starvation is occurring because of politics and greed, not lack of food. With today's production, the world could feed itself. It does not, and our methods would not make a difference. The only change would be whose pockets were filled."

Brian slumped. Don Brown was right. The reality was that neither the amount nor the cost of food would change anything. Too many of those in power furthered their ambition by considering people only expendable tools.

"It is important you understand what we accomplished in the agro area," Don said. "We utilized a lot of the lessons derived from the Biosphere 2 project to create a concentrated and integrated greenhouse system. In addition, we've genetically altered our plants for our protected environment. They are engineered to exist only in our greenhouses. We control the weather, temperature, water, disease, nutrients, and pests. We control photo exposure, extending or decreasing the length of the day as we wish." Don Brown smiled.

"Nutrients are added only as needed. The plants have little resistance to common diseases and little defense against insects. They would not survive a storm, or high wind, or temperature variation. The energy that evolution requires of all plants to survive outside goes into production here." He waved at the projection on the wall. "That is why the yield is so high. We also engineered them to be symbiotic, and many of them could not survive without the others. This is an integrated system that only thrives because we control the environment."

"But how did you do the engineering?" asked Brian.

"That is a question I will not answer. For now, it is our secret. Again, I must caution you about confidentiality. Nothing you've seen or learned here can be revealed. Any other questions?"

"I have lots of questions. Has the nutritional content of the plants changed?"

"Part of the reason we have not proceeded further with patents is because we are testing them now. We want to apply for patents and FDA approval at the same time. For fast-track approval we need to submit test data."

"How are you testing them?"

Don held up his hands, motioning at everything around them.

"You're testing them on yourselves!"

"Yes, for some time now," said Don.

"What about the children?" asked Brian.

"We are all in this together."

"But you're using children for experiments! That is immoral and illegal!" he cried, rising.

Don waved him back to his seat. "That is a gray area. Legally, we are only eating the food we grow, and everyone here is aware and approves of what we are doing. The courts may be cautious in wading in on homegrown foods and regulation. They refused in the past unless harm can be shown." He smiled. "We are much healthier than the normal population."

"But the long term effects are not known. What about that?"

"That is precisely what we are trying to determine. Thus far, it seems to improve our health. Makes you wonder what you're eating out there, doesn't it?" he said sadly.

"I must think on this," murmured Brian, suddenly eager to leave. At the door, he turned. "You put me in a very difficult situation. If I say nothing, and something goes wrong, I would be partially responsible. If I say something, I've broken your confidentiality agreement. Yet, what you've done here is revolutionary." He whirled and strode away, cameraman following.

Don sat perfectly still. *What now?*

Chapter Seventeen

As Katharine drove toward Tucson, she recalled the worrying call from Don Brown last night. Dr. Brian Denton might be trouble. Don remembered him as a rising star at a large private company. He left suddenly amid rumors of scandal. The move into government service was not a happy one. She would speak with John about what choices were open.

When the FBI moved demonstrators and press out to the highway, Dayton and his cameraman became the only newsgroup on site. There was no question of their staying to cover the story. The problem was getting it out. Video footage sent to the station was garbled and useless.

As she pulled into the parking garage under the federal courthouse building she saw the non-descript sedan park near her. Outside Judge Bassit's office, Katharine stopped, smoothed her suit and straightened her hair. Taking a deep breath, she entered.

The attractive woman, smartly dressed in a conservative suit stood behind her desk and held out her hand. "You must be Katharine Levey. I'm Carol Boston, Judge Bassit's clerk." She was of medium height, slight build, with short frosted hair. Her face was smooth and ageless, but her pale eyes showed a wealth of knowledge, and her manner and soft voice spoke with confidence.

"Thank you for arranging this meeting on short notice," Katharine said.

"The FBI has an appointment later, but a few minutes were open before they are due." Her eyes twinkled.

Katharine's brow rose. "How can I thank you?" she asked.

"It's not necessary. The judge will see you," she said motioning toward another door.

Carol knocked. "Your Honor, Katharine Levey to see you. She needs a few minutes of your time." Carol turned and left, closing the door behind her.

Judge Bassit turned in his chair and stood. He was medium height with a neatly trimmed mustache and beard. His black hair had fringes of gray, but his eyes were still intense, giving him a severe appearance. Katharine's hand disappeared in his firm grip as they shook.

"A pleasure to meet you," he said. "I knew your father before he left the practice. I was sorry to hear of his passing, but I understand you have done well. Please sit." His voice was deep and melodious, able to get attention and take control of his courtroom, like the gavel on his bench.

Katharine looked around the neat office, dominated by the large mahogany desk with several files stacked on top. There were leather chairs, with diplomas and pictures on the paneled walls. She met his gaze. "Your Honor, I am here about the warrant you signed for the Bureau of Alcohol, Tobacco, Firearms, and Explosives to search for illegal weapons at Kihhim."

"I thought so," he said. "That was a nice bit of maneuvering you used to restrict it. Judge Emerson called me about it. He spoke most highly of you. What can I do for you?" he asked, cutting straight to the chase.

"We believe the FBI will ask you to expand the search and negate the court order. As I am sure Judge Emerson explained, we operate several research laboratories. These laboratories are sterile. In addition, we use greenhouses to grow our own food, also controlled environment."

"You allowed the agents in to search?" asked the judge.

"Yes, your Honor. They searched and found no illegal firearms. We expect they will ask you to allow them to tear up the floors and excavate as an expansion of the search. This would destroy all of our work and our food supply."

"They found nothing? I signed the warrant based on a tip that illegal machineguns were there. This statement was made under oath to the sheriff's department."

"Your Honor, they will not find any evidence of illegal weapons, nor any move for sedition or secession. There is neither." Katharine could not reveal their knowledge of Bill Broaderick's statement. "Also, your Honor, we believe wiretaps have been installed, and they are attempting to restrict our ability to communicate."

The judge stared hard at her and his eyebrows rose. "Why do you suspect this? Well, never mind, let's discuss this with them. They are outside now for a meeting." He pushed a button on the desk. "Carol, please ask the federal agents to come in." A minute later the door opened and two men wearing dark suits entered. One was Robert McWilliams. He started in surprise at seeing her and then glared. The other agent was introduced as Ted Stevenson. He was average–height, weight, hair, a tapioca human being.

Judge Bassit gestured at the chairs. "Ms. Levey feels you will try to petition the court to negate the court order restricting the search of Kihhim. She also feels you are now, or are planning to interfere with their communications and freedom of movement," Judge Bassit said without preamble. "I am not aware of any order allowing that."

"Your Honor, the restrictions placed on us are preventing a thorough search. In addition, they are trying to garner public support through the media, and that is interfering with our investigation," answered Stevenson.

"How much of the property has been searched?" asked the judge.

McWilliams spoke. "Three fourths of the area, but the greenhouses are only partially complete due to the restrictions."

"Have you found any evidence of illegal weapons or of activity to support this?"

"No, your Honor."

"Could you have received a bad tip?"

"It is always possible, your Honor, but we must be allowed to thoroughly investigate."

"Would you be willing to make yourself and the bureau liable for damages if you do not find any illegal weapons?"

"Your Honor, I don't think we can put this on that level!"

"I take that as a no. Kihhim appears to have cooperated in this search but tried to protect the integrity of their property, minimize any damage, and not impede the search. Would you agree?" he asked, looking at McWilliams.

"They have not impeded our investigation."

"Would you know anything about troubles with their communications?"

"Your Honor, we've experienced unusual sunspot activity," Stevenson said, looking at McWilliams.

"I have seen no request for a wiretap nor restriction of communication. Finish your investigation. If you don't find illegal weapons, get out. Consider this a warning that the liability issue was not rhetorical. Any questions?" All three shook their heads, thanked the judge for his time, stood, and headed for the door. None of them said anything until they were waiting for the elevator.

"You think this is over?" Stevenson asked her.

Katharine said nothing. When the elevator door opened, they went separate ways. As she got into her car, she noticed the sedan and two passengers waiting.

***

On Sunday, agent McWilliams pulled his team out. The demonstrators had left a day earlier, having made their point. Dayton and his cameraman left in the afternoon taking the tapes with them. The station rescheduled the special report on Kihhim for later in the week.

Chapter Eighteen

Dayton called Carol on Wednesday. "I've been going through everything, editing it and putting together another documentary including the search by the FBI. The station is sure it will be picked up by the network for national broadcast I could use help finishing it," he said.

Carol's heart jumped. She missed him terribly, afraid to call him. That pain was something she didn't want again.

"Why don't you come into Tucson for dinner? My treat. You fed me for almost a week."

"Okay," she barely was able to squeak out. Her heart pounded. "What time?"

"Meet me at the station at six-thirty."

"Okay, I'll be there."

***

Carol turned in front of the mirror, her own worst critic. Agonizing over what to wear, she decided on a short black skirt and white tank top that showed her figure nicely. Nobody but Yankees and Easterners dressed up in the summer in Tucson, they didn't know any better. Waving to Rico, she drove out. Once on the blacktop, doubts rode the white lines of the highway into her mind.

She could not leave Kihhim and go back into the city. As before, his career was the most important thing to him. He could live at Kihhim and commute but would he? She was so deeply in thought she hadn't realized she was in the parking lot until Dayton knocked on the window. It startled her.

"Hey!" Dayton said as he slid into her car. "Boy is it still hot! Of course the humidity doesn't help."

"It looked like rain for a while this afternoon, but the clouds stuck to the mountains," Carol replied, keeping to light chitchat.

"Our esteemed weatherman believes we will get a pounding later. The radar showed a large cell to the southeast that might hit Tucson this evening."

"Where to for dinner? This is your turf."

Dayton looked at her. She was dressed well, but casually. Like many newscasters, Dayton's formal wear was only from the waist up. His jeans would not fit in some of the places he wanted to take her.

"I could change into something less casual at home and we could go to St. Phillips Plaza. There's a jazz group on the patio this evening."

"Let's save that. How about Club 21? I haven't been there in quite a while and I'm in the mood for Mexican." The last time Carol had been to Club 21 was with Dayton before the breakup. It seemed appropriate.

"Great suggestion!" he exclaimed. "Afterward we can come back here for your car."

"My car is already cooled down, but I'm having margaritas, so you may have to drive," she laughed.

As they got out of the car at the restaurant, Dayton pointed to the black sky beyond the top of the Santa Rita Mountains. They watched for a few moments then walked through the archway to the entrance. The hostess quickly seated them at a small table near the window.

Their server arrived with water, chips, and the salsas (mild and hot). He took their drink order and left. Dayton immediately scooped the hot salsa with a chip. Carol dipped from the mild. After the second scoop Dayton reached for the water glass with a look of surprise on his face and beads of sweat on his brow.

"I don't remember it being that hot!" he said between gulps.

Carol laughed and thought how good she felt. The server set the frosty goldfish bowls of margaritas on the table. Hers was a golden mango margarita, his was traditional lime. The waiter stood, pencil poised. Dayton ordered the Enchiladas de la Casa and Carol ordered the Chicken Chimichanga. He left. Dayton held his margarita toward her for a toast.

"To you and Kihhim. I hope to be with both of you much more," he toasted, smiling. Carol was taken aback at his words. She glanced down at her glass and used both hands to pick it up. As they touched glasses, his eyes stared deeply into hers.

The frosty cool liquid was welcome as it floated on her tongue and slid down, chilling her throat. It tasted like heaven. They both spoke at once and then laughed. "Go ahead, you first," Dayton said.

"This place brings back a lot of memories, most of them nice," she said glancing at him, then out the window. A burst of laughter came from the family at a nearby table.

"It's really is nice to see you again," said Dayton. He started to say something else as the waiter appeared with more chips and mild salsa. "I have missed you," he said, "more than I thought I would."

These were exactly the words Carol wanted to hear, but now she hesitated. A look of puzzlement crossed Dayton's face. Thankfully, dinner arrived and thoughts of conversation were swallowed along with the food.

Carol stared at her almost empty plate. "I've missed that," she said. "The food at Kihhim is good, but that was great!"

Dayton looked at her as he used a chip to twirl a cheese string around his fork. "You said it!" as he stuffed the last bite into his mouth.

Suddenly, there was a tremendous flash followed by thunder shaking the windows. They both jumped. Someone at the next table knocked over a glass with a crash. The lights flickered then steadied. They looked out the window where leaves and paper were flying around the courtyard in a dervish as the wind started to howl. "That was close!" they both said.

"We better get out of here, or we're going to be stuck until the storm is over," Dayton said. He rose and put five dollars on the table. After paying at the cash register, they went into the entryway. The outside door rattled as the wind struggled to get in. Both of them pushed to open the door. Dust, dirt, and swirling leaves pelted them as they squinted and shielded their eyes while sprinting for the car.

Another simultaneous flash and crash sounded as they got in. The noise level dropped, but outside was a maelstrom. As Carol fumbled the key into the ignition, the first big fat drops splattered on the windshield.

She backed out and pulled into the street to the staccato pounding of rain that soon rose to a steady roar. The wipers first smeared the dirt across the windshield, but within seconds, it washed clear. In her headlights, the rain fell in heavy streaks, exploding on the street like clear meteorites from space. They were driving away from the tempest, and visibility improved as they outran the worst of it.

"Do you really want to drive back tonight?" Dayton asked as they pulled into the almost empty parking lot of the station. "Why don't you wait it out at my place?"

She didn't want to go back tonight and had told Leticia not to expect her.

Dayton smiled. "Come on. Pull over here, and I'll drive. You can bring me back in the morning." Their eyes locked. The pounding in her head was louder than the thudding of raindrops on the car. It quickly became a roar. The tempest caught them.

The twin beams of Carol's headlights dissected the downpour into a glittering curtain that seemed to move toward her. She drew back. Was it fear, she asked herself. Yes, but she could handle it. "It's okay, I can drive." Dayton looked at her. "Really!" she said.

As she pulled out of the station parking lot, she focused her total attention on the rapidly filling streets. In Tucson, the streets were the storm-water drainage. During the monsoon season, the rain came so hard and heavy that only a massive storm system could handle it. That did not happen often, never often enough for desert natives, so it was not a priority in the city's design. She crept through the river with the barely visible curbs her only guide.

A pickup passed them, immersing the car in muddy water. The wipers struggled against the tide, but it was as if they were submerged. She didn't panic, holding the wheel and herself steady as their submarine surfaced, and she could see past the windshield.

An eternity later she pulled under the carport in Dayton's driveway. Suddenly the car was quiet. Carol blew out the breath she did not know she was holding, and her tension left with it. They both got out and walked to the edge where the rain was still a curtain. Gusts tried to reach them with wet fingers, and they stepped back. Even diminished, it was still intense, and they would get soaked. They looked at each other; Dayton's expression was that of a kid about to take on a dare. "On three," he said. "One, two, three!" Carol watched him dash toward the front door, fumbling for his keys, fumbling at the lock. When the door finally opened, he turned toward her, soaked.

Carol put her purse over her head, dashed out and past him into the house, laughing at the surprised expression on his face. They looked at each other, then at the widening puddles of water on the tile.

It seemed so wonderful. The windows of the dark house flashed and a few seconds later the house shook. Dayton closed the door against the storm outside. They moved together as another tempest started, holding each other for several minutes, not saying anything. The lull gave way to growing anticipation. Dayton's breath was on her neck, and the awareness of their bodies pressed together ignited warmth that grew, spreading throughout her body. His hands caressed her back, and goose bumps formed. God, she wanted him! Hungrily, she pulled his lips to hers, craving the flavor of him.

A shiver traveled to her feet, and she hugged him tighter, feeling like she was melting into him. Her tongue brushed his lips, and his mouth opened, inviting her in. She tasted him. He groaned. Her hands caressed the nape of his neck, moved down his back, around to his chest, and she unbuttoned his shirt.

Carol's tongue explored his mouth. "You have changed!" he said.

"I guess now I am more aware of what I want and less afraid to go for it," she said looking into his eyes. They fell together on the bed and into each other's arms. Their lovemaking seemed to go on forever.

There was a flash. Carol wondered if it was the storm outside or the one inside her. A golden bubble, floating independently of the world, surrounded them, blocking out the turmoil outside.

PART 2

BIRTH AND EXODUS

Genetically Modified Pigs to be Bred for Organ
Transplant Harvesting
Monday, January 26, 2009 by: David Gutierrez,
staff writer Learn more:
http://www.naturalnews.com/025414.html#ixzz2E7a
k92KZ

Chapter Nineteen

After the disruption of the investigation wore off, John called a communitywide meeting. Attendees were physically present and on link. He looked at the small group sitting around the circular table, then at the waterfall cascading into the pool. Clearing his throat, he started.

"As you know, the publicity we received resulted in an interest in us. We do not have the ability to respond to all of the inquiries. I don't have the desire either. Requests will soon become demands–for information, for access, for oversight. We have a window of opportunity to decide our future before it is decided for us."

"Our quiet isolated life is at an end. Change has arrived. We were able to build this," he gestured around them, "because of individual effort, teamwork, and lack of intervention. That will no longer be possible. The Kihhim we know will not be the same–may not even exist." He sighed. This was the hardest speech he'd ever given.

"The question is, do we believe in Kihhim the place or Kihhim the ideal? If it is the place, we will stay and be absorbed into the outside world. Many of us came here to escape that." Heads nodded in agreement.

"If we go elsewhere, where do we go? I talked it over with Rich Lewis, and I'll let him tell about this exciting idea."

Rich stood, took a deep breath, and looked up, light gleaming on his balding head. An electronic engineer and a whiz at anything technical, he was responsible for most of the electronic innovations at Kihhim.

"When John came to me with the problem of where we'd build a new Kihhim, we quickly eliminated moving to another country. That would only delay the problem, not solve it. There's no way we could take land from somebody else, we're not strong enough–it's just not us. The root of the problem is the word land." He looked at his notes, obviously nervous.

"So I thought if not land, maybe the sea, offshore. The oceans are not owned by any country. As long as we stay in international waters, there can be no claims." Rich smiled broadly. "Offshore means floating, a ship. What kind of vessel could we use as our home? It would have to be large–among the largest vessels ever built–like aircraft carriers or supertankers. Not many old aircraft carriers for sale. They aren't the best structure for us, anyway. John and I started looking at supertankers."

Rich moved his glasses atop his head and pushed a button on a remote. A holographic image of a ship floated above the table. To give it scale, the Empire State building appeared horizontally next to the ship. The immense size was apparent.

"This oil tanker and one of her sister ships is on the block." The building disappeared. The super tanker image changed to wire-form, like a skeleton, making it possible to see inside.

"This is the ship as it would be sold today. It is huge, over three hundred yards long and more than half of the volume of Kihhim. We'd convert the oil storage tanks into the greenhouses and living quarters." He pushed another button, and partitions formed rooms filled with foliage. The image rotated, giving views from all sides.

"We would also convert the sister ship." A second ship appeared beside the first. "We would couple them together creating the new Kihhim."

A huge arch formed between the two ships joining them together forming a colossal catamaran. The arch was a structure of glass and steel, and as the view moved closer, tiny figures appeared inside amongst lush foliage. As the view pulled back, the ships were visible again with people as specks moving on the deck.

Rich looked up to see awed expressions on the faces around him. "We would use the ships boilers sparingly, building large semi-rigid sails to move us." Several masts arose from the decks. Vertical wing structures formed, like the wings of a Boeing 747. Rich's eyes glittered as he watched his creation spin in the air to stunned silence. The idea of Kihhim as a nation at sea was growing.

Chapter Twenty

John stood. "Where we go is only part of the problem. How we live there is another. Our independence is due to our ability to produce our own food and sustain ourselves. Jamie Wong and his companions achieved this by genetically altering plants to our environment, maximizing food production. He also has been looking at the challenges of this new habitat." John nodded to him.

Jamie Wong was a small plump man with Asian features, black hair, and an erect bearing. He was one of the best genetic engineers in the world. In tan slacks, white shirt and a tie, he was a rarity in today's world, dressing up rather than down.

Jamie stood and looked at his notes on the table and then directly into the monitor. Now a lecturer, he spoke as if beginning a class.

". As you know, some of the foremost genetic engineers in the world are at Kihhim. We worked extensively to make a success of the agricultural program, designing crops specifically for the environment in our greenhouses. We did not stop there." He clasped his hands behind his back.

"We've been working on fauna as well as flora. We have chickens, rabbits, and fish as our sources of animal protein. But we were not satisfied with just raising them as a part of our eco-system. We wanted a direct source.

"We are already able to grow organs by taking tissue from existing organs and cultivating them. We use viruses to imprint individual human DNA, thus making them unique to each individual person who receives them."

A holographic image of a vat appeared in the air above the table. Inside was a tubular mass suspended between two rods in a liquid. The mass contracted, pulling the rods together. It relaxed, allowing them to move apart. "Muscle tissue is formed to work. We can actually harness this as a source of energy. The conversion rate of nutrient to protein is about ninety percent, and it tastes better than chicken." Jamie chuckled, "It's more like veal." He took a deep breath.

"At Kihhim we maintain our immunity to diseases by exposure to illnesses we introduce. With our strong immune systems, we are almost never sick. Our bodies are trained to respond rapidly and fully to foreign intruders." He shuffled his notes.

"But more wonders lie ahead, and we are at the edge of a new era. We modify plants and ourselves to the environment of Kihhim. Someday, we will modify ourselves to meet other environments." Jamie looked at the faces around him.

"Man has always modified his environment to suit him. That is not always best for the environment. We feel it is time for a change in us. Creating a nation at sea offers many opportunities to adapt ourselves to our new home." That statement hung in the air. There was a murmur of voices.

Chapter Twenty-One

John looked at those around him. "Creating a new nation at sea is possible. We sought independence and isolation because we wanted freedom. Here at Kihhim, we will no longer be allowed isolation. When the extent of our knowledge and abilities becomes known, especially genetically altering animals and potentially ourselves, we will be both cheered and hated. We will be different from everybody else, evil to some." John paced a few steps.

"Some will view us as alien though we are as native to Earth as they. Others will see us as a threat, able to change ourselves to meet the necessities of survival. Though most of us will look perfectly normal, doubt will always be present, and we will be ostracized. The true scope of our abilities is not even a notion to those outside. Yet."

"John," said Katharine, "you're giving us a lot of gloom and doom. People have good sides."

"True, but people will see us as not natural, no longer belonging to God's children, no longer human. Fear will bring the scorn and prejudice of the world down on us."

Katharine interrupted. "John…"

He held up a hand to stop her objection. "Katharine, the problem is that if we guess wrong and stay, what we have will be destroyed."

"Well, it will certainly change," Katharine conceded.

"Even if we move to sea, it will take a year to acquire and outfit these ships well enough to live on. Construction and modification will continue after that. We must survive here until then. We are open to discussions and questions."

Sharon Steele's voice came over the speaker. "John, how are we going to pay for this?" As the accountant for Kihhim, hers was the cold voice of reality.

John gave a weak smile. "We need massive amounts of money. We'll seek buyers for our technology, specifically the greenhouse technology and the genetically-altered plants. These sales and our stock shares in other companies will account for three-fourths of what we will need."

"These sales will leave us almost broke," said Carol. "We'll have no assets and yet it's not enough. John, are you sure about this?"

"We'll have our greatest asset, our knowledge and abilities. And we'll have a place to live." There were murmurs, most of approval. "We may have to sell Kihhim to bring in enough to finish the project." There was a gasp from those listening. "We won't be here."

"Once we leave, there is no turning back, is there?" Carol said quietly.

"Our ties to the United States of America and, some will say, to mankind will be severed. We will be on our own," John responded, "and have to establish ourselves as a fully independent and sovereign nation."

"What about security?" asked Leticia. "How do we protect ourselves from the rest of the world when we're on our own?"

"That is a major concern. When the extent of our knowledge and abilities becomes known, there will be pressure to share, perhaps selectively. The potential for misuse would be huge. People may want to steal it, which would lead to attacks, both open and covert."

They looked at each other, stunned, as the full realization dawned. Questions flooded in lighting up the query board. The discussions went late into the night and dominated their lives for several days. After a week John called for a vote. It was not unanimous. When the time came to leave, there would be citizens staying behind, but not in Kihhim. It would be gone.

Chapter Twenty-Two

John Vance called Stephanie Kirchner. Stephanie and John had been much more than fast friends over forty years ago. They lived together as graduate students, but after graduation, each accepted a job at opposite sides of the country. Their romance did not stand up to the long distance and excitement of new careers. Stephanie worked for Engen Corporation, and John watched her career from afar as she steadily moved up.

When several quick mergers created a mega-corporation, Stephanie was catapulted into the lofty position of Director of Genetic Development. She pushed the development of enriched and disease resistant crops, and much of her efforts propelled Dow Engen-Michaels (DEM) into the largest international corporation in the food industry.

The DEM conglomerate was the powerhouse. It was nearly impossible to eat a meal in the United States not touched by DEM.

"John! It has been way too many years since we talked. Where are you? What are you doing?" Stephanie asked in a surprised voice.

John laughed at the rapid-fire questions. They chitchatted for a few minutes about old times and old friends. With a break in the conversation, John swallowed. "Steph, I have a business proposal for you."

There was a silence. "If it was anybody but you, I would pass them on to someone else. You dropped from sight when you left the Biosphere 2 project. I wondered what happened to you, usually over a glass of wine when I am dining by myself and feeling lonely. So, tell me your proposal."

John explained about Kihhim and the work they did. When he stated the crop yields, she was astounded. "If someone else told me that, I would write them off as a crank. From you, it must be something. You certainly have my attention."

"We are looking to sell the technology. Would you be interested?"

"Why wouldn't you develop it yourself? Never mind. Yes, I would like to see you and your proposal. You can tell me everything then. We are always open to new ideas." They talked a little longer, arranging for her to visit Kihhim.

When John hung up, he experienced the first sense of relief in weeks.

***

John met Stephanie's flight three weeks later. Long ago, she had been cute, but did not put effort into her appearance. Her whole attention was focused on her studies except for the nights with John. He was looking for someone plain and older when a stunning svelte woman in a smart business suit walked up to him.

She laughed, pleased at his surprised look. Her face was unlined and framed by dark golden hair–coifed and perfect. She was taller than he remembered, or he was shorter?

"Is it okay? I have had a little help," she said turning around for him.

"You look great!"

As John loaded the bags in the car, Stephanie said, "I was surprised to hear from you after so long. There are times I missed your calm demeanor in the hubbub of corporate America." John held the car door for her. "Always the gentleman," she said. "I haven't been in Arizona in a long time. The skies are still the bluest ever."

"I missed you, more than you know," said John quietly as he guided the car from the airport. "Kihhim has kept me very busy, but there are some moments when I wish things had gone differently. When you got the job offer from Engen, you were so excited you were off the planet. Are you still excited?"

"Of course not," she laughed. "One cannot stay that thrilled for as many years as I've been there, but I haven't found anything else I would rather be doing. How about you and Kihhim? After your call, I Googled it, but all the information was about the mess with the firearms a month ago. Did that come out all right?"

"As good as could be expected."

"We heard rumors you have a high-powered team producing genetically engineered innovations that could change the face of agriculture."

John's eyebrows rose. Someone had talked.

Stephanie continued, "I had no trouble getting the board interested in this visit. DEM is curious about anything that could affect us."

John smiled. Corporate America, he thought. "We made steps that DEM might find valuable. It is more than genetic engineering."

"So you need capital. Are you planning to expand?"

"In a manner of speaking. Rather than say anything more, I would like you to look at what we've developed, and if DEM is interested, consider an offer."

"That's what I'm here for, well, not completely. You have aroused my curiosity."

"I think you'll find your visit interesting, and I hope relaxing." During the drive from Tucson, John filled her in on the history of Kihhim. He felt good as they turned off the highway onto the dirt road and headed west. In the distance, the granite knob of Baboquivari Peak sparkled in the sunshine.

Stephanie silently watched the desert, enjoying a view that went on for miles in all directions. They rounded the last bend, and Rico waved them through the gate. On the drive toward the parking garage, she studied the glinting greenhouses.

"I'll send someone for your bags," John said, opening her door. As they entered the reception area, she looked around. A sunbeam lit the waterfall, and colored light danced across the room, misting the plant life in a rainbow.

"This is beautiful. An interesting array of plants here," she said, leaning close to inspect one. "This fern seems different. What is it?"

"It is one of our own. Are you tired? I can show you to your room to freshen up or for a rest."

"What I really need is something to eat. There was no breakfast on the redeye, and the soy nuts they served didn't do anything, even if they are one of our products."

"Let's go to the cafeteria. They always keep some things out." John held the door. The aroma of food was rich. One of the servers came over.

"Hi, John. What's up?"

"We missed breakfast, what do you have to tide us over until lunch?"

"Breakfast food or pre-lunch stuff, like soup and sandwiches?" asked the server.

John looked at Stephanie.

"What is the soup?" she asked.

"Green gazpacho. How about soup and a fish salad sandwich, or a salad?"

"Soup and sandwich sounds good," said Stephanie. At the coffee dispenser, she glanced around the room. "Is that a window?" she asked, pointing at the west wall.

"It is a real-time projection."

"It's good." The server brought two bowls to their table. Stephanie looked at the chilled green soup and then at John. He smiled and picked up his spoon and started to eat. Stephanie followed, not knowing what to expect. It was great! She tasted cucumber, bell pepper, grapes, and a hint of mint. It was cool and refreshing. "This is great soup! Can I get the recipe?"

"No problem," said John. "Do you still cook?"

"Purely for hobby. I'm always on the lookout for new recipes." When the server returned with the sandwiches, John introduced him to Stephanie. She complimented him on the soup and asked for the recipe. He nodded. "Buen provencha" he said as he left.

"It means bon appetite in Spanish," said John.

The sandwich was excellent as well. The fish was light and firm, with a delicious green chili sauce, and homemade bread. As they finished, John asked "More?"

"No. That will be just right until lunch. Okay, you have kept me away from this place long enough. Show me what you have." They rose and left the cafeteria. "How many people do you have here?" she asked as they walked down a corridor.

"Almost two hundred."

"And you feed them with the greenhouses I saw coming in?"

John nodded. He explained the change room procedure. They met again in the entry lock.

"Pretty elaborate procedures you have," Stephanie commented, looking good to John, even in the shapeless suit.

"You'll see why." He opened the entrance, and the heavy humidity seemed to submerge them. Stephanie inhaled sharply and blew out her breath in a gasp, eyes wide taking in the immensity of the greenhouse. She felt like she had entered an organized jungle! Everywhere were plants, tier after tier, row after row, so thick she couldn't see the end of the building. The light was bright, but not painful. There were no shadows, and plants grew in every direction.

"This is striking," she said, turning to John. She held a leaf in her fingers. "What species is this? It looks like lettuce, but I don't recognize the type."

"Another of our own species created specifically for this environment and maximum production. We call them geneered species. Most of these plants are that way. We created an environment, then geneered plants for it. As long as they are in here, they just produce."

"What is your per acre production?" Stephanie asked.

"More than ten times that of the best agriculture. It's done through a combination of isolation, volume growing and genetic engineering." As they walked through, Stephanie would study one plant or another then look at John with her mouth open. She let out a particularly loud exclamation when she looked closely at the support structure and growing vats of living bamboo.

After the other greenhouses, the sweat was rolling freely from her, and the shapeless white suit hung like a soggy sheet. Stephanie signaled she wanted to go somewhere cool and talk. After a shower, they returned to the cafeteria for lunch.

"Okay, I am impressed. You've made a leap forward in food production an order of magnitude better."

"It is more than genetically engineered plants. Here, the organism is Kihhim, not a group of people, plants, and animals thrown together. The plants here grow to produce food for us. We have taken on the reproduction requirements. The fruit they produce is not the plants making seeds in order to reproduce. It is designed to produce for us, as part of the organism Kihhim."

"That is a pretty radical change in thinking," said Stephanie, slowly.

"The vitamin, mineral, and nutrient content closely match what the human body needs. Just two or three of the products from the greenhouse could make up a complete diet. The variety is more for taste than necessity."

"This is bigger than I thought. It will take some real effort for the board to understand. We've had problems in the past getting acceptance of genetically altered foods by the marketplace, but we've broken that ground. It won't take nearly the effort as the first time. Still, this would have to be on a long-term basis before we would see return."

"Let me make the offer."

Chapter Twenty-Three

Stephanie watched John's face as he began the proposal. He was obviously passionate about Kihhim.

"We are offering the entire package. That includes the plants, environment design, and more importantly, years of study and test data, including human tests for FDA approval. To date, the health benefits outstrip those of foods grown any other way. DEM could be at market with this in two years."

She would need to proceed carefully. Her experience was that the glacial pace of government was half of the projections.

John leaned toward her. "This is better than organic quality. Some of our foods are specifically engineered to fight human diseases. As produce, this could make serious inroads into the drug market. This is an area DEM could not enter after the Securities and Exchange Commission ruled against your merger with that large pharmaceutical company—antitrust violations. This is the back door."

Stephanie raised an eyebrow. This could be huge. "You have done your homework. Okay, you've set the hook, what's the rest."

"Kihhim wants $750,000,000 for the package." Stephanie's mouth fell open. John hurried to explain.

"The estimated value of the geneered plants and environmental design is $275,000,000, the tests for FDA approval are worth $225,000,000."

Stephanie nodded. Optimistic but feasible, she thought.

"On your own, it would take three years to get approval from FDA. The first two years at market are worth $750,000,000. After that we project market growth at thirty-five percent per year for the first seven years. Here are the studies," he said handing her a drive.

She sat back stunned. She thrived on mega-projects, and this represented a quantum change in DEM's direction from support of the food industry to production. It was possible they would end up competing against themselves for the food market, a sure winner. Stephanie's mind whirled. "I would like time to go over this. Afterward we can talk more. And I need to speak with my board. When do you want an answer?"

"You are the first person I called. I would like to not call any others." At her room, he told her, "I'll be back in a few hours to pick you up for dinner. I can answer any questions then. Use the terminal here or your own. Call me with questions."

"The computer," John nodded toward the workstation, "is voice activated. Ask the phone for me any time." He looked at her for a few seconds. "Steph, thanks for coming." He closed the door as he backed out.

Stephanie was awed by it all. The rumors were true! DEM had to be the one to take this, even if only to squash it. No company would want to compete against it in the marketplace. And all the work was done! She inserted the drive and sat.

Chapter Twenty-Four

In John's room, he and Rich watched a hologram of a ship form above the work station. Barry Jackson the president of Maorimax Marine, the company they had settled on, took them on a virtual walkthrough, showing them the modifications.

Rich and Barry had toured the two ships a month before. Both agreed they could be satisfactorily modified. Kihhim bought them and the Maorimax engineers and work crews had flown up to take over. They had begun work on the voyage to New Zealand.

John and Rich approved the design offered by Barry. It was time for a milestone payment and the beginning of construction.

"Remember," said John, "secrecy is critical. It is the one thing that will cancel our contract. All of us are depending on you for that."

"No worries, mate," said the Kiwi. "We're going to move everything down to the South Island. We've a remote yard there, and as far as anyone here is concerned, we're building a pair of research vessels."

"That is exactly what you are doing," said John. "You see no problems in coupling the ships together at sea?"

"Nobody in the world has the port facilities to handle construction on two supertankers simultaneously. After we complete the modifications to the individual ships, we'll move them out into the harbor. Nothing like this has ever been done, so we want to be careful. It wouldn't do to muck it up. We can handle it."

"We'll be looking for your work schedule in the next week."

"It'll be posted to you." They rang off.

"Whew! It's such a relief to be moving on that," said John.

The image floating in the air slowly rotated. Tiny specs were moving through transparent walls and over the decks of the ships. It gave meaning to the term immense. They both stared at the creation they would call home.

"You know, as soon as DEM agrees to our conditions, there'll be rumors we've sold some new technology. If the FBI considers the genetic technology something that could be used for bio-weapons, they will be back with arrest warrants."

"You think DEM is going to buy?" asked Rich.

"There's not a doubt. DEM is big enough to fend off government harassment. They already have the licenses for research. Price is the only question. We'll both haggle and settle for what is fair. Our technology will change DEM from one of the largest international corporations into the economic power in the world. The wheels are in motion."

"So we're good to begin moving. We've been able to rent a warehouse in Puerto Peñasco," said Rich.

"Be sure to work with the lab staff. If we must run in the dead of night, the important stuff has to be gone."

Chapter Twenty-Five

John called Stephanie from his quarters. "Are you ready to talk?" he asked.

"I have questions."

A few minutes later, he knocked at her door.

"This is quite an offer," she said pointing at the screen. "Why not take this to market yourself? Why are you selling it?"

"DEM is already set up to market this, and we aren't. We would be at least a decade away while you would do it in a matter of two or three years."

"What about Kihhim itself? We want that as part of the package."

"Kihhim would make a good research platform. It could be included. As soon as you sign the purchase agreement, we'll arrange for you to bring in teams. All of our research and development, all the agricultural equipment and the labs go with us, but we'll train your people in every aspect. You'll own everything." So, all that is being sold are the plants and some training for 750 million?

"You're leaving?" Stephanie asked, brow furled.

"That's why we need the capital."

A puzzled expression appeared on her face. John offered no further explanation.

"I think I can get the board of directors to approve, but what's your timeframe?"

"How long to raise the capital?"

"It would go in the next budget." Stephanie shrugged. "Our fiscal year begins in January."

"That's not fast enough. How long before the rumors you heard become public knowledge?"

"Once we start the purchase, it won't matter."

John frowned. "It will matter a great deal to us. This has to remain completely confidential until it is complete. To do that, it has to happen fast. Everything must be finalized by June."

"That timeframe changes the picture. Let's work out milestone payment schedules. We'll send in teams as we submit applications to the FDA. The confidentiality is a problem. It's impossible to keep that many mouths closed."

"Bring your teams to Kihhim? We have control of communications."

"John, we cannot sequester these people for months. They do have outside lives. I don't understand your need for secrecy."

Not commenting, John handed her another disk. "Here is all you will need for the greenhouse construction bids. Included are the modified plants growing the internal structures. If you can meet the schedule, this package is yours. In addition, there's the application package for FDA. We'll provide consultants."

"I think I can get the approval from our Board of Directors within a week and a letter of intent within two weeks. An initial good faith payment would be due then."

"There is one other thing. All payments must be made to this company," he said handing her a slip of paper.

"Who is Maorimax Marine Ltd.?" John just looked at her. "So mysterious. Okay, I don't see any problems doing this," said Stephanie. "Let me get the ball rolling."

"Call when you're ready for dinner." John excused himself.

Chapter Twenty-Six

At Sharon Steele's apartment John asked, "What's our financial status? Short version."

Sharon turned to her computer and spoke quietly for a few minutes. She looked at John. "Kihhim has $200,000 in liquid assets, and stock in several companies worth an additional $5.5 million. The money can all be available in a few days."

John nodded. "Start buying stock in Maorimax Marine immediately. Use the Cayman companies we formed last year. Buy in small enough blocks it won't draw attention. We'll need controlling interest within two months. In a few days I'll give you the name of stainless steel and fiberglass suppliers and fabricators in New Zealand. Buy stock in them."

"I gather you want me to cover our tracks as well as possible?" she said.

"We need time. Everything we do will eventually be discovered. Any investigation must take at least a year. I'll pass this by Katharine."

"If this investigation is for insider trading, they will take their time, dot their i's and cross their t's. If this is for other reasons, it may move faster, depending on who's investigating and how quickly they want to pursue. I'm sure we can delay submissions, but our assets might be frozen during any investigation."

"Let's start asset transfers to the shell companies regularly. There can be no direct tie between Kihhim and Maorimax Marine. That name must not even be mentioned. Form other companies as needed."

"I'll give you a report in five days," said Sharon.

John's phone rang. "Let's go to dinner," Stephanie said.

Walking toward the dining hall she said, "I spoke to several members of the board. They believe we can do this, but we will need a full presentation to the whole board to get the votes for approval. How soon can you prepare one?"

"With your help, it will be ready tomorrow," said John.

"You have been preparing for this! It will take me a little while to get this on next week's agenda as a confidential addition. We can move fast when we must. John, I believe in this, because I never stopped believing in you. I want this to happen."

Unlike this afternoon, the dining hall was now crowded. At a table, he introduced Stephanie to Katharine, Leticia, and Don Brown. Katharine gave Stephanie an appraising look while Leticia watched Katharine. Stephanie appeared not to notice.

"John mentioned he knew someone high up at DEM, but failed to mention it was a she and attractive," said Don.

"Don, you are shameless!" said Leticia. They all laughed, and the ice broke. "Have you taken the tour?" asked Leticia.

"We visited the greenhouses this afternoon, but that's all I've seen," said Stephanie.

"What do you think about our technology?" asked Don.

"This is really exciting," said Stephanie. "It's the first time I've seen the merging of genetic development and environmental control to this degree. You basically turned vegetation and your environment into a food factory for maximum production. The nutritional technology is fantastic."

"I'll give you a tour of the rest of the facility tomorrow," said Katharine. John nodded. "I'll come get you for breakfast."

Stephanie smiled at John and then said to Katharine, "I'll call when I'm ready. Today has been a long day, starting at 2:00 am your time."

"Okay," Katharine said, getting up with her tray.

Leticia and Don stood also. "If you want to see more of the greenhouses, just let me know," said Don.

Leticia groaned, and Stephanie laughed. "For in-depth explanations, no doubt." John and Stephanie finished their meal in silence while the buzz of conservations hummed around them.

As they left, Stephanie commented, "The food here is superb, the flavors seem to come out. I must get recipes."

When they reached Stephanie's quarters, she was all work. "Let's get started on some background of the board members." She took out an annual report. John brought the presentation up on her workstation, and together they created a strategy for each of the specific members needed to support the project. The presentation would be done via secure videoconference, with Stephanie supporting him in the Chicago office boardroom.

Included would be a virtual tour of the greenhouses and the labs. John would answer questions and show them things upon request. They both felt prepared.

Several hours later John stood and stretched, his head fuzzy. "I'll go over this and call you tomorrow after your tour."

"Are you sure you're ready to go?" asked Stephanie, a husky tone in her voice. She reached around him to close the door. The press of their bodies was electric.

Chapter Twenty-Seven

Dr. Adriana Getzwiller stared at the wall in her office at the Center for Disease Control. Normally a neat person, her government-issued desk had several piles of unfinished work. The monitor glowed in front of her unseen. The search for information about Kihhim and any medical publications had turned up zilch. She found the licenses granted for biological and genetic studies. On the surface, it looked as if they maintained the license to do genetic work, but didn't do any. She knew better.

The images of what she had seen at Kihhim would not fade. For her, it was personal. Marie, her mother had a failing heart and was in the hospital, probably her last trip on earth. Far down on the heart transplant list, she would never survive until one was available. It seemed so unfair! Marie was a good woman–a very good woman.

Even though Marie was comfortable with the fact she was going to die soon, Adriana would not let go. Her mother had supported her through medical school after a terrorist bomb killed her father in Israel. Marie was all she had, her best friend. Adriana was not ready to be alone.

After the hospital visit this afternoon, she couldn't stop crying. With desperation and determination, she called Kihhim, asking for Dr. Ruben Sanchez.

"Sanchez here," was the curt reply.

"Dr. Sanchez, this is Dr. Adriana Getzwiller of the CDC."

"Oh yes, I remember. What can I do for you?" he asked guardedly.

"Doctor, I cannot get what I saw out of my mind. My mother is dying from a bad heart, and without a transplant, she has no hope. How does one get on the recipient list for your organs?" Might as well just cut to the chase and not bull shit around.

There was a long pause at the other end. "Dr. Getzwiller, there are a number of reasons we keep our work here a secret. This call is one example. Another is that this work is still experimental. If your mother were to receive one of our organs, questions would arise. We would lose the protective veil of secrecy we need."

"I will sign a waiver. I will promise not to say anything!" she practically shouted, sounding desperate, even to herself.

"Adriana, I am truly sorry."

"Look, I will make this easier for you," Adriana interrupted. "Your confidentiality agreement is binding, but I am willing to face the consequences of violating that. I want your help. I demand it!" she sobbed. There was a silence on the other end. Had she blown it?

At last, Dr. Sanchez's voice came back very softly. "I understand. Of course. Let me discuss this with others. Give me your home number. Please forward me your mother's medical records."

"You'll have them today," said Adriana, as a slight glimmer of hope appeared.

"I cannot promise anything, but give me a day. I will call you."

Adriana looked around her plain office. There were diplomas, awards, all the memorabilia of her career, but only one picture of her mother. She stared at it for a long time as the evening darkness surrounded her. She was alone in the quiet building.

***

As soon as he hung up, Ruben made a call. "John, we may have a problem."

"We'll be right over," said John, recognizing the urgency in Ruben's voice.

In a few minutes, Ruben explained the situation with Adriana Getzwiller and her demand. "If we refuse, she is willing to go to prison, or pay fines. Basically, she would ruin her career, so she is not thinking clearly," said John.

"She is willing to pay the consequences," said Katharine, "like a terrorist willing to die for his cause."

"Either we reveal what we have or supply the heart," said Ruben. "We would do the surgery here."

"That is how I see it, too," said John.

"The mother will have to stay to recuperate," said Katharine. "Perhaps we should offer to make her a resident. We would have Adriana's mother here, and Adriana says she will risk everything for her mother. Good insurance."

John stared at her. "Katharine, your mind never ceases to amaze me. Remind me not to get on your wrong side."

"I will call Adriana back after I check over the records. The main risk may be getting her mother here. We could operate next week if she is strong enough."

"Make sure Adriana understands her mother must stay here several months. She will become part of our study. Adriana cannot refuse under those conditions," said Katharine. "Tell her you are taping the conversation and make sure there is a statement about her not revealing confidential information in exchange for the operation."

Ruben called Adriana and explained the arrangement. She readily agreed, her voice laden with gratitude. Ruben began preparations.

Chapter Twenty-Eight

FBI Special Agent Robert McWilliams squirmed in his seat. When he returned to Washington from Tucson a month ago, he understood he would be walking out of this debriefing either fired or with five pounds less ass. He didn't think it would hurt this badly. Assistant Director Janet Kilgore's words still echoed in his head.

"In four days of intensive searching, you found nothing?" the derision dripping from each word. "Do you have any idea how much this whole fuck up cost? I'll tell you!" Her voice rose to a screech. "It cost us $500,000, but that is not the worst! This screw up cost us creditability. It cost us our image! It cost us prestige! Since you do have a few friends left, I cannot fire you, but I can make your life miserable." Her sharp features, framed by her short brown hair, twisted into a sneer. "Now, get out!"

Christ! What a mess! He had only inherited it. The BATFE rushed in with shaky information. There was something at Kihhim. That scared him. They were clever enough that four days of searching turned up nothing. If they were that smart, then the danger was even greater. He could not drop it.

Only by the grace of God was he still in Washington, but now with a lot of time on his hands. In a proper search, the floors would be excavated, the walls torn down, and everything in those greenhouses dug up. Computers would be confiscated and searched until they found something, and if they didn't find anything, they would keep going, until they did.

If those goddamn cameramen were not recording their every move, he would have made sure something was found. He demanded copies of the videos from Kihhim and viewed them looking for something. With all the investigators being followed, he had over eight hundred hours of videos, and for three days he looked until his vision blurred. All he saw were plants, tanks, and vats.

The search of the computer firearms files was equally frustrating. Everything was legal. Firearms were not the problem.

These people were not the usual separatist, but they shared similar attitudes. They did not conform. If they did not have firearms, what weapons could they have? Bombs? They didn't act like bombers either. The sniffers (both electronic and the dogs) did not detect any explosives. Vats and tanks! It was chemical or biological! That had to be it!

He pulled out the videos, and after several frustrating hours, found the disks of the greenhouse search. He fast-forwarded to the search of the nutrient preparation area. Chemicals. They had chemicals labeled nutrients. Maybe those were actually components for nerve gases. He called Dr. Brian Denton.

"Dr. Denton, this is FBI Special Agent Robert McWilliams. Do you remember me from our search at Kihhim?" He did not wait for the answer. "When you did the search of the greenhouses, did you look at the nutrient preparation area?"

"We looked at it carefully," said Brian. "They had the expected chemicals needed for fertilizers, but not in quantity. Recycled wastes are biologically broken down to make the nutrients they need. There were not enough nitrates to make much of a bomb if that's what you're asking."

"What about chemical weapons? Nerve agents?"

"The chemicals needed to manufacture those are toxic themselves. We did not find any toxic material. Nothing that could be used for nerve agents, and very little chlorine-based material. They did have the capability to make ozone and hydrogen peroxide to use for disinfectant. It breaks down into oxygen and water, you know. That could be used for explosives, but we never saw concentrations high enough for that."

"Okay, thanks," said McWilliams, the disappointment obvious in his voice. "If you think of anything, call me."

Okay, if not chemical, biological. He watched the disks of the lab search carefully. The camera was almost always directed at the agent, making the background difficult to see. With the viewer slowed, a vat came into view behind an agent. Dr. Adriana Getzwiller entered the picture and stared intently into the vat at objects being stirred around. She started, then turned, quickly walking toward the cameraman. Her mouth opened but she said nothing, while behind her, the agent shrugged, his search complete.

McWilliams watched carefully as the agent and Adriana cycled through the air lock. She moved toward the cameraman, then turned, walking out of the picture. The agent moved to another area. McWilliams stopped the video. Cameramen followed everybody. There had to be one of Adriana when she wasn't in this picture. The agent searched through the stack. Nothing. She went somewhere without her cameraman, or that video had not been turned over.

McWilliams called Dr. Getzwiller at the CDC. The phone rang several times before her answering machine picked up. He left a message for her to call and then called the CDC operator. "This is FBI Special Agent Robert McWilliams. Is Dr. Adriana Getzwiller in the office today?" he asked.

"I will connect you with her office," said the voice. A soft feminine voice with a distinct southern accent came on the line. "Dr. Getzwiller's office."

"This is FBI Special Agent Robert McWilliams. Is Dr. Getzwiller there?"

"She's checked out until tomorrow. I believe she is at the hospital visiting her mother. Is this an emergency? Do you want me to try to reach her?"

"Yes, please have her call me as soon as possible." McWilliams gave his direct number. He turned to the viewer, watching the sequence again.

This time, he ran the section before they entered the chamber, paying particular attention to the admonishment about confidentiality.

Adriana's phone started vibrating as she walked into her mother's room. The only sound in the darkened room was Marie's soft snoring. She ignored the phone. It had to be the office, and Shirley would leave her a message. She had to talk to her mother.

The lights from monitors cast wavering shadows on the wall. Marie looked so small and frail under the sheets. Adriana watched her mother's chest rise and fall. She did a lot of sleeping lately, having only enough energy to go to the toilet. Adriana tiptoed over to the bed and kissed her mother's forehead. Her mother's eyes fluttered open and moved over the room then settled on Adriana's face. She broke into a weak smile.

"Don't try to talk, Mom. Save your strength. I may have something that will help us, and you're going to need it for a trip."

"Addie, please. I don't want..."

Adriana put her finger to her mom's lips. "Shh. I'll be back when you're stronger. We'll talk then." Her mother's eyes closed. Not one of her better days. Being this weak, she would never be able to make the trip to Tucson, much less survive the surgery. Adriana left the room just as her phone vibrated again. This time she answered.

Chapter Twenty-Nine

In response to Shirley's message, Adriana called McWilliams from home.

"This is Dr. Getzwiller."

"Doctor, I have been reviewing the videos of the search of Kihhim labs. There is one incident that concerns me. In this search, you and the agent entered a chamber. There is a vat you examine closely. Do you remember?"

Adriana's heart stopped. What should she say? If they knew what she had seen, the whole thing would blow open. She would have no leverage over Kihhim. If she lied to cover it up, she could not say anything later.

She had to protect her mom, at least give her the chance to live. "There were several vats we looked at. Which one are you are referring to? Can you be more specific?"

"It was the one in a darkened chamber. After the search, you walked somewhere out of the camera view. In fact, there is no video of where you went, and those goddamn cameramen followed us everywhere, even into the bathrooms. Do you remember a time when no cameraman followed you?"

SHIT! The discussion with Dr. Sanchez! That conversation had been recorded. The video hadn't been turned over to the FBI. Think!

"There was a short time when the cameraman changed disks and didn't catch up as I stepped outside. Could that be it?" She struggled to keep her voice from shaking.

"That doesn't sound like enough time, but I'll review the disks. Do you remember what you saw in the vats?"

"Several contained plant organic material. Plant material for the greenhouses was being processed. I'm not sure about the process, but the setup was for growth from genetically engineered zygotes." Lies had to be kept simple and to a minimum. "I don't remember anything other than that."

"Please think about it. I will call you back in two hours."

With shaking fingers, she dialed Kihhim. "Dr. Sanchez, this is Dr. Adriana Getzwiller. The FBI just called me. The agent asked about the search of the lab and the organ area. He has been looking at the videos and noticed there's a section of video missing. It's time we spoke in your office." The words came out in a rush.

"Calm down, Adriana. What did you tell him?"

"I said I remembered nothing other than plant materials in the lab."

"What about the video?"

"I tried to cover saying there was a short period when the cameraman had to change disks and didn't catch up. I don't think he believes that would account for the lapse." She heard the alarm in her own voice.

"It's okay, Adriana. We'll take care of it. Just say you went into the hall for a break."

"I will, I will." She took a breath.

"I saw Mom today. She's very weak. I'm not sure she will be able to make the trip, much less survive the surgery."

"Let me review the files. Do not call here again. I will call you. What is your private cell number?" She gave it to him. "Do not worry, Adriana. This will come out all right. Thank you very much." They hung up. Tears spilled from her eyes.

"Our bargain with Dr. Getzwiller seems like a good one," John told Ruben. "If she can stick to the story, she should be fine. Let's send Jamie to get her mother and keep our contact to a minimum. He was not here during the search, and he's not as well known as you. Where is he?"

"He is attending a conference in New York, but he can be in Atlanta tomorrow," said Ruben.

"Let me know if there're any problems."

Ruben called Jamie Wong, the genetic engineering genius behind the actual designs. Dr. Ruben Sanchez applied them medically. Dr. Don Brown applied them agriculturally. Ruben was leaving a message when Jamie answered. "I was having dinner with friends."

Ruben explained the situation. Jamie called Adriana to introduce himself. He explained he would arrive in Atlanta to visit her mother tomorrow in the hospital.

"If she can be moved, I will need your help with the clearance. I'll arrange to get her to Kihhim, but you need to stay in Atlanta. Things must appear normal."

"I need to be with my mother," she insisted.

"Any interference by the FBI will destroy her chances," said Jamie. "Meet me at ten o'clock tomorrow morning at the hospital."

Adriana called her mother's doctor to inform him Marie would be leaving the hospital tomorrow. The doctor was extremely unhappy with her decision to override his advice. Only after her dogged insistence and credibility as a physician was she able to obtain his consent. Her fabricated story of having Mom home for a family reunion was weak, but she insisted. Without a doctor present, he would never have agreed.

Chapter Thirty

Carol looked out over the sparkling waters of the Sea of Cortez from the shaded deck at Fabio's Restaurant. The warm air caressed her face, as she watched the pelicans in their vee formation, wingtips skimming the low swells. It was one of those early spring afternoons, with a steady soft breeze interrupted by gusts dappling the smooth blue surface of the bay. She had to return to Kihhim soon, but for now, the peace of the sea, mild temperatures, and shush of the gentle surf was relaxing. Forgetting about the rest of the world was easy here. She closed her eyes.

Carol, with her soft but persistent demeanor, worked with the Mexicans to gain the warehouses and the help they would need loading and boarding the ship. Leticia supervised disassembly of the labs at Kihhim. Things were hectic for a while, but once she got to know the right people, it went smoothly. The slower pace of life in Mexico was contagious. She adjusted to it.

The first ship refitted by Maorimax Marine was scheduled to arrive in Puerto Peñasco in June. Rich was leaving for Auckland to oversee the special outfitting. Nothing like this had ever been built before and the stainless steel and fiberglass construction overran the estimate. Their lives depended on the construction, so it had to be right.

The ship would cause quite a stir as it would be the largest ever to visit Puerto Peñasco. One concern was the port itself. The tidal changes in the Gulf of California reached over twenty feet, second only to the Bay of Fundy. Special knowledge and care were required to navigate the Sea of Cortez.

If only Dayton could visit for the weekend she wished, but nobody could know they were leaving. With closed eyes, she fantasized about them both sitting here. The waiter interrupted her thoughts.

"Señorita Carol, something more? A margarita?"

The neatly dressed young Mexican waited expectantly. She shook her head. They knew her here as she frequented the small restaurant. Time to get started back to the United States.

Carol paid the bill and walked down the stairs climbed into her car. Three hours later she waved at Rico, and parked the car in the garage. As she got out, she noticed the ambulance. Entering, she nodded at EMTs as they were leaving, their gurney empty.

Carol called Marcus Washington, the head of the medical facilities, but he was checking in a patient and would call her back. An outside patient, she thought. How unusual. She called John to bring him up to date on the Mexican end of the move.

"Everything's done." Carol said. "We can accelerate moving the equipment any time."

"Some of the labs won't be able to shut down until the last week," he informed her.

"Changing the subject, I saw the ambulance. Who is the celeb?"

"We had to cut a deal with Adriana Getzwiller, the CDC consultant the FBI used during their search. Her mother needs a new heart, and she remembered and understood what she saw here. In return, she'll keep quiet and inform us of any developments."

"Have there been any?"

"Not yet, but Special Agent McWilliams does not seem satisfied and is still smarting from the failure to find anything. We can only hope he gets a new interest before we become his mission in life. I got the impression he could be worse than a jilted ex-wife with a war chest of settlement money."

"His boss probably has a huge chunk of his buttocks in his office," chuckled Carol. "How about the technology transfer to DEM?"

"There's a team here now. Kihhim must be sucked dry of information within the next sixty days, because DEM is scheduled to start construction in thirty," said John.

"Anything else happened?" asked Carol.

"I've contacted people who want to buy Kihhim if DEM doesn't. Their offer was much too low. I'll send them a counteroffer next week. We can keep the negotiations going until we've moved out, but I hope DEM wants it. Things would be much easier that way."

"I gather Environmental Sanity has been quiet," said Carol.

"Nothing. A huge number of requests for visits flooded in since Dayton's special was broadcast. So far, those have been delayed, but the pressure is mounting. By the way, Dayton has called several times. I don't think he believes you're still in the shower."

Carol heard the smile in his voice. "I'll give him a call."

"Things are quiet here for now. Take a couple of days off."

"I might do that." She hung up and sat quietly. Maybe she and Dayton could go to the White Mountains for the weekend. She called him at work. He sounded genuinely glad to hear from her. They agreed to meet for a late dinner.

Chapter Thirty-One

Carol was torn having not told Dayton anything about the move. She couldn't ask him to come with her. He had his career and life, and it was not at Kihhim. Nor could she stay here. Carol remembered none of the trip to Tucson, but here she was, in Dayton's driveway.

She found this renewed relationship much easier. Now, she felt a twinge of sweet sadness as she rang the doorbell. Musical chimes played, and in seconds, the door opened. He was barefoot, wearing shorts and a Polo shirt. She saw his face light up. Another twinge.

Dayton stepped back sweeping his hand. "Please come in."

Carol smiled, stepping over the threshold. The tide of rising emotions within her were not all light.

He seemed puzzled by her coolness. "Something to drink?"

Carol's mind started moving again. "Wine, please." She followed him to the kitchen. "What are the cruise plans?"

"I made dinner reservations if you want to go out, and I have fixings here if you want to stay in." He peered at her. "In or out?" "In?" Carol nodded. "I'll start dinner." He filled every bit of counter space with a variety of utensils and food.

"What's for dinner?" she asked.

"Marinated tuna steaks. The rice pilaf will only take about fifteen minutes. There is tubule chilled, a nice Pinot Gris in the bucket there, and a special dessert surprise," he said with a twinkle.

Dessert surprise! I bet, she thought and laughed. Her spirits lifted. Dayton watched her face, laughing with her. "What can I do?" she asked, noticing the table was set nicely, even with candles.

"Just sit for a minute." Dayton headed out the back door for the barbecue grill. He returned a minute later. From the refrigerator he got the wine, opened it and poured a glass for her. He set the tubule salad and a basket of fresh bread with olive oil on the table. Picking up his wineglass, he held it out toward her. "To us."

The clear ring from the glasses hung in the air threatening to shatter her composure. She looked into his eyes. It would be so easy to fall in there, she thought. The dream of years past, a life with Dayton rose within her.

Yanking her glance away, she forced that vision down. Smiling, she took a sip of wine. It was good! She focused on the flavor to change her train of thought. "Nice wine."

"I was saving it for a special occasion. So let's make this special." Dayton got up and took the platter of tuna steaks from the refrigerator. "Dinner in twelve minutes," he said, heading out to the grill. "Check the rice, would you?"

Carol lifted the steamer lid and forked a few grains out. An image of her grabbing Dayton and dragging him to the bedroom formed. She hurriedly pushed it away.

The rice was perfect. She finished spooning it into a bowl as Dayton came in with the platter of steaming tuna. He placed a steak on her plate. "It smells heavenly."

Dayton lit the candles and turned off the lights. The ambiance was perfect–the table, the wine, the food, everything. She forced the squirming worm of guilt down. Dinner became a flood of sensations, with little conversation.

"You seem distant tonight. Want anything more? Tuna, salad?"

She made a decision. "How about the special dessert?" she asked.

As Dayton came to her side to pick up her plate, she tenderly put her hand behind his neck, pulling his lips to hers. He responded immediately, and without breaking the kiss, set the plate down. His arms moved around her, he knelt enfolding her into his embrace.

The comfort of his closeness enveloped her. She had to make this good–one to remember–for it might have to last her a long time. The warm glow of passion began inside her, building into a hot fiery desire.

She wanted him close, to feel him burn with fire for her. Her lips started moving over his face, lightly on his eyes, almost probing around his ears, slowly down his neck. Dayton trembled. As she opened his shirt and her lips moved over his chest, his heart sped up.

Carol stood, backed away and pulled him up and toward the bedroom.

Afterward, as she lay beside Dayton in the dark listening to his soft snore, tears rolled down her cheeks.

Chapter Thirty-Two

Dr. Brian Denton sat at his old metal desk picking at the chipped paint and fuming. A friend of his at DEM called to fill him in on the latest. Years ago Brian had worked at DEM where he'd been on the fast track, until Stephanie Kirchner fired him. The report stated "falsifying report results," but in reality, it was because he tried to get her job. She caught him undermining her position and building up the results of his project. No offer was made . Just bang! Out the door!

Because of her reference, or lack thereof, he had not been able to get work in the chemical industry again, finally settling for a position with the Department of Agriculture.

Now, through her, DEM was about to make a huge step in food production. Brian was one of the few people who understood. He was even more cautious about the confidentiality agreement since things would be in the hands of Stephanie Fucking Kirchner.

As he fumed, a thought struck him. There might be another way. He punched in McWilliams' number, composing what he would say. The phone rang three times, and the answering machine came on. This is FBI Agent Robert McWilliams. Please leave your message at the tone. The beep sounded.

"This is Dr. Brian Denton. I need to talk to you about Kihhim." Suddenly he heard a breathless voice.

"This is Special Agent McWilliams. I stepped away, but heard your message."

"This is Dr. Brian Denton," Brian repeated. "I've been thinking about Kihhim and what I saw there. We didn't find any chemicals, but they certainly have the potential to make other agents. A number of plants that produce toxins are cultivated there."

"What do you mean?" asked McWilliams.

"They have genetically modified plants, mushrooms, and toadstools. Some may be capable of producing highly toxic substances. Also, and this is much more serious, there is no way of knowing what would happen if the genetically modified plants were released into the outside world."

"Go on," said McWilliams.

"Genetic research is overseen carefully so that our environment is protected from creations made in the lab. Though they seemed cautious, there is no official oversight. They have elaborate procedures, but nobody is watching. I find that troubling."

"You mean something like Jurassic Park could happen?" asked McWilliams.

"This could be worse. They're not on an island, and things could spread before anybody knows. Then it would be too late. A release might not be an accident."

"Who do you know able to assess the potential danger here?" asked McWilliams.

"That doctor from CDC should be able to help you."

"Thank you for your call, Dr. Denton. I will get back to you on this." McWilliams hung up and stared at the phone. Why had Getzwiller said nothing? Had she not recognized the potential danger? Of course, she'd been in the labs and may not have seen any plants. He dialed her number.

"This is Dr. Getzwiller."

"Doctor, this is Special Agent McWilliams."

"Yes," her voice sounded cautious. "What can I do for you, Agent McWilliams?"

"During your search of Kihhim labs, did you observe any potential danger that their genetic research presented?"

"Agent McWilliams, they do genetic engineering work, but had numerous safeguards to prevent any problems. That was the reason the search was so restricted. Safety procedures had to be followed."

"I was told it was to prevent destruction of laboratory work and greenhouse property. There was no mention of danger."

"Okay, safety was one of the reasons," Adriana amended.

"Did you see anything that would represent a threat, if released?"

"I did not, though that is always a concern with any work of that type."

"Could anything potentially become a threat?"

"I saw nothing dangerous there, only the ability, but there are hundreds of labs with that capability," said Adriana carefully.

"Don't you oversee those labs?" asked McWilliams.

"We monitor most of those labs, because they are doing work with various levels of government involvement. It has become one of the tasks for the CDC in the last few years, under the Expanded Domestic Terrorism Act. Monitoring of independent labs is difficult, as there are no requirements for reporting, So far, no one has chosen to test a requirement in the courts. With government contracts or grants, reporting is required. When the government has some type of contract with a lab, we can monitor them."

"There are no contracts with Kihhim?" asked McWilliams.

"I've checked all the records. They never accepted a government contract or grant. Not even as a subcontractor. Why this interest in an arms investigation?" she asked."

"It may be more than that. Perhaps Kihhim is our test of the EDTA," said McWilliams. "I may need you to give testimony. I'm going to send you the tapes of the lab search. Would you review them? If something doesn't look right, call me." It wasn't a request.

"You are welcome," said Adriana to a dead phone.

Chapter Thirty-Three

Special Agent Robert McWilliams scribbled notes from his conversations with Drs. Denton, and Getzwiller. Standing in front of his supervisor's office, he hesitated, then knocked. Assistant Director Janet Kilgore looked up from her overloaded desk.

"Do you have a minute?" he asked. When she nodded, he stepped in. "Something has come up on Kihhim." An annoyed look flashed across her face.

He knew she'd taken a lot of heat from that busted search. "I thought we put that issue to rest. Are you still working on this?"

Robert McWilliams swallowed. "I received a call from one of our technical advisors at the site. Dr. Denton has reservations about the benign nature of the biological work being done." Janet Kilgore's thin eyebrows arched upward.

He plunged ahead, summarizing the conversations. "Kihhim is a community that has isolated itself and has the capability of making biological weapons–weapons of mass destruction. There is no oversight of their labs or of this group of people. If they felt threatened or provoked, they could mount a disastrous attack potentially killing thousands."

Assistant Director Janet Kilgore sat back in her chair and steepled her fingers. Something might salvaged from this after all. "What do you want to do?"

"When we searched Kihhim, we were looking for illegal firearms and explosives. There weren't any. It could be much worse," said McWilliams. "There are lots of potential threats, and the key word here is 'potential.' The Bureau can't go after everybody with the ability to manufacturing a threat, but we need oversight." Kilgore nodded.

"Kihhim has separated itself from most of society, with their own schools, hospital, teachers, and scientists. Operating under a barter system, they avoid taxes."

Kilgore frowned.

"The real problem with these people is the magnitude of the threat they represent. As an unmonitored biological and genetic research facility, Kihhim may have already violated UN sanctions. They are capable of manufacturing weapons of mass destruction. That is why we have to do something."

"You want us to use the Expanded Domestic Terrorism Act to do what?" asked Janet carefully.

"We must place monitors on their activities to have oversight. Or we need to eliminate the labs," confirmed McWilliams.

"Okay, I understand why you want to do something with this group, but I am not sure what we can do." She reached for the phone and dialed. Turning her chair away from McWilliams, she spoke quietly for a few minutes, and then turned back around as she hung up. "Grab your files and let's go over to Justice. This may be the test case we've been looking for."

She rose, signaling the discussion was over. He returned to his office, grabbed the thick file, and met her in the hall. Together they went to the Department of Justice.

Chapter Thirty-Four

With shaking hands, Adriana dialed Kihhim and was connected to Ruben.

"I know you said not to call, but something happened," she said with no hesitation.

"Hi, Adriana. It's okay, I was about to call. Your mother is fine. She made the trip without a hitch and is a little stronger. The surgery is scheduled for next week after we imprint the donor heart with your mother's DNA codes. We do not foresee any problems."

Adriana laughed at the good news, the darker purpose of the call momentarily forgotten. "You made my day."

She paused, "I got another call from the FBI. McWilliams is asking pointed questions about possible bio hazard and bio terrorism. The FBI may be considering another investigation."

There was a silence on the other end. "What exactly did they ask?"

She related the conversation.

"Thank you, Adriana. I will pass this along. You must be careful about calling in the future. If we act in any way that shows foreknowledge, they will look for a leak. Phone records are easy to track. Something will be worked out so you can stay in touch with your mother."

Adriana worried if Kihhim came under investigation again. What would it mean for her mother? By being more involved with the investigation, she would know more, maybe even be able to help. If McWilliams didn't call her in the next week, she'd think up a pretense to call him.

***

John met Katharine, Leticia, and Carol in his apartment. He quickly related Ruben's conversation with Adriana. Katharine sighed. "The Justice Department has been trying to find a test case for the Expanded Domestic Terrorism Act. We may be that case. The government needs a high profile case to rebuild support."

"What does this mean to us?" asked Carol, worry in her voice.

"Under this Act, potential for terrorism, having the ability to produce terrorist weapons or acts and having antigovernment sentiments is enough for arrest and prosecution." Katharine grimaced. "To prove their case, they must show the ability to produce bombs or devices for mass destruction. They must also show the probability that antigovernment sentiments will lead to planning and carrying out these acts."

Katharine frowned. "From what Adriana said, they will try to prove we have the ability to make biological weapons. The bio war we just went through will make this pretty easy in the public eye." There were glum faces around the table.

"They must then show we harbor separatist sentiments–feelings strong enough to raise the possibility we will use weapons. That will be the hard part for them. They must show our isolationist feelings are separatist and antigovernment, and they will have to show that we represent a significant threat."

"But we haven't made any threatening actions," said Carol.

"We only need to represent a threat, not do it," said Katharine.

"We can be prosecuted for what we might do?" asked Leticia. "Is that constitutional?"

"That is what this case will be about. The case will drag out for years, and hundreds of thousands, if not millions, of dollars before it gets to the Supreme Court. Make no mistake–that is where this must go. If they win, it is a huge loss of individual rights and a large step toward a police state. This is basic to the idea of the United States of America. It is only a small step away from the era of the thought police."

"And of course, the public has to be frightened about the idea of biological weapons," Carol said. "We are in trouble, aren't we?"

"This is a battle that needs to be fought to preserve the foundation that made this country," said Katharine. "But I don't believe we want to fight it. Whatever the outcome, we will be destroyed. In this case, we may win the war, but Kihhim will not be around to celebrate."

"What can we do?" asked John, his voice calm, but his look intent.

"Can we speed up the move?" asked Leticia.

John shook his head. "The ship will not be ready. I'll call Rich and see what we can do about the delivery schedule, but we've already pushed it."

"I'll start accelerating the equipment and lab schedule," said Leticia.

"How will they go about proving we are separatists?" asked Carol.

"Our records will be subpoenaed looking for evidence of organized tax evasion, political involvement with separatist organizations, and any writing or literature supporting that position. They will also pry into the background of everyone here. We will be under the microscope."

"I'll start going through our files and records," said Leticia. "How much time do you think we have?"

"They will move carefully on this, making sure each step follows the law. Warrants will probably be issued within two months," said Katharine. "If they move quickly, they could be issued as early as the end of next week."

John hung his head. "I don't see how we're going to get through another search. They'll see evidence we're moving."

"This time, they will take all the records–business, communication, medical, agro, and lab," said Katharine. "They will take the computers or the hard drives along with any hard copy files. Another big problem will be the human genetic work. They can show we are skirting–if not violating–both the United States regulations and the UN sanctions."

"What happens if everything is gone by the time they get here?" asked Leticia.

"Somebody will go to jail for contempt until the subpoenaed information is produced," said Katharine.

"Either we give them everything, or we must be gone," said Carol.

"In a nutshell," said Katharine.

"We must assume we are being watched now," said Leticia. "I'll start transferring the backup files. Do we still have the link to the unit at Dayton's house?"

"We can reestablish it. We need someone at the other end to keep things going smoothly," Leticia looked at Carol and winked. Carol felt her heart throb and then sink. Could she take another visit?

Chapter Thirty-Five

"Sorry John, we cannot move the schedule up that far," said Rich. "We could charter a commercial freighter, shipping everything to another port then transfer to our ship when it's ready."

That would work, thought John. They had to escape first. "We might have to stay somewhere for a while. Where could we go that would not extradite us?"

"There is a Venezuelan shipping company we did business with," said Rich. "Let me check to see if it has a ship somewhere on the west coast. We'll reroute them and pick you up in Puerto Peñasco, but it will be expensive."

"None of our money will do us any good in jail. Let me check. Concentrate on getting our ships completed."

Rich gave him the name of the company and wished them luck. John called and explained he wanted to charter all cargo space and passenger space for a departure from Puerto Peñasco, Mexico going to Puerto Cabello, Venezuela.

Venezuela maintained an adversarial attitude toward the United States. Many blamed the U.S. for the death of Chavez and the political turmoil that roiled the country. There was some validity to the speculation. Under United Nations pressure,

Venezuela would relinquish a ship and contents, but not quickly.

The shipping company was extremely eager to assist them when he offered fifteen percent more than the charter rate. A ship, presently offloading at San Diego would be rerouted. It could arrive in Puerto Peñasco in five to six days. He felt a little relief and called Carol to tell her of the new schedule.

"John, we can't have everything ready in six days!"

"While we're loading the ship, we'll keep moving things from here. Since Puerto Peñasco is such a small port, loading will take a few days. We just have to do what we can. We'll be fine, Carol." He could only hope.

Chapter Thirty-Six

Sweat beaded the brow of FBI Special Agent Robert McWilliams as he finished relating the events concerning Kihhim to Assistant Attorney General Lawrence Kennedy. Average height, average weight, average looks, Kennedy was the epitome of a bureaucrat on the way up. As McWilliams spoke of his feelings that Kihhim represented a huge threat, they intensified even more. It was frustrating trying to get others to understand.

"Let me summarize to see if I have this right," said Kennedy. "This Kihhim is a secluded but hi-tech community with their own school and medical facilities. They grow their own food. Their laboratories engage in biological and genetic research without monitoring or oversight. Though not outwardly separatist, they maintain isolation. Little is known about them."

His fingers formed a steeple on the desk as he looked from Assistant Director Janet Kilgore to Special Agent Robert McWilliams. "The Center for Disease Control, who normally monitors facilities capable of working with or developing biological agents, has not done so since they never came to the attention of the agency." He looked at McWilliams. "It is your belief that if provoked, they might mount a terrorist act using biological weapons. Does that accurately portray this issue?"

"Yes sir," said McWilliams.

"The problem with going further is there's too much of your feelings here and not enough fact. Admittedly, the bio qualifies as a potential weapon of mass destruction, but that is not enough. The courts already gave us some direction in ruling that the threat must include the potential and the disposition to use it. The disposition is the problem here."

"There is something else I picked up while looking over the files," said Janet Kilgore. "Their genetic engineering program appears to be mostly on plants, but without oversight, they may be violating the United States and UN sanctions against human genetic modifications."

"Are there any records of genetic work?" Kennedy asked. "Was there anything to make you suspect genetic modifications or cloning?" looking at McWilliams.

"Our warrant didn't allow access to their research records, but I asked our CDC advisor to review the tapes."

"Call her," said Kennedy, handing him the phone.

"Dr. Getzwiller, this is agent McWilliams. Do you have time to answer a few questions?"

"Uh, yes, but I haven't much time."

"This will only take a few minutes," said McWilliams, cutting any excuse short. "I'm in the office of Assistant Attorney General Lawrence Kennedy with Assistant FBI Director Janet Kilgore. We have questions about the Kihhim search. Can I put you on the speaker?" he said not waiting for a response. They introduced themselves.

"Doctor, I asked you before about bio hazards and genetic work. Did you review the tapes?"

"I did," Adriana lied. "Nothing represented a bio threat,"

"Could they build something that might be a bio threat, either intentionally or by accident?" asked Janet Kilgore.

"A lot of labs have that potential," started Adriana. "Kihhim's safety procedures were good. Agent McWilliams saw that."

Slightly stung, McWilliams asked, "We would also like to know if there was anything indicating human genetic work."

Adriana winced. "Nothing I saw made me think they were violating any sanctions, if that is what you are asking."

"Doctor, this is Lawrence Kennedy. Did you see anything that could have been human genetic engineering or cloning?"

She steadied herself. "Mr. Kennedy, we were looking for weapons. I was there to assure that the agents were not subjected to hazards, and that any work Kihhim labs were doing was not compromised during the search. I was not looking for human genetic research. I did not see anything like that." Adriana said her voice hardening.

"Thank you, Doctor. If we need anything else, we'll call," said Kennedy as he broke the connection. He looked at McWilliams. "She's hiding something."

"Why would she do that?" asked Janet.

"Maybe I should take a closer look at her," said McWilliams.

"Just do a quick and dirty," said Lawrence. "If you find anything odd, we'll get a warrant. Start with CDC phone records. We should be able to get those easily enough."

"So you want us to pursue this?" asked Janet.

"I'm beginning to get a feeling similar to Agent McWilliams," said Kennedy. "These guys seem all right. The problem is if we are wrong, the damage could be catastrophic. Can we afford to push this to one side? I think we must prove there is no threat in order to sleep at night," he said. "Get back to me in two days."

Chapter Thirty-Seven

Adriana sat, staring at the phone and trembling. Despite her resolve to become more involved with the FBI investigation, she realized she didn't have the nerve for it. The questions hit too close to the mark. Adriana looked around her office, feeling trapped. She had to get out of here now.

Her legs wobbled as she gathered her purse. At the door, she turned to see if she had forgotten anything, but her eyes saw little. As she hurried through the outer office, she told her assistant she had an errand and would be gone for the rest of the day.

At the pay phone, she dialed with shaky fingers. Ruben answered almost immediately. "Ruben, this is Adriana. Call me back at 555-628-1442." When the phone rang a few seconds later, she grabbed it with both hands and held it to her ear, saying nothing.

"Hi Adriana," Ruben started. "What is up?"

"I just got a call from the FBI and the Justice Department," gasped out Adriana. "They asked about human genetic research at Kihhim. I'm afraid I wasn't very cool," she added in a weak voice.

"Hold on a sec," said Ruben. "Okay, Adriana, I have Katharine Levey and John Vance on the line with me."

"Tell us about this call, from the beginning," said Katharine.

Adriana related the conversation. Nobody interrupted her. She was relieved to pass this on but worried. What would they do?

"The name of the Justice Department official was Lawrence Kennedy?" asked Katharine.

"Yes. He asked me about the human genetic engineering."

"Don't be surprised at more calls or questions, but don't worry," assured Katharine. "You did fine. We will set up another number that is not associated with us for you to call in an emergency. Buy a burner phone. Do not call from the CDC or from your home or cell. The FBI will access phone records."

"This sounds so secretive," said Adriana. She glanced around to see if anyone was watching.

"Let's not take chances," said Katharine. "The calls you already made to us will be noticed. If you are asked, tell them that after the search, you were missing a watch your mother gave you. You called to see if it had turned up."

"Are you OK with all of this?" Ruben asked.

"I think I can take care of it," Adriana said, not sure at all.

"By the way, your mother's doing fine. The surgery went well, and she's recovering quickly. We should be able to move her from the intensive care to recovery therapy tomorrow," said Ruben.

"We'll call you as soon as we have anything. Thank you for helping us," John said.

As Adriana hung up, she was trembling. What would happen if there were another search? What would happen if they tried to shut down Kihhim? Where would her mother go? In fact, could she really ever come home?

Chapter Thirty-Eight

Carol and Leticia explained to John that transport schedule of months could not be done in days or even weeks. "Okay," said John, "let's prioritize to see what we need to move, then how to do it." He turned to Katharine. "What has to be out of here when they return?"

Leticia spoke up first. "I have experience here. This time, they will secure the whole area. Nothing will enter or exit. They will also secure the communications so that no information goes in or out."

"How will they be able to secure the whole area? The fence line is miles long," said Carol.

"They'll put a cordon around us, bring in enough agents and equipment to keep the road blocked and keep the whole area under surveillance. Unmanned drones from border watch will give aerial support. They will lock everything up and take their time to investigate. There will not be any court orders or limits this time." Leticia concluded.

"Remember," said Katharine, "they will be looking for anything to indicate subversive activities and anything that could be used as a chemical or biological weapon. They already know we have the ability to build them. We probably cannot stop them from finding enough to file charges. The only question is can they prove intent?"

"Our customer list, the full extent of our genetic design capability, our medical advances, and all references to the ships must be kept confidential," said John. "Once they get the personnel roster, they'll be looking at our research staff, our medical staff, and anyone associated with the labs. We can delete some of the names, but the people need to be gone, not available for questioning." Looking at those around him, he said, "I must stay here."

Katharine nodded agreement. "It would probably be best if I remained, too. Let's make up a priority list and see how far we can get."

They nodded glumly. By noon they had everybody listed by priority. The names of those choosing to remain in the United States were purged from the system. Leticia was programming to download and wipe the information they had to cleanse. Carol was arranging for the first rotation of transports in the morning. The mood was grim.

Chapter Thirty-Nine

The phone rang as Adriana was stepping into the shower. She scowled. With her towel around her, she listened as the answering machine picked up. "This is your mother's doctor." Relief washed over her. "Marie is doing well. Please call us in an hour." Adriana wiped the message and sat on the bed, her face in her hands. She had to trust Ruben and Kihhim, she thought as she headed for the shower, still worried.

Adriana, in jeans, tee shirt, and wet hair arrived at the coffee shop and deli a few minutes early. She ordered a bagel and mocha. Right on time Adriana called the number Ruben gave her. The phone rang once, followed by several clicks, and then Ruben spoke. "Adriana, it is good to speak to you. Here is your mother."

"Adriana?" her voice stronger than Adriana had heard in a long time. Relief washed through her.

"Hi, Mom. You sound really good."

"And I feel good. Dr. Sanchez is taking care of me. I'm sore from the surgery, but I'm so much stronger. I was hoping to come home, but they tell me we will be moving."

"Moving! Mom, where are you going?"

"No one has said yet, but Dr. Sanchez knows what he's doing."

"Mom, let me speak to him for a moment." Ruben came on the line. "What is this about a move?"

"Your information about the Justice Department requires we take precautions in case another search warrant is served. We are moving your mother, so she won't become involved."

"Why can't she come back here?" asked Adriana, already knowing the answer.

"Adriana, we'll arrange for you to visit her soon, but for now, we need to keep her. This is to protect you, too. Any questions and you would be implicated, and we would all be in more trouble."

"How long will this take?"

"We don't know, but we won't keep you apart any longer than we have to. Please trust me on this," said Ruben.

"Let me speak to my mom again."

Her mother's voice came on the line. "Adriana, you need to trust these people. They certainly have done what's best for me. It's so nice here. I'm perfectly safe in their hands."

"Okay, Mom. Let me talk to Dr. Sanchez again, please." The phone passed. "I guess I really have no choice, but where are you taking her?"

"It is best if you know nothing for a few days. We will call you as soon as we're settled. Expect another call from the FBI. They may even want you to assist again in the new search. In case they suspect anything, I sent you a package containing a watch. The package should be there next week. Adriana, be careful what you say. Volunteer nothing if they question you.”

“I will, Ruben. Thank you for Mom.”

“Thank you for your help, Adriana.” She hung up. As she walked back to her table, each step seemed to lift her. She trusted Ruben Sanchez and not because she had to. That night, she slept better than she had in months.

Chapter Forty

"Getzwiller made two calls to Kihhim since the search," said Assistant Attorney General Lawrence Kennedy. "Any ideas about those?"

"We had no taps on her," said FBI Agent Robert McWilliams. "We do now."

"Let's see what she has to say. It may be nothing," said Assistant Director Janet Kilgore.

McWilliams called.

"This is Dr. Getzwiller."

"Dr. Getzwiller, this is Lawrence Kennedy along with Assistant FBI Director Janet Kilgore and FBI Special Agent Robert McWilliams. We would like to ask you a few more questions about Kihhim."

She expected this. "Yes, how can I help you?"

"Since our last communication, have you recalled anything we should know?"

"I thought about everything we saw there. I reviewed the tapes again. Nothing represents a threat."

"Since the search of Kihhim, have you had any communication with anybody there?" asked Kennedy.

"A watch my mother gave me was missing. I called Dr. Sanchez to ask if he would look for it. Later I called to check if he found it. Why do you want to know?"

"Had he found it?" asked McWilliams, ignoring her question.

"As a matter of fact he did, and he's sending it."

"Dr. Getzwiller, several things in the labs appeared to be quite advanced yet you did not find it strange nothing was known or published?"

"Some of what I saw surprised me, but they insisted we sign a confidentiality agreement to preserve proprietary rights. It is not uncommon," Adriana said, guardedly. "There are many labs we do not track."

"Thank you, Dr. Getzwiller. We may be in touch with you again." Kennedy hung up.

"She does not strengthen your position of a threat at Kihhim," said Kennedy, "so you need to convince me to proceed. If I am not convinced, a judge wouldn't be. We cannot afford to stub our toe on this. A loss for whatever reason would be a big setback to the EDT Act. Call me when you have something," he said, dismissing them.

In the hall outside, Janet Kilgore turned to McWilliams. "Bring in Brian Denton. We'll need him. I now believe Kihhim represents a potential threat we need to control, but we will proceed as Kennedy sees fit."

***

McWilliams' request that he come to Washington D.C. surprised Brian Denton. He hadn't been positive this would work, but it appeared something was going to happen. McWilliams met him at Ronald Reagan International Airport and drove to FBI Headquarters.

They spent the rest of the day in Janet Kilgore's office reviewing what he saw, what he thought, and how to tell Kennedy. He found Kilgore intimidating. They did not offer to accompany him to dinner.

After a fitful night, he was, tired but eager. The three of them went to the office of Lawrence Kennedy. After the introduction, Kennedy got to the point.

"Dr. Denton, you told Agent McWilliams after thinking about the search there was a possible danger from the genetically altered plants in Kihhim. Please explain."

"Since we were focused on firearms, I didn't think about dangers. To be honest, I was caught up in the wonder of the genetic work they had done. I didn't see any records, so I don't know the extent of the alterations performed on the plants. I was told they were modified to increase food production, but several had obviously been modified for other purposes."

"Explain," said Janet Kilgore.

"As an example, they altered a strain of bamboo to form the structure supporting the different tiers of plants. They modified the melons to grow more like a tree than a vine. These are obvious examples. Their greenhouses are isolated to keep out insects, pests and disease, but it is not possible to be 100% effective. I noticed several species of plants that produce toxins, insecticides and pesticides. I'm sure forms of water plants are used as bactericide to control disease, but the water treatment portion was not explained."

"Could these be a hazard?" asked Kennedy.

"If they were to get out of Kihhim, there's no way of knowing what effect they would have on the environment. With no natural enemies, they may well grow without check. That would be a disaster." Okay. Denton started the ball rolling, yet no one asks why he didn't bring this up immediately. Do they just assume he's a super patriot—with no other motive?

Lawrence Kennedy smiled thinly at him.

"Did you see any indication they were separatists or had seditious tendencies?"

"They were obviously secretive about their genetic work. I keep up with changes in the agricultural field and there has never been a hint of their work. Kihhim has done everything outside of our agricultural community so they would not be subject to criticism or controls. They also made a point of emphasizing the confidentiality agreement we had to sign. I find this disturbing, and in combination with the secrecy threatening."

"You cannot think of another legitimate reason for this secrecy?" asked Kennedy.

"If they were awaiting patent approval, I could understand, but I did a patent and application search. I did not find where they had applied. If they intended to go to market with this technology, they would have applied for patent."

"Why would they not apply for a patent?" asked McWilliams.

"The patent process is supposed to be secret, giving protection and opportunity for inventors to realize profit for their efforts. The patent process is not absolutely secure. Illegal things cannot be patented. Also, there have been instances where patents were taken, when in the national interest."

Brian sat back, hoping they would draw the conclusions to justify further investigation. The agents and the Assistant Attorney General all looked at each other. There were a few more questions and discussion, but they involved minor topics and clarifications. After ninety minutes, Brian was thanked and ushered out.

McWilliams put him in a taxi to the airport. Back in Lawrence Kennedy's office, Kennedy said, "I find Brian Denton's story somewhat biased. Certainly, we would have no problem showing capability, but again, intent is weak. The jump from secrecy to insurrection is big."

Kennedy looked from Kilgore to McWilliams, "We must be sure this will fly. Getting shot down would weaken our whole anti-terrorist effort. We need to be able to show clear-cut intent to use weapons for terrorist purposes." McWilliams started to argue, but shut his mouth. He would keep looking.

PART 3

THE ATTACK

First Lab-Grown Organs Implanted in Humans
Richard A. Lovett
for National Geographic News
April 4, 2006

Chapter Forty-One

Since the search at Kihhim, Bureau of Alcohol, Tobacco, Firearms and Explosives agent David Moldovan had not slept well. His strong faith and the church were normally a refuge for him. Though he attended services several times a week, the comforting words did not last past the exit.

The recurring nightmare of horribly distorted figures spreading across the Arizona desert from Kihhim woke him in a cold sweat. In the dream, everything they touched withered and died or was engulfed. Black clouds and lightning rolled over the land. David had seen the Apocalypse, and it scared him badly.

"I had to confide in someone," said Moldovan, looking into the dark-bearded face of his pastor, Deacon Smithson. "What does it mean?"

David Moldovan, one of his truest believers and best supporters was clearly disturbed by the unnatural things he saw at Kihhim. Deacon Luke Smithson, founder of the Guardians of the Light Church looked at the trembling parishioner.

These last few years, his fiery sermons fell on fewer and fewer ears. Raining fire and brimstone from his pulpit had not brought him new followers. He needed a cause, and this might be it.

This Kihhim group tinkered with God's natural ways. He closed his eyes and pictured the sermon. He looked at the obviously uncomfortable man in front of him. "David, I want you to go through everything again, leave out nothing." Mentally he sang hallelujahs that God had sent him a lightning rod to bring people back. As the miserable David Moldovan recounted the search of Kihhim, the Deacon wrote furiously.

David finished and sat, head down. "Let me summarize," said the Deacon. "This Kihhim is an underground city hidden in the desert. There were secretive greenhouses filled with unnatural plants producing unholy fruit to be consumed by these heathens. Is that right?"

"Well, it was not really hidden; they just lived underground."

"But these greenhouses were secretive, not open for people to go in, and they used children to work and toil in these hothouses. Is that right?"

"Well, yes," said David hesitantly.

"And these people—even the children, consumed the unholy fruit produced in these hothouses?" The Deacon asked, warming to the subject.

"Yes," confirmed David.

"This Kihhim is surrounded by a fence with a guardhouse, and arms inside?"

"Just some old rifles, nothing illegal," mumbled David.

"But you sensed something evil there." said The Deacon. "Satan's work was going on."

David squirmed at The Deacon's description. "Well, not really evil, just not right.".

"Satan's works are not always obvious, even to the faithful. In your nightmares a plague spreads over the land. This is a sign, a warning." said The Deacon. "As with any black evil creature, it shall be destroyed by bringing it into the light of goodness."

***

The Deacon's Sunday sermon, the loudest, harshest in years, described the nest of vipers in the Arizona desert. He called for battle against this scourge–this Kihhim, and the forces of evil residing there. The fear rose in David again, along with hatred for the unholy, but also shame. Kihhim was not everything that The Deacon said.

In the ending prayer, The Deacon called upon the Lord to guide them in the fight against this unnatural movement. He prayed for help from the heavenly host to bring down this threat against God's natural way. There was a loud "Amen" but the congregation did not leave, waiting for more.

The following week, a trickle of donations came in. After a fiery tirade about the ungodly threat and a call to oppose this evil, the trickle became a gush. In the weeks that followed, the radio audience responded. Donations poured in. The next Sunday his congregation tripled, leaving few empty pews. Other fundamentalist leaders called him for information, and the movement against Kihhim spread rapidly.

On Saturday, three weeks later, the sheriff's car appeared at The Deacon's church. A round man in a light tan uniform, buttons straining, his belt buckle invisible, got out of the driver's side. He raised a hand in greeting as he moved ponderously toward The Deacon. Behind him in the car sat a man in a suit, black sunglasses trained on The Deacon.

As the deputy neared, The Deacon turned to face him, his own eyes looking back from the mirrored sunglasses under the tan hat. "Luke, I have to talk to you about this trouble your raising about this Kihhim place. Do you understand that you and The Guardians of the Light Church would be in trouble if there is any violence at Kihhim?"

"Sheriff, this Kihhim is an abomination and a threat to Christians and the natural progression of life worldwide. It has to be destroyed before it destroys us. I cannot control who listens to my sermons. Good or evil is their choice. I only present the facts and explain the Lord's way."

The sheriff took off his dark glasses, and his eyes flicked back toward the car and the shadowy figure within. He stared hard at The Deacon. "Luke, urging your followers to attack Kihhim is like yelling 'Sic um.' to a pit bull. It's dangerous. Prayer is one thing, attacking them is another. It is against the law."

"Against the law!" shouted The Deacon, his arms rising as his voice went up. "I'll tell you what is against the law, is this Kihhim. That's against God's and nature's law. Satan is at work trying to destroy us."

"Then let God handle this and stay out of it. If I hear you urging your Soldiers of God to attack Kihhim again, I am going to have to arrest you."

"Sheriff, you were elected by the God-fearing people of this county, and if you allow this Kihhim to continue, you are betraying them, and you are betraying your Christian faith."

The sheriff's eyes flicked toward the car. "I was elected to uphold the law, Luke, and that includes conspiracy and inciting violence. I'm warning you now, if I hear any more, I will have to come back." He got into his patrol car and left. The Deacon watched as he turned the corner and disappeared.

The Deacon returned to the house. A medium-height, thin angular man came up from the basement. He had brown hair, a large nose, olive complexion and black eyes. "You get all of that?" asked The Deacon.

"Most of it," said Ralph. "I thought the sheriff was a friend."

"He is. The suit in the car was probably FBI. That's the reason the sheriff was here. I thought that went well. He did his duty, and I did mine. His visit let me know they're watching. Can we move the schedule up?"

"Yeah, but we will have to go with a smaller group. Six guys can be there in a few days, but six won't make much of a demonstration."

"It's not what they do, but that they do something. Our true aim is to bring attention to our cause, and believers will flock to us once they know what we're fighting. If we appear too radical, it will hurt us. Since what we want is publicity, we do not attack, we blockade them."

"Some or maybe all of us will be arrested you know," said Ralph.

"We can handle misdemeanor charges," said The Deacon.

Ralph could not handle an arrest. He had baggage. "Okay, but these guys of ours are not passive. If there is any resistance, they might get out of hand."

"We have to be the good guys here. It's up to you to keep them under control. Let's get this show on the road." He laughed at the wordplay.

Chapter Forty-Two

The Deacon waved as Ralph Whitney and his men maneuvered down the driveway in the old Ford van. It looked like an old pinto horse with flaking paint and gray primer. But hidden under the hood sat a primo big engine, it looked bad, ran good.

Though Georgia was a long way from Arizona, they would be a third of the way by tomorrow night. In his mind, the opening prayer for his next sermon formed. Nothing directly advocating violence, it would be a clear message.

***

Ralph Whitney (aka Musamma Ajud) guided the old van along the almost invisible track in the swampy mire. The engine had a deep rumble that silenced the forest around him like a huge predator on the prowl.

Raised in the dusty and dry desert of the Middle East, the swamps of Florida were too close, too heavy. The moisture-laden air was the hardest to get used to. He missed the long vistas now robbed by the trees, and the crisp dry air. As a deep agent for the al Qaeda, he saw his cell destroyed as the pursuit of the United States government devastated all semblance of organization.

With the death of Osama bin Laden, al Qaeda had fallen from grace within the Muslim world and funding became scarce. Ralph saw this as a sign he needed to watch out for himself.

After his deep al Qaeda cell was wiped out, Musamma Ajud became his cover, Ralph Whitney, full-time and dropped from sight.

Understanding religious fanaticism, Ralph found The Guardians of the Light Church. The Deacon offered to let him stay with them, training his Soldiers of the Lord in survivalist tactics and doing occasional work. It was a safe haven.

He now sold his talents and information to anyone willing to pay—anyone needing services. The right customers were always open to getting WMDs. Nuclear weapons cost too much, were monitored too closely. Chemical weapons were hard to deliver. But bio-weapons could be delivered by one infected person. Never was it better exemplified than the bio war a few years ago. Kihhim's description caught his attention. They could develop things that humans never faced before, had no resistance to. They might already have them. WMDs sold for very high prices.

Chapter Forty-Three

As the sun dropped, the shadow of Baboquivari Peak moved across the still valley, shading John and Katharine in a soft cloak. All Kihhim personnel and equipment left two days ago, and the last DEM team had left only hours ago. They caught a break, and the expected search had not occurred.

Kihhim was a ghost town. The fully-loaded ship would depart tomorrow afternoon with the arrival of Katharine, Leticia, and John.

Ron Emerald, a prominent developer in Southern Arizona, bought Kihhim. They had inked the deal this afternoon.

John and Katharine looked up at the massive peak with the sun setting behind it. How ironic that the native Tohono O'Odham people considered Baboquivari Peak the navel of the Earth and the birthplace of humanity. In their legends, the People issued forth and spread out to populate the world. Kihhim started here, and now they were departing to start a new nation.

Leaving was a bittersweet sensation. It was time to move on, yet he felt like a youth leaving home— both fearful and confident.

Next week the management at Maorimax would learn their largest customer now owned the majority of stock. There would be no personnel changes.

Once Maorimax Marine crews completed the final ship assembly, they would return to port, but the ships never would, redefining the meaning of nation.

John did not try to stop the memories flooding through his mind like a disjointed film. He tried to imprint the emotions that flowed through him. He suspected Katharine was doing the same, making an emotional photo album before they had to leave this place, this world. Neither said a word when Leticia's shout pulled them back to the here and now.

"John, it's the FBI calling."

Alarmed, he looked at Katharine. "If it's serious, they would not call first," she offered.

He smiled grimly, whatever it was, how could it be good? He entered the office and picked up the phone. "Hello, this is John Vance," he said.

"This is FBI Agent William Black of the Arizona Regional FBI office. How are you this evening?"

Puzzled, John asked. "What can I do for you?"

"It is what I can do for you. We received a tip that a group of armed men is heading your way with bad intent."

Was this the new ploy? "Bad intent. What is that?" asked John.

"This is a serious threat from a credible source. We believe they intend to capture Kihhim. In fact, we're taking it so seriously that there are agents on their way to Kihhim now."

"Who are these people? Why do they want Kihhim?" John asked, signaling Leticia to get Katharine.

"I can only say they are part of a religious militant group. The copters should be there any minute to protect you."

"What if we do not want protection?" asked John. "Is this a ploy to take us over?"

"In this case, you have no choice," responded Agent Black. "If our presence becomes an issue, we would rather be there and lose later in court. Mr. Vance, your technology could be used for strategic purposes, and we do not want it in the wrong hands."

"We have nothing here that could be used for a weapon," said John.

"I spoke to Assistant Director Janet Kilgore and Special Agent McWilliams as soon as we learned of the threat. We believe there are no WMDs at Kihhim, but with your gene-modifying technology, bio-weapon components could be built. This decision came from high up. Until the agents get there, we would like for you and your people to stay inside. Lock up. Our agents are in the air now."

John said nothing. If he told them everything was already gone, it would raise questions. "We will look for your men," he said. He turned and quickly related the conversation to Leticia and Katharine.

Chapter Forty-Four

Within thirty seconds of the thumping noise of the helicopters, they settled, kicking up clouds of dust and obscuring the gatehouse. A fully outfitted Special Agent Robert McWilliams got out, instinctively ducking as he walked under the whirling rotors. He approached John, the wind whipping his cammies as he held out his hand. An M-4 was slung over his shoulder. As they shook hands, he said "I'm sorry we had to meet again under these circumstances."

"On our way in, we spotted a van parked off the road three miles away. Know anything about it?" John shook his head. "I didn't think so." He spoke into a small microphone on his collar. Other similarly clad figures spread out, moving into the dusk. Dust and noise from the rising helicopter battered them. "We're going to look from the air. It may be smugglers, but we'd like you to go inside until we see it's clear." It was not a request.

The opportunity presented by the news of Ralph Whitney's group was too good to pass up. They had no trouble getting an order to take Kihhim into protective custody. The Soldiers of the Lord were a militant ultra-right separatist group at war with the federal government.

McWilliams glanced around. A puzzled look came over his face. "Are there fewer people here now than before?"

"A lot of our residents left since you were here." John confirmed, saying no more.

McWilliams stared, but John looked back coolly. "We'd like to use your security system, the motion and infrared detectors around your perimeter fence. If anyone attempts to get near, we should be able to tell," the agent said.

"The greenhouses are cleared," John said, not wanting to offer any more information than he had to.

"The labs?" asked McWilliams.

"Cleared also," said John.

"Mister Vance, the last time we were here you had a lot of work in the labs, work that required isolation. Are you saying that work is over?"

"There is no work going on in those labs at this time."

McWilliams glared at John. The first bead of sweat formed on his brow. The people were gone and the labs shut down. Kihhim had been misjudged again, and someone's head would roll, almost certainly his. Evacuated and empty, Kihhim had nothing to steal, no threat.

***

Ralph Whitney knew the ground around Kihhim from his intense Google Earth study of maps and photos. His men were carefully dug-in surrounding the compound, covered by thermal blankets, and completely invisible. From his position on the hill, he didn't see much of a defense set up, not many people and no patrols–until the helicopters landed.

Large FBI letters on the backs of the men gave him pause. He sent a coded message to his men to be as still as rocks until they heard from him.

The Deacon only wanted to publicize Kihhim in order to lead a crusade, but Ralph had his own plan, and it did not include blockade. He watched the FBI place their sensors, detectors, and men. They did a good job, but it was too big an area. He learned patience years ago and was satisfied to sit and watch for now.

***

"Mr. Vance, would you join me in a conference call to Assistant Director Janet Kilgore and Lawrence Kennedy of the Justice Department," said McWilliams.

"I would like Katharine Levey with me, please," said John. McWilliams nodded. Within minutes, he had Kilgore and Kennedy on the speaker phone. Quick introductions were made.

McWilliams spoke. "I need to give you a summary of the situation here. Mr. Vance can comment or add as necessary."

John nodded.

"We arrived an hour ago and have evidence there are unknowns in the area. Our assumption is they are SOL. We've found nothing yet. Mr. Vance informs us Kihhim has been sold. The greenhouses and the labs are shut down and all material removed from them. In addition, it appears most personnel have left, including the research staff. Does that about sum it up, Mr. Vance?"

"Yes," said John.

"Mr. Vance," Lawrence Kennedy spoke, "where have you moved your operation?" His voice was sharp.

"Mr. Kennedy, I do not have to answer that," said John.

"Mr. Vance, let me explain our situation. We consider your technology strategic. We are not the only ones who think that. There are those who would use that technology to attack and weaken the United States and aid the cause of terrorism. That position allows us to take you into protective custody and secure Kihhim. If we cannot secure the critical items and information from Kihhim, we will charge you with withholding evidence and jeopardizing national security. There will be no bail. Mr. Vance, I repeat, where have you moved your operation?"

"I will not answer that," said John, staring ahead, head up, lips pressed together. Katharine started to speak, but John made a slight shake of his head, signaling her to silence.

"Agent McWilliams," said Janet Kilgore, "please take Mr. Vance into custody and withdraw your men."

"Wait!" Katharine yelled. "You said we were in danger here, but you're going to withdraw your men. How can you do that?"

"With the technology and the personnel gone, so is the threat. Mr. Vance is refusing to cooperate, so I suppose we will see you in court, Ms. Levey," said Kennedy.

"I would like to confer with my client for a few minutes," said Katharine.

"You are not in court yet, but go ahead," said Kennedy.

John and Katharine moved away. "Katharine, all we need is a few days. After that there will not be any use in keeping me."

"But you will be in jail." exclaimed Katharine. "As a potential witness, they can keep you indefinitely without charging you."

"Katharine, you and Leticia finish this up. Get everything away and then worry about getting me out." He stood and walked toward the door with McWilliams. Katharine looked at his back.

Chapter Forty-Five

Ralph Whitney was stunned as the agents gathered their sensors and boarded the helicopters. A handcuffed man from Kihhim was taken aboard as well. With a clatter they lifted off. He watched patiently for another hour.

The two women he'd seen remained inside. To be sure it was clear, they waited. One hour later, he moved his men into Kihhim.

Leticia and Katharine sat in the security office too stunned to move by the progression of events. The sound of perimeter alarms startled them.

In the monitors, Leticia saw a figures move furtively toward one of the greenhouse doors. Within seconds a door alarm sounded. She dialed 911.

"This is Leticia Gardner at Kihhim. We have intruders breaking into our facility. Send someone at once. Call FBI, Agent William Black. We are preparing to defend ourselves."

The line went dead. She pulled her Beretta 96 out of the desk drawer, racking a round into the chamber with a loud snick. Katharine locked the door and backed away glancing at Leticia. Seconds later the power went out, and the emergency lights clicked on.

Someone tried to open the door. Katharine stifled a scream, clapping a hand over her mouth. Eyes wide, she turned toward Leticia.

Hushed voices came from outside, then the door shook as someone put a shoulder to it. It did not yield, but Katharine fell back.

A raspy voice yelled, "Open the door. We know you're in there."

Katharine's panicked face offered Leticia no help. She pushed Katharine into a space between two file cabinets. "Just keep quiet. Don't make a sound," she whispered. "We'll be okay," but she didn't believe it as she moved the cabinets together, hiding Katharine completely.

She took cover behind the desk. A thunderous explosion splintered the door. With her ears ringing, Leticia positioned her arms on the desk, gun pointing at the center of the dust cloud where the door had been. A figure appeared. She snapped off two quick rounds.

The first bullet caught the figure high in the chest, knocking him backward. The second shot was higher. As his head snapped back, the 180 grain bullet entered under his chin with a meaty smack. He dropped like a sack of flour.

Someone stuck an Uzi around the corner and opened up. The muzzle flashes caused the smoke to strobe as Leticia hunkered behind the desk, and the bullets stitched a path across the wall behind her. With her gun above her head on the desk, she fired once at the doorway.

Somebody shouted. "Cease fire. Cease fire." The silence was deafening. In a soft persuading tone, a voice spoke.

"We do not want to hurt you. Put the gun down, so we can talk."

"I can talk and aim at the same time," yelled Leticia. "What do you want?"

"Can we come in?" asked the voice.

"Sure, come ahead. I'll shoot your lame ass."

"We do not want to hurt you. All we want is the biological data on the pathogens and the test samples. Tell us where they are, and we will go away."

Sure they would. They obviously didn't know everything had been cleared out. "Everything's been moved out. There is nothing here," Leticia said.

"You're a stupid lying bitch." shouted a different voice.

"I am in here, and you are out there. Go check. So who's stupid?"

There was some discussion and the sound of retreating feet. The voice came back, conversational and soft. "So if it is gone, where is it?" That voice chilled her.

Leticia was quiet, but her mind raced as she lay behind the desk. The heavy smell of cordite hung in the air with the dust and smoke. If these people would attack like this, they would go after the group in Mexico without hesitation. The silence stretched out.

"You might as well tell us. We are not going anywhere, and if you make things easy for us, we will do the same for you."

The voice was seductive, but Leticia said nothing. Did making things easier mean a quick death? How long before someone responded to her call? Would they respond?

"As soon as the alarm sounded, I called the sheriff. It takes forty-five minutes to get here from the substation at Kenny Road. You've used up most of that."

"We cut the lines." said another voice. "Quit lying, bitch."

"The perimeter alarms went off first," said Leticia. "That's when I called."

"Just tell us what we want to know, and we will go. It is as simple as that. No one else will get hurt."

What shit. They couldn't take the chance she would lie to them and leave her. She heard the sound of returning feet and whispered conversation.

"Okay, so there is nothing here. Are we going to do this the easy way?"

Leticia said nothing. There was a soft pop and a hissing canister flew into the room. Gas! Several shots rang out and struck the wall, behind her.

Leticia instinctively ducked under the desk, trying to cover her face with her shirt, but the gas seeped in, burning her eyes and gagging her. She held her breath as her heart hammered, but she choked as her lungs tried to reject the burning fumes. Stomach heaving, her sinuses let loose. She retched.

At the sound of feet, she blindly fired several shots from under the desk toward the door. A scream rang out. She felt her collar grabbed, and she was yanked out. A foot stepped on her gun hand. A gas-masked figure loomed before her teary eyes. She heaved and brought the gun up. Something struck her head as the gun fired. Everything turned black.

Chapter Forty-Six

"Damn." exclaimed Ralph Whitney. "Kyle's dead and we have to drag Billy's lame butt around." He wiped the side of his face. The flash burn from Leticia's last shot hurt like hell. "Take a quick look around and let's clear out. She might have gotten a call off, and we gotta be gone before anyone gets to the turnoff at the highway or we're trapped."

Ralph quickly secured Leticia's hands with a nylon wire tie. "Darren, take her out and radio Joseph to bring the van, quick. Gordie, you help Billy. I'll bring Kyle." The van roared through the abandoned gatehouse a few minutes later.

They bounced down the dirt road to the highway. As soon as they got on the blacktop, Ralph told Joseph to slow down. They had only been traveling north for a few miles when flashing lights sped past them, heading toward Kihhim. That was too close, thought Ralph. They had to get something out of the woman. He applied burn salve to his face and let Gordie bandage it.

***

Katharine used her legs to shove the file cabinet away, so she could crawl out. She had her sleeve over her mouth and nose, but her eyes burned fiercely. Tears and mucus streamed down her face in the reek of the gas. She moved toward the doorway in the half dark, stumbling over the debris of the shattered door. She had to get out before she threw up.

In the hallway, the air was cleaner, and she took in deep breaths–bending over and trying to clear her head. The only sound was her gasping breath and sobs. She looked into the office for any sign of Leticia. The room was a shambles; papers and pieces of desk and door lay everywhere. Bullet craters walked across the wall.

Katharine stepped into the hall. On the wall, she saw a large wet stain, red rivulets running down from chunks of gray matter. Gorge rose in her throat before she could think. Trying to run away, her feet slipped in the sticky red puddle on the floor.

Katharine was violently sick as her legs collapsed and spilled her into the whole mess. Sobbing, she crawled down the hall, barely able to move her arms and legs, until she got to the underground parking entry.

She gulped deep breaths of fresh air. The heaves subsided, but the image still burned before her eyes. The sound of a wailing siren overcame the ringing in her ears. A figure darted toward her. Deputy Harry Kisto had his arms around her.

With her face buried in his shoulder, she shook. "They took her, Harry. They took her," she repeated over and over. He held her, saying nothing as she quieted. When the tears and shakes subsided, Harry asked, "Can you tell me what happened?"

Katharine sucked in deep breaths, trying to organize her thoughts from the jumble of images that kept blinding her. Finally, she told him the story, starting with the departure of John and the helicopters.

"They left us, Harry. They left us knowing we would be attacked. As soon as the alarms sounded, we called 911. Leticia shoved me behind the file cabinets. I panicked, but I could hear. When the door blew in, it sounded like all hell broke loose, with them shooting and Leticia shooting back." She shuddered.

"When it stopped, they tried to talk to her and bargain with her, but she knew better. They gassed the place and took her. I think she hit at least one of them." The vision blinded her again, and she retched.

The other deputy emerged from Kihhim. "We got one serious hit, brain tissue on the wall. There's blood in the office too, maybe from another person." Katharine closed her eyes and tried to fight the nausea. God. Don't let it be Leticia's. "They took her. They took Leticia," she repeated.

"What did they want?" asked Harry.

"They asked about the bio stuff and some pathogen test work we did last year." The two officers looked at each other. Harry held Katharine's hand while the other deputy called in the information and requested an ambulance. The thumping roar of an approaching helicopter broke the silence of the desert. Amid a cloud of dust, it settled into the yard.

Agent Robert McWilliams and John Vance got out, bent over and ran toward them through the swirling debris. Harry helped Katharine stand up on wobbly legs in time for John's arms to enfold her. She trembled violently as he hugged her. The shudders went on and on, the tension racking her like a dog trying to shake off water. At last she stopped, but the sobs did not.

"John, they took her, they took Leticia. What's going to happen to her? What are we going to do?"

"Who were they?" asked agent McWilliams.

"You know better than I do," Katharine snarled. "You left us to them, knowing they would come, you bastard." She glared at him.

"We first saw them on the monitors when the alarms went off. They broke in looking for bio agents, just as you suspected. We called for help, locked ourselves in the security office, and Leticia hid me. They blew the door, and she held them off for a while, but they gassed her and took her," Katharine sobbed.

"How long ago did they leave?"

"It's only been half an hour," said Harry. "We may have passed them on the highway coming in. A van was heading north towards the Ajo highway. Didn't notice the color or make."

"Damn, they were fast." McWilliams turned and ran toward the helicopter signaling to take off. "They have a hostage," he said into his mic. Climbing in, he yelled instructions over the rising noise of the whirling rotors. Within seconds, it leapt upward and headed north.

John hugged Katharine again, trying to shelter her from flying dust and the tragedy. "We have to wait. There is nothing we can do," he said, trying to comfort both of them.

Chapter Forty-Seven

As the van sped toward the Ajo highway, Ralph broke the ammonia capsule under Leticia's nose and waved it until she struggled to get away. She tried to push his hand back, discovering hers were bound. Her eyes flew open.

"We need to have that little talk now," said Ralph, his voice just loud enough to be heard above the whining engine. Joseph turned from the steering wheel and looked back, but Ralph barked for him to watch the road. "Where are your labs, your results? Where are the pathogens?" Leticia said nothing, her heart pounding, a cold knot forming.

Ralph shrugged and slowly opened the blade of a large folding knife. Her irises dilated in fear as her eyes followed the point of the curved blade. She looked up. Too fast to follow, his hand flicked out and sliced her left cheek. Blood filled her mouth, gushed down her throat.

The knife was so sharp that there was little pain— at first. Leticia's eyes bulged at the wetness soaking her shirt. She looked down at the blood already pooling in her lap.

"Now we are even," he said, turning his face so she could see the bandage. Pointing the knife at her face, he said, "That cut will leave a nasty scar unless it is treated soon." A smile appeared on his face.

"You will be quite ugly. Do you want me to continue?" Leticia shook her head. "Where?" was all he asked. She closed her lips, pressing them so tightly together they became a thin line, not wanting anything to escape. Air whistled through the open cut in her cheek, and the knife flashed again. More blood flowed, this time from her lips.

Joseph turned from the driver's seat, saw widening pools of blood and moaned, but Ralph screamed at him. The van swerved several times, throwing Leticia back and forth. Only Ralph's grip on her shirt kept her from rolling away.

Pulling her up until his face inches from hers, she looked into his black eyes. His eyebrows rose questioningly. Closing her eyes to escape this scene, the razor sharp blade cut the right side of her face from cheekbone to chin. She fled toward a sweet blackness that embraced her.

Chapter Forty-Eight

As the helicopter lifted off, Robert McWilliams keyed the radio. Arizona Department of Public Safety and Pima County both dispatched forces, in the air and on the ground in response to the emergency call. A roadblock was set up on eastbound Highway 86 while Tribal Police from Sells put units on the highway heading west toward Ajo.

Traffic was light on the Ajo highway at this time of night, but it took McWilliams a while to spot the van moving west with its lights off. They must be driving with night-vision glasses. They tracked the van from high altitude.

Without knowing what the terrorists had learned, they had to stop them. McWilliams supervised a hastily built roadblock–an overturned car and fire almost blocking the road near the village of Quijotoa. It was the best they could do on short notice.

The sound of the van's engine broke the night silence before it crested the hill and then was upon them. Tires squealed, and the van skidded from side to side before it straightened out as the driver got control. It stopped, waiting.

Nobody moved. Voices shouted inside as the van edged off the road to get around the car. As foreseen, the front wheels dropped into the small brush-covered ditch. The driver gunned the engine, the wheels spun. Amid more shouts, the passenger and van door opened and two figures got out moving to the rear of the van to push.

McWilliams signaled, and the agents sprang from concealment. Within seconds, guns were at the heads of the three men. It was over.

McWilliams looked inside and saw a body and a wounded man, dried blood caking his pants, his eyes wide in shock. Crouched in a dark corner, he saw another figure, shirt and pants blood-soaked. When he reached out and removed the blood sodden towel from the face, he thought it was Leticia. The hair looked like Leticia's.

"Leticia? Can you hear me?" he asked. The face turned toward him, eyes glazed in terror, the cheeks flapping loose, flesh hanging down, lips gone. Her teeth shone through a hole of a mouth, and she moaned, the sound coming from the depths of her soul. He turned and yelled to the other agents. "Get the chopper down here and get an ambulance to meet us."

Chapter Forty-Nine

Carol sat on the patio of the *El Capitan* restaurant with Jamie Wong and new friends Rick and Kay Robinson. The Venezuelan ship was loaded and ready to sail, only awaiting the arrival of John, Katharine, and Leticia tomorrow.

The Robinsons had sailed into Puerto Peñasco on their trimaran three days before. Rick went to Casa Grande to see his mother in the hospital. He'd returned to Peñasco to take Kay back with him.

Carol was nervous. Kihhim would not contact her again. They were so close to succeeding in their escape. Her tenseness showed.

"Carol, are you okay?" asked Kay.

"Just worried," she answered. In the short time she'd known Kay, Carol trusted her. She'd confided to Rick and Kay about their escape from the U.S. The Robinsons had told her they, too were refugees, and not for the first time. They gave no details but advised that the Kihhim group leave as quickly as possible. She'd been glad for the support.

Back on the dock after dinner, she hugged the Robinsons goodbye. They would probably never see each other again. She wondered if Rick and Kay were their real names, but dismissed any concern. It really didn't matter.

Returning to her room, she was determined to get some sleep.

The sound of the phone jarred her. Only Kihhim would be contacting her. The call could not be good. Before she said anything, Katharine spoke. "Carol, are you there?"

"Katharine. What is going on? Where are you?"

"No explanations. Leave now, as fast as possible. We'll catch up with you in Venezuela. No calls or communication. Run absolutely silent. We'll be okay."

Carol stared at the dead phone. What happened? In a fog fumbled around the room, picking up her things. A call to a sleepy voice arranged for transport to the ship. A radio call to the ship alerted them to prepare for immediate departure. She gave a last check of the empty storage building. In a daze, she texted Dayton. *'b out of touch 4 while. will get msg 2 u when i can. already miss u trbly. I luv u.'*

She hung her head, wiped her face, grabbed the last of her things, and hurried out to the waiting launch crew. The mooring lights of the ship sent wriggling rays of light across the water to her, but they were blurred by her tear-filled eyes.

Dayton sat on the edge of his bed staring at the phone. The text tone had awakened him. This had to be a dream. What had happened? He had to wake up. Carol could not have just texted this. Calls to her phone went to voicemail. He left a worried message and called Kihhim. There was no answer, just the lonely ring.

Chapter Fifty

Leticia awoke to a white world, her face covered in bandages. Silence surrounded her, punctuated by occasional hospital sounds; monitor beeping, announcements, pages, squeaking shoes.

She tried to remember. An image formed of someone with a knife, asking questions. The flash of the knife caused her to jerk at the memory of searing pain in her cheek. A door opened.

"Miss Gardner," a woman's voice, soft, sympathetic. "It's all right. You're okay. This is hospital. Agent McWilliams should be here within a few minutes."

Her mind cleared rapidly. She tried to speak, but her mouth was immobilized within the bandages.

"Agent McWilliams will explain everything to you. Please try to relax. You've been injured, but you're safe here." Leticia tried to get control of her mind as it leapt from image to image in drug slowed sequences. She lost time and awakened to another voice.

"Leticia, this is Agent McWilliams. Can you hear me?"

She tried to nod, but her head felt as if it was in molasses, her eyes unable to focus.

"You are in a hospital after a bad time with those terrorists. I want to say how sorry I am we left you. I had my orders. I knew they were wrong and followed them anyway. That is no excuse." He was silent.

"I'm going to ask you some questions. You can't speak, but blink once for no, twice for yes. Did you know who the people who kidnapped you?"

Leticia tried to shake her head. The world rolled with her. She blinked once.

"The people who attacked you were called Soldiers of the Lord, an ultra-right terrorist group. They were after information from Kihhim. Did you tell them anything?"

Her mind was clearing. She blinked once.

"Did you tell them where the rest of your group is?"

She blinked once.

"Leticia, these guys will not stop until they find what they want. Your people are in danger. Let me protect them. John and Katharine are with us in protective custody. Katharine is your attorney, and maybe in a few days you can meet with her, but you have to help us. Think about what these people did and what they can do to your group. Let me help you."

She didn't blink.

"I'll be back tomorrow." His footsteps receded as the door closed. Muffled voices came from outside.

Her mind felt like it was racing through mud as it started to work. Katharine and John were under protective custody. They would be held incommunicado for as long as deemed necessary.

Being held as critical witnesses in a terrorist act meant even if they told everything, they still would be prisoners. My fate too, Leticia thought. She had to get away. Carol and the Kihhim group had to leave as soon as possible. Leticia tried to sit up, but the restraints on her arms pulled her back. She struggled with them, but lay quietly when she heard the door open.

"Just try to relax, dear. You have terrible injuries, and you need to give them time to heal. Something rustled, and Leticia felt warmth spreading within her. Her mind shut down.

Chapter Fifty-One

FBI Agent Robert McWilliams faced John Vance and Katharine Levey across the table in the interview room. "I want to tell you the same thing I told Ms. Gardner. I am sorry we left you. It was wrong, and I cannot hide behind an excuse of bad orders. I do not expect you to forgive me. I have to live with it myself." Katharine looked at him. His sincerity surprised her.

"You know we can hold you as long as we deem necessary." He looked from John to Katharine. "In the national interest, we cannot afford to let you and your technology fall into the wrong hands. You and Kihhim will not be allowed outside protective custody as long as you have this information and continue work in these areas. Please help us. Where are the people and the technology from Kihhim?"

Katharine and John glanced at each other. Katharine said, "I would like to speak with my client alone, please." Robert McWilliams got up to leave, but Katharine said, "Outside, if you don't mind. This definitely falls under attorney client privilege."

"That does not apply under the Expanded Domestic Terrorism Act, but I will give you a few minutes." He took them to the door and told the waiting agent to take them outside. After passing several doors, they entered a small enclosed patio area.

The agent moved a short distance to one side. The day was warm with the sun completely hidden by heavy clouds. Humidity pressed them down and made the clean desert of Kihhim seem a universe away. Pangs of the loss ached within them.

"It will not get any better, will it?" John asked.

"Probably not. They haven't gotten anything from Leticia yet, or they wouldn't be so intent on us. I've asked to see her for the last week, but they say she is still unconscious in ICU. She may not be anywhere near here."

John held her gaze. "If we tell them what they want, they will go after Kihhim. Everybody will be brought back."

Katharine nodded. "Carol, Rich, and the rest will have to carry on without us. They are quite capable of that. You chose them well." They looked away from each other. Unsaid was they would remain here, perhaps forever.

When they reentered the room, Agent McWilliams rose. Their faces told him nothing would be forthcoming. As they were escorted to their rooms, he spoke to the one-way glass and Assistant Director Janet Kilgore. "We should let them think on this for a while and then try again, perhaps appealing to national patriotism."

"These people do not have feelings of patriotism to the United States," she snarled. "They look at the government as an impediment to their way of life.

We cannot re-educate them in the short period we have. What other avenues are you pursuing?"

"There aren't many places they could go. We are trying to get information from the Mexican government after tapes showed other members crossing at Lukeville. We should have that within a few days. A Venezuelan freighter left Puerto Peñasco a week ago, the same night as the attack. Venezuela has not been quick in giving us destination information."

Janet Kilgore spoke. "The other possibility is they've gone to Idaho or Montana and sought help from the secessionists. Their scrambling system has made telephone records worthless." Janet looked at him. "Let's check the records from the other ends, the organizations likely to take them in? Let's see who's called them. It's a list of those we really hope they haven't talked to."

"We'll get on it right away," said McWilliams.

"What about the one in the hospital?"

"She is in bad shape, but she should be able to communicate in a few days. She was cut up so badly she may not be able to talk for a while. Can I use drugs?"

"Give her a day, then start. She doesn't need to be well for this. She can write the answers to our questions. Whatever you do, do not let her see that attorney."

"I will get back to you in two days," said McWilliams. "We should have something by then."

"Two days at the max."

Chapter Fifty-Two

Leticia's face ached terribly. She was self-medicated but needed a clear head. Yesterday a nurse helped her to the bathroom, her first time out of bed. She'd been weak and wobbly, but today she walked on her own.

She had not seen her face, still swathed in antibiotic bandages and cream. She had to get out, but how? With the bandages and a guard at her door, she couldn't just walk out. The weakness made her shaky as she eased to the window using every piece of furniture for support. Opening the blinds, the high clouds created a shadow-less brightness that hurt her eyes. More tears welled up.

A first floor room, but where? The TV didn't work. Outside she saw trees and bright green grass. This didn't look like Arizona. In the parking lot, a man got out of a car with a Georgia plate.

How did she get here? How long had she been here? Suddenly too weak to stand, she sat on the bed. It seemed only moments later a man stood at the bedside telling her to wake up. She struggled up from unconsciousness, totally confused.

"I'm Dr. Williams, your surgeon. How are you feeling today?"

"Where am I?" mumbled Leticia through the bandages. It hurt, and her jaw and mouth did not work well, but the doctor understood the question.

"Don't talk too much. A little is fine but we don't want to tear open the sutures. You're in a hospital where we specialize in plastic surgery for crash and accident victims. It's lucky you're here, because we're the best at patching people up."

"Where?"

The doctor glanced at the open window. Leticia watched him. The daylight outside was fading. The earlier view had been morning. She had slept all day.

"This is Atlanta," the doctor said. "You arrived here in a helicopter, and I wasn't told from where."

Something in his voice warned Leticia she wouldn't get much more information from him. She had to try. "How long?"

"You were transferred here three days ago. Your doctor at the first hospital did some repair because you arrived so soon after the accident. What you need to do now is get more rest. The damage was severe and will require several operations, but we're starting the day after tomorrow."

"Calls?"

"I am afraid not. You received some bad treatment at the hands of some very nasty people. Rest now and I'll see you after supper." He turned to leave, smiling.

"Dressed?"

"Because of all the blood, your clothes were not salvageable. I will have one of the nurses get you something." He left.

Leticia sat thinking. Several surgeries so she wouldn't frighten children or make adults sick. Tears rolled down her cheeks as she allowed herself a few minutes of self–pity.

Atlanta. How could she get to a phone? she wondered, glancing down at the hospital gown. Might as well try it. A large man in a blue suit stood as she opened the door. "Can I help you?"

"I need to talk to a nurse about clothes," mumbled Leticia.

The man looked her up and down trying to translate what she had said. "I'll get someone for you." He turned and walked down the hall. Leticia noted the direction.

In a few minutes, he returned with a slender haggard nurse about Leticia's size. The nurse introduced herself. "I have a spare pair of jeans and shirt in my locker. I know you'll feel better in regular clothes. Use those until we get you to a store." She turned and left. Leticia smiled at the man and backed into her room. He closed the door.

Leticia looked at the window frame. It was not a secure one. After dark, she would have to get out and to a phone. She would call Dr. Adriana Getzwiller. It was time for both of them to leave the U.S. and catch up with the Kihhim crew in Venezuela.

PART 4

REJUVENATION AND REUNION

Scientists to Pause Research on Deadly Strain of
Bird Flu
By DENISE GRADY Published: January 20,
2012
The scientists who altered a deadly flu virus to
make it more contagious have agreed to suspend
their research for 60 days to give other international
experts time to discuss the work and determine how
it can proceed without putting the world at risk of a
potentially catastrophic pandemic.

Chapter Fifty-Three

FBI Agent McWilliams visited John Vance and Katharine Levey weekly after the first two months as "guests." A year later, his visits had dropped to monthly, Quarterly these last three years. The lost laboratories and scientists from Kihhim had disappeared from the face of the Earth. He traced the freighter carrying the group to Venezuela, but once there, they disappeared.

Robert was sure neither John nor Katharine communicated with the outside, so the message from the Director surprised him. Instead of more threats, badgering, cajoling, and begging, he was here to take them to meet with the President of United States.

"It is your lucky day," Robert McWilliams said to John as he entered his room. The imprisonment had aged John. "You and Ms. Levey have an important meeting, and you need to dress." He handed John a new dark blue suit. It almost fit.

They walked through the hall past closed doors. John always wondered how many were occupied. He hadn't seen Katharine or anybody else except the staff in a long time. McWilliams knocked on a door.

A muffled voice inside said, "Come in." McWilliams held the door open to let John pass. Surprise crossed Katharine's face. She ran to John, and they hugged each other tightly.

Katharine, dressed in a smart dark gray business suit looked great but then she always looked great to John. There were a few lines on her face, and her hair was lighter, but she looked the same.

"Three days ago," said Robert, "President Carson received a message from Leticia Gardner requesting a meeting."

John and Katharine's faces showed shock. They hadn't even known she was alive.

"She specifically requested you both be present. This is the first time we heard from her since she and Dr. Getzwiller disappeared."

More information they didn't know.

"Our meeting is in thirty minutes. Are you ready?" asked McWilliams, holding the door open.

Chapter Fifty-Four

The rich green Virginia countryside flowed beneath the helicopter. It was the first time in four years they had seen more than a walled courtyard.

Washington D.C. appeared below them. The unmistakable lawn of the White House neared quickly, and they wasted no time landing. An immaculately uniformed Marine escorted them through a side door and into an empty office.

John and Katharine's mouths fell open, as Leticia Gardner, looking younger and better than ever came in. The spell broke, and they rushed forward hugging each other, all talking at once. The man behind her cleared his throat.

Leticia stepped back from them. "May I introduce you to the president of the United States, Ronald Carson. Mr. President, this is John Vance and Katharine Levey."

Ronald Carson looked every bit presidential. He was just over six feet tall, slender build with dark hair graying at the temples. His handsome face showed the hints of lines certain to deepen as his first term in office lengthened.

After shaking hands with John and Katharine, the president introduced Janet Kilgore and Lawrence Kennedy. John remembered them, not fondly. The president gestured toward the table and seats.

"Last week I found out about a problem I unknowingly inherited from the previous administration." He looked at Lawrence Kennedy. "Ms. Gardner sent me a message a few days ago making me an offer. After a briefing about this situation by Mr. Kennedy and Ms. Kilgore, I could not refuse to at least meet and discuss it." He glanced at Leticia.

"In this message, she revealed Kihhim has now declared itself a sovereign nation, one at sea. As such, Kihhim has become Kahchk Kihhim. As I understand, in the native O'Odham language it means Sea Village."

John and Katharine looked at each other, smiles on their faces. They'd done it.

The president continued. "Kahchk Kihhim is asking for recognition from the United States, and it is requesting the United States of America assist in their protection. Not until I was briefed about the history of Kihhim did I give serious consideration to this." He glanced at Leticia.

"She has made it clear there are compelling reasons for a bond between Kahchk Kihhim and the United States. Recognition and the opening of relations with us will have to pass Congress, and we are prepared to offer aid."

Leticia held up her hand. "As I mentioned to you before, our security is in both of our interests."

The president nodded. "We realize the protection of your technology is best for not only the United States but the world. To get any treaties and recognition approval through Congress, we must have to have fact-finding visits and a presentation for discussion."

"Mr. President," said Leticia, "I'm not sure fact-finding missions will work. At this time, we would like to address only the issues of recognition and an alliance for defense. As a very small nation, we are afraid of being overwhelmed and subverted. What we possess could be a threat to the United States or any nation if it falls into the wrong hands."

"Exactly." exclaimed the president. "The term 'wrong hands' bothers us too. For any defense agreement, we need to know a lot more about Kahchk Kihhim. Sooner or later expenditures of the United States must be justifiable to the people."

"Mr. President, this is what we believed would be your position. We understand it."

John watched Leticia as she conversed with the president. She seemed so assured, capable of playing at this level. Why? How? he wondered.

"It is vital we live independently without outside interference and influence," she continued. "That is why we fled the United States. Inspection by outsiders would subject us to judgment of our lifestyle. Whether that judgment was negative or positive, eventually it would lead to pressures to change because we are different."

"Are your differences so great you could not adapt or the world might not adapt to you?" asked the president, trying to understand.

"Our differences define us," said Leticia.

John did not understand either. How had Kihhim changed?

"I am afraid I cannot move forward under these conditions. Without the approval of the people of the United States, support for you is not possible," said the president, "no more than we would support slavery or child abuse."

"As you already said, it is vital that our technology not be misused. If you cannot support us, and you cannot allow our knowledge to fall into other hands then you must destroy us." Leticia's face took on a joyless smile. "We foresaw this dilemma. I hope you understand what I am about to tell you." Leticia glanced at Katharine and John then back at the president.

"Do you understand the term 'dead man's switch'?" The president nodded. "Make no mistake. Like any nation, including the United States, we will do anything to preserve our existence and independence. We signed no treaties limiting any of our activities, including what we can use to protect ourselves. We will sign none. I want no misunderstanding. If we are attacked or even destroyed, the destruction of civilization will follow. That is now out of our hands."

There was a stunned silence around the table. John and Katharine looked at each other, then at Leticia. She coolly looked back.

"Ms. Gardner," said Assistant Attorney General Lawrence Kennedy, "what kind of threat are you trying to make here? How do we know there is any truth to what you are threatening? Do you have some kind of bomb?"

"We do not want to ever resort to any demonstration, so we prepared this description which your own people can verify." She handed him a data cube. "To explain," she continued, "we introduced a virus into the world's human population. Presently, it is inert."

The president stared at her, a knot of dread forming in his gut. "Ms. Gardner, as Secretary of the Interior under President Davidson, I saw the results of both the bio and cyber-attacks that destroyed the economy, and effectively the United States. Only now is the recovery taking hold. If this threat is real, the potential damage would be much greater."

Leticia continued, "Yes, sir. It will become active sometime in the future. The effects resemble Ebola, but it is even more virulent." Mouths fell open around the room. "The virus is fully resistant to any antivirus agent available today." There was a collective gasp.

"Kahchk Kihhim will release an antivirus in time to avert the virus becoming active. The antivirus will not kill the virus, but keep it inert. We will continue to release the antivirus as long as we can. Our sampling shows virtually the whole human population is already infected."

"This is extortion." shouted the president, as he stood and banged his fist on the table.

"It is, Mr. President, this is also our existence. There are no rules for us. As a quid pro quo in return for your protection, we offer some of our developments to the United States."

She handed over another cube and a vial. "This is a micro-algae that uses sunlight and water with a few nutrients to grow and produce hydrogen as a waste product. It is much more productive than any in existence today. As you know, a hydrogen-based energy system is the ideal that scientists sought for decades. It offers pollution-free cheap energy. We believe this," she held up the vial, "will give the United States the potential to become a world supplier of energy instead of the largest per capita consumer. It could substantially improve your economic position in the world."

"On one hand you put a gun to our heads," the president snarled, "and then you offer us candy?"

Leticia hurried on, "In addition, we have this." She held out another data cube and vial. "This is another plant to be used in making a living paint, a special paint. When exposed to sun and air, it lives and sustains itself, forming a strong protective coating over roofs and buildings. It uses sunlight to break up carbon dioxide and release oxygen, existing solely to clean up the air. If used on city buildings and roofs, we predict it will drop the carbon dioxide content below pre-industrial revolution levels within fifty years. In simple terms, it will clean up the air." Again, there was silence around the table. "These gifts are to help mankind, but more importantly, they will help the Earth."

"What a challenge," said the president "On one hand, you offer gifts to improve our world, and on the other, you threaten to destroy us. Why are you so averse to joining the world community? Do you think you are so different? It seems you are ostracizing yourselves, not attempting to become a part of the world with us."

Leticia smiled. "I hope to show you why we needed to take these precautions someday. Now is not that time. First, we need protection in order to survive, protection, without a presence in Kahchk Kihhim itself."

"Why do you object to a presence?" asked Kennedy.

"I am sure you are already getting hints that our way of life is different from yours. We have not abided by the United Nations directives regarding human genetic research and development. Some would say that is immoral or against God's law. We cannot afford to gamble our existence on the tolerance of humanity. That track record is not good."

Here it is, thought John. Kihhim has continued with genetic development. How far? he wondered.

"We will not change," stated Leticia. "When you cannot control or influence us, there will be a clamor for our destruction."

"You sound paranoid as if you have separated yourselves from the human race," said the president.

"Is it possible to exist alongside the world community without joining? Can the world allow anyone to be separately independent?"

"Of course we can," said the president.

"Name an example," said Leticia, softly.

The president said nothing for a few minutes. "The world is a community. We must live together. No country is independent of the rest."

"It is tolerance that is in short supply," pointed out Leticia. "Differences in race, religion and economics have driven all of the world conflicts. What would be the reaction to something seriously different? History makes us feel threatened, and we are trying to survive. We seek your assistance in doing that."

"Not a good way of asking," sneered Kennedy.

"The weak are absorbed or conquered. Without this gun to your head, you, too, would be tempted to use us to promote your way of life in the world. You would do this through coercion, gradual infiltration, outright force, or a combination of all of these. It is what you do."

"What is wrong with that?" asked Janet Kilgore speaking for the first time. "We maintain one of the best representative governments in the world, and our way of life is the envy of most of humanity."

"Not everybody in this world thinks your way of life should be the only one," said Leticia. "Many do not think the majority rule is best, but we are straying from the purpose of my visit. In addition to those," she nodded toward the cubes and vials, "I came to take John and Katharine home."

She pointed at the data cubes. "Take thirty days to analyze the contents and respond. I will remain with you as your new guest to answer any questions and communicate back to Kahchk Kihhim," she said smiling. "Consider me an envoy of the new country."

Kennedy shook his head in disgust, muttering the word, "envoy."

"Assure yourselves everything I told you is true," continued Leticia. "Formulate your plans and decide how to enact them. I am here to assist you in any way I can."

She looked at John and Katharine. "I would like to spend time with John and Katharine. We will take my car for a short trip." Janet Kilgore started to object when Leticia continued. "We expect you to place cars around us the whole time."

"We have rooms for you to use," said Kennedy, but Leticia looked at him and raised one eyebrow. "Give us a few minutes to... have your escort ready," he weakly finished. The others rose, not sure what had happened. Was this meeting at an end?

Chapter Fifty-Five

As they walked out to the car, Katharine studied Leticia. According to McWilliams Leticia sustained severe disfiguring injuries in the kidnapping, nothing about the extent. Leticia looked healthier than ever. In a few minutes, they were in a car waiting for the FBI cars to move into place. "Can you really do what you said?" asked Katharine.

Leticia put her finger to her lips. Within seconds, a car pulled up behind them, and they started driving. Leticia removed a small box from her purse and flipped a switch. "It's clear to talk now. First, this is the real me, not a clone. After I called Adriana and explained my situation, she agreed to help. She wanted to be with her mother again and was ready to leave."

"Adriana helped you escape?" asked Katharine.

Leticia nodded. "She's now a doctor on Kahchk Kihhim."

"We were told you were severely injured in the kidnapping. You seem fine," noted Katharine.

"I'll show you pictures someday. That bastard carved me up. It'll take a strong stomach."

"But how…?"

"You'll see when you get home. We've made remarkable progress in many forms of genetic control. And yes, we spread a virus that shows virtually 100% saturation within one year. This is not an idle threat. They would detect it. It will do everything I said. The president will not take long to wonder about our design abilities since I gave him the gifts and the virus."

She smiled at them. "Things changed faster than even you could foresee. Once we were able to design and direct genetics to grow what we wanted, we accelerated all of our programs changing life at unbelievable rates. Residents within our ocean nation would not be considered human by the rest of the world."

Katharine didn't understand. "Not human? What does that mean?"

"Kahchk Kihhim citizens are of the sea. We design ourselves for our environment. Many of us don't look like humans. You'll learn more when you get home."

John and Katharine sat silently trying to absorb everything. Leticia continued. "In an evolutionary world based on competition and survival of the fittest, the human race reached their lofty status by being the strongest. Humans today cannot throw off that genesis. Confrontation would be inevitable. We cannot take the chance they might not accept that there is enough room on this earth for both of us."

"But there will be teams of scientists trying to produce an antivirus," said Katharine.

Leticia nodded. "We're only buying time. In ten years we'll have the resources to ensure our existence. Until then, we'll use all means necessary to protect ourselves."

"Including wiping out civilization," muttered John.

"John, we are citizens of the ocean. We modified ourselves to live on the sea, and we modified sea creatures to live symbiotically with us. The bigotry of sex, different races, skin colors or religions is nothing compared what would happen to us, people who are fundamentally altered?" Leticia looked from John to Katharine.

"We are no longer land creatures, and thus not part of the human race. They must destroy us. Humans are not tolerant enough to accept us."

"Don't you think you are selling them short?" asked Katharine.

"We can only use history to judge. Do you want to take a chance?"

"Would you really destroy civilization?" asked

Leticia grimaced. "Though we hid the virus in the basic DNA of humans, they will find it and eventually find a cure. We do not intend to war with anyone, only protect ourselves. In doing so, we refuse to be bound by the rules of war that favor those who have always won. All is fair in survival, and this is not a game."

"You know they will test you. They must," said John.

"There are lesser options, most non-lethal. Each time we use something it will point up our weaknesses."

"Time," said John, "something Katharine and I have had too much of the last few years. I feel so behind."

"Kahchk Kihhim needs a protector with an incentive stronger than good will or friendship or one subject to the political wind."

"Very neat," said John. "You realize that you have become the nightmare they foresaw–the very thing they fear. You have justified their fear. Do you really think you can extort the United States government?"

"How long did the threat of mutually-assured destruction keep nuclear war from happening? The ultimate club is the best insurance we could come up with. It's our survival. Where we differ from the nightmare is that survival, not dominance, is our only intent."

John and Katharine were astounded by this whole turn of events. This was too much and too fast. They were going to be free, not because they had been wrongly imprisoned, but because of threats made against humanity. They could not understand what had happened at the new Kihhim. How could this change have taken place so quickly?

Chapter Fifty-Six

Back at the White House, an escort returned them to an office. Janet Kilgore and Robert McWilliams sat at the table, but the President was absent.

Robert stared at Leticia. This could not be the ruined face he pulled from the kidnapper's van four years ago. Absolutely no sign of the vicious slashing she had sustained. Were they that good at cosmetic surgery? Was it the same Leticia? Perhaps there was something to be afraid of.

With effort, he looked away from her and toward John and Katharine. Both he and Janet Kilgore had a hard look about them. They did not like no longer being in control.

Janet Kilgore left with a curt goodbye.

The agent's cell phone sounded. "Your things are here. You two are free to go."

"Ms. Gardner," he said facing Leticia, "I want to say how glad I am that you're okay. I'm so sorry we left you, and I have lived with the guilt that I was the cause of your terrible injuries. Your recovery is more than remarkable. I am happy for you."

John and Katharine hugged Leticia. "You will understand much better when you get home," she said. "I'll be joining you in a few months."

"I feel we are abandoning you," said Katharine.

"Not at all," said Leticia. "I have the capable agent McWilliams to take care of me. I'm sure he will see no harm comes."

McWilliams quietly said to them, "It was not just your threat that secured your release, but there is now no reason to hold you. I follow orders and take my job and my responsibilities seriously. I harbor no animosity toward you, and in some ways, I admire you. We were just on opposite sides. I wish you luck."

Katharine and John smiled. "Thank you, Robert," John said. "We wish you luck as well." They turned and hugged Leticia a last time and walked through the door toward a new world.

Chapter Fifty-Seven

A helicopter took John and Katharine to a general aviation airport where they climbed into a small jet. Despite the excitement of being free, they both fell asleep, awakening as it landed. The sun shone brightly, the air warm, like the best of summer days.

A tall thin man introducing himself as Albert Jackson met them. He had an easy smile, a weathered face, thinning hair and an unmistakable Kiwi accent. He led them across the sunlit tarmac to a helicopter. Talking without taking a breath, he went through the preflight checklist. Albert seemed to know everything about them, but within minutes, the whine of the rotors winding up drowned him out.

As they became airborne, he signaled for them to put on the headsets, and the one-sided conversation resumed.

"Call me Jacko. Been a resident of Kahchk Kihhim for longer than two years. I gotta say it's a bang-up great place to be. Before I joined, I had a one-man transport company, flying people and equipment around the South Pacific. Damn company grew, and before I knew it, all I flew was a desk."

John and Katharine laughed at his measure of success.

"I tell ya, mate that wasn't for me. When this secret contract came along flying equipment to Kahchk Kihhim, I took it. My first view of that place dropped my jaw. When they asked me if I would join, I couldn't get my knickers out of the office fast enough."

Four hours later, over sparkling blue waters, a dot appeared on the horizon. Jacko pointed. "Home," he said and let the quiet grow. He watched them strain to resolve the tiny speck into an object. The helicopter dropped close to the water, and the waves flew by in a frenzy of motion.

When they looked up, their mouths opened and their eyes widened as the floating city rushed at them expanding until it filled the windshield. Jocko laughed at their reaction. "See, I told ya."

Before them floated the gargantuan catamaran. The two supertankers each had a row of five wing-shaped sails towering from the decks, like wings from a Boeing 747 standing on end. A wide arched skyscraper lay on its side, stretching between the two hulls. It extended half the length of the ships, the top a checkerboard of glass windows, plant filled green squares and solar panels. They were still much too far away to see any people.

Jacko circled, and the enormous arch resolved into an arced segment six stories thick at the top. The ends connected into the ships with monstrous pins, forming a huge hinge. The decks had gigantic open hatches with more greenery and the occasional glint of mirrors inside.

Trailing behind the catamaran in the blue Pacific floated concentric rings of what looked like small buoys. These circles extended to a diameter of over two miles. John opened his mouth to ask about them, but Jacko was into his landing sequence. The helicopter swooped down feathered out and landed on the deck with a gentle bump. Jacko flicked switches and the whine of the rotors diminished into a welcome silence.

As Katharine and John removed their headsets, the door opened, and warm fresh air wafted across their faces with the smell of the sea. It felt wonderful.

Chapter Fifty-Eight

Eager hands assisted them into the sunshine. Carol and Rich were close, their arms around them. Tears streamed freely as more people pressed in. At last, they were home.

As they disentangled, Rich turned and held their hands up like winners in a prizefight. A cheer arose. Vigorous hugs jostled them with everyone trying to speak at once.

"Welcome home to the sovereign nation of Kahchk Kihhim," said Rich. Another cheer and both Katharine and John waved. They both looked up, letting the brilliant sunlight bathe their faces. Free at last. Above them, the monstrous sails seemed to touch the blue sky. They ducked through a doorway.

"Are you tired?" asked Carol. "Do you want to rest?"

"We both slept on the plane. Jacko kept us awake on the trip here," said John,

"He does that," she laughed.

"Is there somewhere we can sit and talk for a while?" asked Katharine.

"Tea garden," said Rich. He guided them through a series of halls and doorways until they stood before a covered ramp that arced up into the distance. On one side, windows overlooked the sparkling blue ocean. The ship's hull curved out of sight while the protected area between the massive ships was like a hot summer day at the public pool. Activity was everywhere, people, dolphins, fish, everything moving. They watched for a few minutes.

Lush thick greenery crowded from the other side of the ramp, arching above and shading them from the sun through the glass roof. The air held the fragrant moist heaviness of a greenhouse with the tang of the ocean. The temperature was warm but not uncomfortable as a breeze pushed its way through the verdant life.

"Many of our greenhouses are open, since we don't need to worry about dryness or insects. All can be closed to prevent storm damage."

"The climate is warm enough for everything?" asked John.

"John we're mobile. We follow the climate most favorable for us," said Rich. "We move from the southern hemisphere to the northern in a great oval path that allows us to maximize our sunlight. For us, it's forever summer."

Where the arch leveled off, they found themselves in a beautiful shaded glen, with trees and grass surrounding several tables. On one side was another greenhouse filled with fruit-laden trees. Blooms added their fragrance to the fresh sea air. Through the glass wall on the other side were the twin hulls of Kahchk Kihhim reaching back into the sea behind. As they sat, John and Katharine watched, silenced by the peace and beauty. A teenage girl came over and gave first Katharine then John a hug.

"I'm Megan Steele. It is so nice to have you back. We were planning a party tonight to welcome you, but Carol said tomorrow."

"Megan." said John. "You've grown up so I hardly recognize you. What a lovely young woman you've become."

She blushed. "Thank you. There are so many of us who missed you." She started to say something more and stopped, seemingly flustered. Walking away, she glanced over her shoulder as if not believing she was seeing them again.

Rich touched the table. It displayed a menu. "Scroll through or pick a category. You can check or sort by ingredients if you want. When you make your selection, the kitchen receives it. Let's start with drinks."

As Katharine scrolled the beverages, she saw teas and coffees, but also beers. She ordered one.

"Our menu will include wines by the end of next year," Carol said. "We've developed grapes that don't need the cold weather, but it's taking a while to get the flavor right." They made their selections, and in a few minutes, Megan was back with their drinks and snacks.

John looked out at the expanse of sea and questions flooded in. "What are all of those buoys with the sails?"

"Those are modified Portuguese Man of War, part of our aquaculture. They're strung together to form the concentric circles you probably noticed from the air. The sails on the jellyfish keep the nets spread out. Their long tentacles form a mesh barricade and each circle holds a different size of fish. The outer net is the finest mesh, holding the smallest fish, the fry, and protecting them from things outside the ring." Rich looked at John and Katharine.

"We've developed strains of algae, plankton, and brine shrimp that grow rapidly in our vats. It's our feed for the fry. The next circle in is a larger mesh, which keeps the larger fish from getting into the smaller, but the smaller fish stray into the larger and are food for them. This continues to the center section where we harvest our food fish. It all trickles down." He smiled, obviously proud of the design.

"If you look closely, you'll be able to see our Dahlfins working the circles. At first, we domesticated dolphins, like sheep dogs. Soon after, we modified them. Now the Dahlfins are fully as intelligent as we are. They are a young species, still children but learning so quickly. We enjoy them and they us as partners. They're full-fledged citizens of Kahchk Kihhim."

"How did you change them?" asked Katharine.

"We modified their gene structure to increase brain capacity in the abstract and reasoning regions. Once their language expanded, their learning accelerated at an astounding rate. Now they teach each other and sometimes us. We'll go meet some later."

"How many live here?" asked John.

"The number varies between 100 and 150. They have much more freedom to live outside of Kahchk Kihhim proper. Some groups stay for a while, move on, and then return. Though Kahchk Kihhim is their home, they are nomadic. Our resident Dahlfins are territorial, as are we and all species."

"What about the natural dolphin population? Are they affected?" asked John.

"We discussed this extensively with the Dahlfins and agree intermixing would be bad. They do not do it," said Carol.

"Aren't you afraid they will increase in numbers?"

"We both limit our populations for now."

"What kind of work do they do?" asked Katharine.

"They work in defense, fish farming, herding, and even feeding. Some work as scouts fanning out into the sea. Others keep predators away, both the finny variety and the two legged variety."

"You have trouble with people?" asked John, surprised.

"Some fishermen consider us invaders into their territories even though we stay away from the large fishing grounds. At first, some harassed us by getting close, sometimes snagging our growing circles. A few even tried to raid us."

He grinned. "Many of the fry we feed are left behind, enriching the waters. Those fishermen working with us have no trouble with successful catches, especially when our Dahlfins herd the wild fish toward them. Conversely, those who do not work with us come back strangely barren."

"In a few cases, we have to sabotage their boats and nets when they become aggressive," said Carol.

"Six months ago," said Rich, "Chile sent out a naval vessel to move us away from what they considered their fishing grounds. We pointed out that we were far into international waters, but they threatened us. The ships props became fouled with material they could not cut. They had to be towed back to port. Unfriendly fishermen have fouling problems as well with their own nets being a large part of the problem. It's embarrassing, and many consider us bad luck."

"The Dahlfins helped you with this?" asked Katharine.

"They are very protective," said Carol nodding.

John watched the activity below with new understanding. He now was able to pick out people riding Dahlfins or being towed by them attending the nets. His thoughts were interrupted by Megan's return with their food. John and Katharine ate, welcoming the chance to assimilate what they had been told. It was only the first few hours of their first day.

Chapter Fifty-Nine

President Carson hurriedly called the meeting with his Secretary of State, Wesley Hamilton, Secretary of Defense, Craig Nelson, Secretary of Navy, Admiral Harold Cochrain, and Health Consultant, Dr. Karol Benz. Review of Kahchk Kihhim's ultimatum did not take long.

"This whole thing has disturbing issues," started Wesley. "First, the forming of a sovereign nation at sea opens up troubling possibilities. What if every disgruntled group around the world started doing this? Where would the international waters go if every little floating barge declared a twenty-five mile limit?"

Heads nodded.

"Second, they rebuffed all invitations to join the United Nations and the international community. This new nation has no treaties with anyone nor do they intend to adhere to international laws, including weapons of mass destruction–biological, chemical, maybe even nuclear." He frowned.

"Third, we know they are actively pursuing research in areas forbidden by international treaty. This puts humanity at risk and has moral implications. They represent a rogue force, and what we should do is wipe them off the face of the earth."

"This is exactly the attitude they foresaw," said President Carson, "and they tried to counter with this blackmail proposal. Is this a genuine threat?" He turned to a severe-looking woman, her black hair cut short. "Dr. Benz?"

"I studied the information in detail. The consensus of our task group is this is a real threat. Without going into a lot of scientific jargon, they created an artificial virus by utilizing parts of the deadliest diseases mankind has ever faced. They took the worst traits from each and made a nightmare."

"You mean it is true?" asked the president in an uncharacteristically soft voice.

She nodded. "The data they supplied is a step-by-step process for testing for the virus. It's true all right." "We've tried to confirm the virus presence independently with other tests, but it masks like a lot of other benign types. Somehow, it's wrapped up intimately in our cells. Complicating the search is that it's inactive. Our test procedure activates it and it becomes virulent. We had fatalities. People we tested with their procedure were positive one hundred percent."

"Now that you found it, can you do anything?" asked Secretary of Defense Nelson.

"We haven't been able to isolate it, we don't know how they are keeping it inactive, nor when it will become active. When we think we've found the virus, it mutates, being specifically designed to resist our efforts. We are further hampered by the precautions we must take during examinations. At this stage I cannot even give you a projected schedule."

"Surely you have some idea. A week, a month?" asked Nelson.

More chilling than an answer, she pressed her lips tightly together and shook her head looking him straight in the eye. "It changes while we are observing it. None of the changes seem to do anything harmful yet. But at some point the virus may become deadly."

There was silence as the information sank in. "Thank you, doctor. Please keep us informed through the Secretary of Defense," said the president, dismissing her.

"They did indeed do something, and it may be a while before we know what. Can we assume this virus will continue to be harmless? No. Can we stall for time? No. Can we go after them? NO! Worse yet," he was shouting now his hand banging the table, "we cannot let anyone else go after them. I do not like this." he blasted.

Seeing his frustration and anger reflected from each face brought back the calm leadership that sustained and moved him through his years of service. Leadership was what he was elected for.

He pushed the frustration and rage aside. It was time to lead again, to get them focused on the problem and away from the emotions and reactions.

The bottom line was they had to go along, figure out how to protect a new nation while keeping the actual reason secret. If, no he corrected, when, it was discovered that the government of the United States of America, a hyper-power in the world was being extorted, public reaction would be a disaster.

He had three more years to go in this term, and discovery would be a catastrophe for his political future and perhaps for mankind. This had to be spun so they were seen as benevolent guardians of a new and budding nation. He had to buy time. Those agreements required more than the Executive Branch. This could cost him all of his political favors and then some. Interesting times lay ahead.

First, he had to get his own people past the rancor generated by the threat. "Okay, gentlemen, we have to accept the situation for now and take control of the things we can. What are we going to do?" he asked.

"We will do what we always do in these situations," said Wesley. Stunned silence was followed by a nervous twitter as those around the table looked at the sardonic smile on the Secretary of State's face.

The president started to laugh. "I don't believe we have ever had a situation like this before."

"No sir, we have not, but that does not alter our plan. We'll make them our best friends, bide our time, get them to depend on us, and all the while work behind the scenes. Best deal all around politically too. Maybe they can become a protectorate. Will Congress buy that?"

"How long can we fund something like this without somebody getting curious?" asked the president.

"Of course they will get curious," said Wesley. "But that takes time. Time for us to figure something out. We must put someone on Kahchk Kihhim. We must insist on that."

"I agree. How long can we patrol and protect a particular section of ocean before serious questions became a problem, Admiral?" the president asked Cochrain.

The Admiral pulled himself erect, smoothed his silver hair with his hand. "We could get by for a while, unless we actually had to stop someone. What do we do then?"

Aye, there is the rub the president thought.

Secretary Nelson spoke up. "What if we stationed a carrier group in the area? We can always protect a perimeter area around them."

"Good." said the president. "That is the how, now the why. How do we make this seem insignificant enough to not arouse undue concern but justify our carrier group?"

Admiral Cochrain spoke. "We'll designate the usual hundred mile circle as a training area for our carrier groups and rotate them in and out on a regular basis. It wouldn't seem too unusual except the patrol range would encompass Kahchk Kihhim. We could control the area. Besides, they are continuously moving around the Pacific."

"I like it," said the president. "Low key, high degree of response possible, and under our control. Let's get Representative Leticia Gardner in here."

Chapter Sixty

Within minutes, Leticia Gardner was introduced to those around the table, shaking hands with each and meeting their icy stares. She took a seat as the president rose to speak.

"Ms. Gardner, we checked your threat and considered your offer, if that is the right word. We have a proposal for you. We can meet your need for protection by using the area around your new country as a training area for our carrier groups. There are details to be worked out, but we will require a representative at Kahchk Kihhim. We will give that person any title you find acceptable, but we do not consider that item negotiable."

Leticia looked at him and then around the table trying to read expressions. "We must have approval power for this representative."

"Done." said the president.

"Mr. President, we want an agreement that will last past our time. We are in accord," Leticia said.

Past our time meant after my term, thought the president. "If you will meet with Admiral Cochrain and Secretary Nelson regarding details of the patrolling and protection, you can start drafting it. We will issue a joint announcement of recognition of Kahchk Kihhim after the agreement is signed."

The president rose with an expression on his face as if he just spit out a mouthful of sour milk. Those around the table rose as he left the room.

The admiral nodded toward another door, and the three of them left for an office down the hall. Nothing was said until they were seated around a small table. "Do you want anything–coffee, tea, something to eat?" the admiral asked as an aide hovered at his side. She shook her head, and with a flick of his hand, the aide disappeared.

Secretary of State Nelson stared at her with penetrating black eyes and spoke. "The method of protection we are offering you will involve military presence–ships, aircraft, and personnel. We'll control them, but we will need latitude for flyovers, air corridors, and patrol lanes for our ships and subs."

Leticia nodded. "Because we have sensitive areas, we need a ten mile 'No enter area' around Kahchk Kihhim. Outside of that circle you will control the airspace and seaways. All of our comings and goings will be coordinated with you to assure safe passage."

Secretary of Defense Nelson looked at Admiral Cochrain. Neither of them liked a blind spot, but it was at the center of their control zone. In reality it would not be blind. Besides satellite coverage, there would be subs, practically undetectable. No reason to let this detail muddy the waters. "Agreed," said Nelson. The door opened, and they rose as the president entered.

Leticia smiled at him. "I'm surprised at how quickly you moved. We anticipated a much more drawn-out process."

A sardonic smile crossed the president's face. "It is amazing how fast things can be done when a small group is involved, and the press is not allowed to make news out of every little detail. Do not be fooled. There will be a lot of interest, and a clamoring for investigations. We expect you to handle things to protect us as well. If my administration is called to task on this, we will all be in a real mess. Are we close?"

"We have reached accommodation regarding protection and patrol," said Cochrain.

"Why don't you and Admiral Nelson go pass everything on to Wesley. I want the draft agreement in our hands. I would like to spend a few minutes with Ms. Gardner." They both turned and left, closing the door.

"Ms. Gardner, I focused my people on meeting the necessary goals for us to reach accord, but the anger at being threatened, at having a gun put to our heads remains. We will both continue to deal with that resentment."

"Mr. President, without that threat, we would never have been taken seriously. Time would pass while the danger to us grew until an incident would force us to defend ourselves. Like a cornered animal, we would use anything to survive. The danger to the world is real. As distasteful as this method seems, we could think of nothing else with any chance of success."

The president frowned. "It took me a while to reach the same conclusion. A number of my staff have not accepted the fact yet. We must make this appear positive. Your help is critical or control will slip away, and that could be disastrous for all of us."

"Mr. President, this arrangement must appear the most friendly possible." Leticia said smiling. "I propose you plan a visit perhaps to attend the celebration of our recognition as an independent nation."

The president focused his gaze on her. "At this stage, it may be better if I send a representative in my stead, Vice President Sanchez. You understand all that will entail?"

"We need time to prepare for the retinue, but we will accommodate them. How soon can we make the announcement of recognition?"

"Within two days of the signing of our agreement, Vice President Sanchez and his staff will make arrangements for the visit, but we will let the exact date float for now." He rose and smiled, one that Leticia took as genuine. "Now, I must get back to the rest of the world's matters and petty problems."

As Leticia shook his offered hand she said, "This has been a pleasure, Mr. President."

"Maybe more so for you than me, certainly more than for my staff. Let us hope this is the beginning of a long amicable relationship." He turned and was gone. As he walked down the hall, he had to admit admiration for Kahchk Kihhim. Without killing anyone, they formed a new nation and achieved security. What balls! And they were right about civilization too. With all the bells and whistles, the world was still made up of tribes squabbling over territory and trinkets, trying to get power over the next tribe.

Leticia sat and exhaled. This had gone well. Within seconds, Secretary of State Wesley Hamilton entered. Leticia rose again.

"Ms. Gardner, please be seated," he said brusquely. He walked over and handed her several pages of paper. "Please read this over and make changes as you see fit. If you need to speak with your government, I will show you to the communication room."

"Thank you," she said taking the papers from him. As she started rapidly scanning the pages, she was aware of his intense study of her. His rangy body seemed to quiver beneath his tailored gray suit. She ignored him.

There were actually two documents. The first was recognition of Kahchk Kihhim as an independent nation and the establishment of diplomatic ties. It had notations reading "Insert proper formats here," in many places.

The second document was an agreement for "Mutual Protection" of each other and the human race from all threats, and attacks. It was also a mutual agreement for research and development of technologies for the benefit of mankind. There was no statement about joint efforts. It was simple, leaving little room for misunderstanding or guile. Attorneys would hate it. She looked at Wesley Hamilton. "Please formalize these, and I will sign them." It was that simple. Now the reality.

Chapter Sixty-One

When word of the accord and the announcement reached Kahchk Kihhim, the response was explosive. They were legitimate. They were real. For the first time since they moved to sea, they had a holiday–a real independence day. The celebration included feasts and speeches. Katharine gave the final speech.

"Through a long and sometimes torturous path, we built our own nation, one based on freedom: Freedom to move about, freedom to do as we wish, but more importantly, we have freedom of thought. This will lead to a spirit of growth and development in ways we only now are starting to conceive. Never forget we are a part of everything around us, not separate. With our growth comes the responsibility of ensuring humanity's existence, for it is our existence also. We are all in this world together."

As Katharine watched the citizens of Kahchk Kihhim retire for the night, Rich approached her. "We're not equipped for the Vice President's visit and everything it will require. No one here has any experience in this type of thing."

Katharine looked at him. "We'll probably be getting more help than we want. Someone needs to be in charge of it, so start thinking of who is going to get the job."

***

Dayton was shocked to see Leticia Gardner on the podium with President Carson, recognizing the new nation of Kahchk Kihhim. The mystery of the complete disappearance of Kihhim fell into place. He tried to reach Leticia.

After several hours, and using all of his press credentials, her voice came on the phone. "Leticia, this is Dayton King. I just saw the announcement. Congratulations," he said in a rush.

"Dayton. How nice to hear your voice. Thanks."

"Leticia, how can I reach Carol?" he asked without preamble.

Leticia chuckled and gave him a number. "Do not give this number to anyone," she admonished. "We'll release a public number soon, but we will need to keep at least a few lines private."

"Thanks, Leticia."

"I'm pretty busy right now, Dayton. I have to go. Nice to talk to you," she said, hanging up.

Dayton felt emotions wash over him. Carol was alive! He could talk to her again. Quickly he entered the number. The phone was answered immediately.

"Hello." His monitor showed Carol's face as he heard her voice. His breath caught in his throat, and he was unable to speak. "Hello? Dayton, is that you?" she said again, peering at her monitor. At last he made himself speak.

"Carol?" he croaked out.

"Dayton!" she shouted. Then they were talking at the same time. They both stopped. "You first," Carol said.

"When you left, I didn't know what had happened. I didn't hear from you, and the phones at Kihhim just rang. When I went out there, it was abandoned. I've been worried sick." It all came out in a rush.

"Oh, Dayton. I am so sorry. We had to get out, and we couldn't take any chances on being stopped. We didn't dare communicate with anyone in the United States, even after we left the country. I wanted to let you know I was all right, but we were gone for good. Since you had your life and I had mine it seemed like…," her voice trailed off.

"I missed you so much, Dayton. If we hadn't been so busy, I don't think I could have taken it. We were afraid anyone we contacted would be interrogated, maybe even arrested. Katharine and John have been locked up since we left. We only recently brought them to Kahchk Kihhim."

Dayton spoke. "The FBI did talk to me several times. They may have followed me at first. I got that feeling sometimes. I think they monitored my calls too. After a while the feeling went away."

"We were sure they would try everything to find us. I tried to follow your career, but it was too painful. Now that we are a nation, the secrecy doesn't matter, and I want to see you again."

"I want to see you, too," Dayton said, realizing how much he meant it.

"The Vice President is coming to visit, and we are going to need a lot of help coordinating the entourage. Do you know anyone who would be interested?" She added quietly, "Are you?"

Dayton's mind leapt. Of course, he was interested. It would put him in the driver's seat for this whole thing. More than that, he would be with Carol again. "Do you want me to come there and work for Kahchk Kihhim?"

Carol nodded, "Yes."

His mind balked. He could get out of his contract with the news service, leaving the position he had worked so hard to achieve. But the thrill was already starting to wane. Perhaps he was ready for a career change. "Do I need to look first?" he asked.

"You liked Kihhim. You will like this even more," Carol said.

"How do I get there?"

Carol exhaled the breath she had been holding. She gave him directions and a schedule for the chopper ride out. Dayton scribbled furiously.

Chapter Sixty-Two

After seeing the presidential announcement with Leticia Gardner, Ralph Whitney watched a documentary about Kahchk Kihhim. So that's where Kihhim had gone. A smile crossed his face. He'd given up on them. Their technology must have improved even more in the intervening years. The appearance of the bitch was remarkable. He'd left her a ruin. Now here she was not only whole, but as young as the night he cut her up. He still rankled at his failure to get her to talk.

Since that night, the world's increasing hunger for energy created explosive unrest in the areas supplying that need. In the "Arab Spring" the Islamic nations suffered internal uprisings and fought among themselves. Riots broke out, with the people demanding more representative government. The traditional leadership did not react well, viciously suppressing the demonstrators. In several Middle Eastern countries, the United Nations intervened on the side of the rebels, but the puppet democracies were soon taken over by the organized Islamic fundamentalists. The governments became even more oppressive and belligerent toward the world or unstable again.

China was recovering after the disastrous bio-cyber war. Quietly they continued to expand influence across Asia. Without the checks and balances in Europe and North America, their infrastructure was modernizing quickly. They remained the number one polluter throughout the world, impervious to criticism and international regulation.

Ralph watched these changes with glee. Unrest was his stock in trade. He paid close attention. With a new nation being formed with unknown capabilities, new contracts could come his way.

A map of the Pacific Ocean showed a red circle, an X marking the location of the new nation of Kahchk Kihhim. A dotted line indicated the projected course the nation followed throughout the year. The scene switched to an aerial view of the huge ship.

The colored specs in the water resolved themselves into boats, bobbing alongside the gigantic structure bringing the size into perspective. It was more like a harbor than a ship.

The camera circled, and closed in on the curved segment spanning the two hulls. Amid the windows and greenery, tiny dots became people. The helicopter glided toward a landing pad on the superstructure of one of the ships, the football-field sized gray-green decks and silvery sails rising to meet them. Faces filled the screen.

Leticia welcomed them to their nation. How had she done it? Her face aglow, the mocha skin showed none of the scarring that should be there. He remembered enjoying the look of terror combined with his artistry to make a truly hideous mask of that face. Yet, now she looked whole, even better than before.

Picturing Leticia again in his mind, he compared the face on the screen to the one he filleted on that disastrous night. These Kihhim people were good. What else did they have for him to sell? Could they change someone's appearance? The phone rang, and he looked at it, not surprised. A feminine voice smooth as silk spoke. The black video screen showed nothing, but he recognized the voice instantly. He took no notes and engrained every word in his memory.

The caller offered him a contract for something else Kahchk Kihhim had to sell–their lives with a huge bonus for collateral damage. He agreed to think about this. If he did it, he must disappear for a long, long time. He would be the most sought after man in history, maybe more than Osama bin Laden or Sadam Hussain. Was it enough? He must know more and fast. There was a timeline.

Chapter Sixty-Three

General Kai watched Helen Chein hang up the phone. General Kai looked the picture of Chinese military leadership, ramrod straight, severe facial features, unsmiling. For him, Kahchk Kihhim represented an unknown and perhaps perilous threat to Chinese expansion plans in the Pacific.

China and the United States, the two superpowers in the world had been devastated by the bio-cyber war China had orchestrated. The United States had lost half of its population to the smallpox attack and the cyber-attack that shut down the electrical grid. Their economy collapsed.

China had lost half of it military ground forces to the smallpox epidemic they tried to use as a bio-weapon. Chinese leadership was wiped out in a nuclear attack by a stray North Korean missile. Though unproven, Kai was sure the United States was behind these misfortunes.

The U.S. and China were in a race—who could recover faster. Kai believed replacement of the leadership and the military forces would outpace the regrowth of the U.S. economy. He wanted to be the man behind the new leader directing China.

The American recognition of Kahchk Kihhim occurring so quickly and the protection offered them greatly bothered him. Why? Did they have valuable assets to be used to advantage? Was this a mobile base to be moved around the Pacific?

All efforts to find out more met with failure. The secrecy encountered troubled him most. Time to poke the nest and see what flew out. They needed a sharp stick–one that would open up Kahchk Kihhim–so they could peer inside.

Ralph Whitney was to be that stick. Properly pointed, more than this new country could be damaged.

The American Navy represented one of the few military powers in the world posing a threat in the Pacific. A properly planned operation would perhaps serve more than one purpose.

The United States Naval presence in the South China Sea had again thwarted China's latest attempt to bring Taiwan back into the fold. The Taiwanese elected government announced independence, a nation, separate from China. That would not be allowed to stand. Taiwan was Chinese. The Chinese Navy sank a Taiwanese Navy destroyer after it shot down a Chinese fighter plane, claiming it strayed over Taiwanese territory.

Only the presence of a United States carrier task force near the Straits of Formosa prevented escalation and the military solution to this rebel territory. China wasn't ready for a shooting war with the U.S. They held too many U.S. assets.

This thinly veiled story about naval exercises around Kahchk Kihhim was a protective shield.

Why? What was so important that America would stretch its resources to cover Kahchk Kihhim?

General Kai saw an opportunity, but he must know more. The Chinese failure to take over the Russian oil fields was a costly mistake. China was on the hunt for resources.

Kahchk Kihhim's emergence, their declaration of nation status, and the immediate recognition and protection by the United States had been a surprise. Requests for visits, establishment of diplomatic ties, and trade, though not openly refused, met delays, a familiar tactic to General Kai.

Offers for Kahchk Kihhim to join the United Nations also met with postponements. Kahchk Kihhim was in no hurry to join the community of nations on Earth.

When China lodged accusations of environmental damage caused by Kahchk Kihhim, they demanded an inspection, and a UN resolution was passed. The United States vetoed it. The much-publicized visit by the Vice President of the United States became an international event. Kai looked upon it as a once in a lifetime opportunity.

Chapter Sixty-Four

The initial awe of being at Kahchk Kihhim had not worn off, but? Dayton settled himself into life aboard the new nation. A new country being formed out of wilderness, in this case the ocean, was riveting. It brought back dreams of adventure and pioneering. It reminded people of the legend of Atlantis–an image boosted by the press.

Preparations for the vice presidential visit proved a Herculean task consuming almost all his efforts. He and Carol had little time together, both busier than they thought possible, organizing the visit in ninety days. It seemed impossible to accommodate the Secret Service, the entourage, and the press. Dayton gladly accepted the offer of help by the White House Press office. Major Travis Clawson, USMC retired, arrived after a briefing about confidential aspects. His ramrod straight stance and shaved head bespoke his military background, and his commanding demeanor in coordinating the various groups involved proved to be invaluable.

Standing on the deck, Dayton and Carol listened while Major Travis explained the arrangements. "The security team will arrive two days before the vice president to check out the ship and personnel. They will be escorted wherever they need to go to satisfy security requirements. Vice President

Sanchez will first arrive aboard the aircraft carrier U. S. S. Carl Vinson, on station five miles away. He will hold a press briefing there, then he and his Secret Service team will fly to Kahchk Kihhim. Security by the United States Navy will be tight." Major Clawson looked from Carol to Dayton to be sure they understood.

"The press corps will remain on USS Carl Vinson. Coverage will be supplied by a single news team accompanying the vice president. This team provides audio and video feeds to the corps on Carl Vinson. Questions will be relayed from the corps to the team."

He glanced around the deck. "Kahchk Kihhim cannot accommodate a full press corps entourage, and this solution was the fairest. This also meets the security needs of Kahchk Kihhim. After the ceremony, the vice president will return to Carl Vinson accompanied by John Vance, for a full press conference."

Chapter Sixty-Five

The rank odor from the dark bowels of the fish processing ship seemed to have permeated Ralph Whitney's senses. He strained to find the massive shadowy outline as it disappeared behind the cigar shape of the submarine slowly easing through the oily black water. Even in the open water, the reek of the fish gagged him.

He agreed to take the contract against Kahchk Kihhim for two reasons. First, the money. The offer of $4,000,000 U. S. would enable him to live his days out well. Second, the escape and return of Kihhim still rankled him. His record had few failures, and he corrected those. This was one to correct.

There was no doubt they possessed technology and information for biological weapons. It was not the value as much as the power of possessing a weapon of mass destruction, but he would forgo that for the money and the revenge.

Whitney carried the single data cube with all the intelligence his employer gathered. Most interesting was what information they did not have and why. Kahchk Kihhim allowed no visitors. No ship above or below the water could approach Kahchk Kihhim with the carrier group guarding it. Carrier planes warned aircraft away, even fired warning shots.

Satellite photos revealed nothing threatening or useful but Ralph knew there were things there someone in the world would find handy.

Ralph decided to let Kahchk Kihhim come to him. An unmarked plane flew him to a small island off the China coast where a small boat took him out to a fishing fleet. There, hidden within the processing ship, was a mini-submarine and crew. This sub's purpose was for clandestine movements in other nation's waters. It was nuclear powered and very very fast. Armaments consisted of two torpedoes and two small cruise missiles.

They sailed to the interception point and waited. The sub had been inert for two weeks while Kahchk Kihhim crept toward it.

Inactive, giving no detectable signature proved more than tedious. Ralph had learned patience. Not so with the crew. Even though experienced submariners, they needed activity.

Keeping the sub at constant depth with no noise took little activity. Only the portly captain spoke English, and the crew feared him. That helped to keep them in line, but Ralph saw the toll of boredom as the ship became sloppy. The captain had to harangue ever harder, moving through the ship like an orca lashing at the lethargic men to perform their duties. Their health seemed to suffer, and several reported bouts of nausea and intense headaches. Even the food was tasteless.

He finally allowed them to spend time outside underwater SCUBA diving as long as they stayed at least ten yards below the surface. Though not much of a reprieve, it was something. The sub never surfaced as it hung in the water waiting. At night, they exhausted the foul air through the snorkel, while Ralph and the captain vigilantly scanned the horizon and the skies through the periscope. Satellite messages updated them on Kahchk Kihhim's position.

When it seemed they would sink under their own sluggishness and even Ralph felt listless, a satellite fix-ranged Kahchk Kihhim. They would be well within the range of his small cruise missile–so close any attempts to defend would be impossible. Escape would be the problem. His spirits rose, but he felt slow, heavy, and weak. Was the crew's malaise contagious? He saw the moisture drip from the hull, and the plop plop sounds rang in his head.

Chapter Sixty-Six

Monitors around Kahchk Kihhim showed Vice President Vincente Sanchez's pre-visit press conference on Carl Vinson. Those not scrambling to complete last-minute tasks watched. He was due in two hours. The Secret Service made their final sweeps.

Deep within the ship, Dayton coordinated the non-human groups in their security patrols. At first he found the Dahlfins easier to accept than the Altereds. It was easy to think of the Dahlfins as non-humans, but the Altereds were extra-humans.

His conversation with Sean Steele exposed him to the capabilities of Kahchk Kihhim. As an Altered, Sean looked like the monster in the B-movie horror flick, Creature from the Black Lagoon. At seven-feet tall, Sean's thick body towered over Dayton. Heavily muscled arms and legs ended in webbed hands and feet. His dark and mottled skin looked more like a dolphin's. The dual lenses on his large eyes gave him a double blink. It took time for Dayton to accept the figure before him had once been a normal human. In a deep rumbling voice, Sean related his story.

"Two years ago I asked to join Kahchk Kihhim. My sister Sharon, with Kihhim in Arizona, got me an interview. There was refusal in Dr. Wong's eyes as I had none of the needed skills. I told him I'd take any opportunity, anything. I was desperate." Dayton could hear the despair in Sean's voice.

"'Would you consider having your body altered?' he asked me. In school I was the class joke. Tall and awkward with a bad complexion and worse teeth, my social life consisted of being continuously harassed. The acne scars pitted my face like a grapefruit, but the scars on the inside hurt the worst. Only Sharon kept despair from overwhelming me." The massive head dropped as Sean looked down. Dayton wanted to put a hand on his shoulder to reassure him.

"I lived with Sharon and her family after our parents were killed by a drunk driver. Her marriage foundered, partially because of me, but she refused to let me go. She was my family, my only friend." He sighed.

"Sharon got an offer to move to Kihhim after her divorce. The offer only extended to her and her kids. At first she refused to leave me, but I convinced her to go. I lived in her old house alone, hiding from the school that I was living alone so they wouldn't put me in foster care. On the rare occasions when I visited her, I saw how happy she and my niece and nephew had become, but Kihhim was not accepting new people." Sean clasped his webbed hands together.

"Sharon's disappearance left me despondent, near suicide. I stumbled through existence in a blur of school-eat-sleep. Her message telling me she and the kids were alive and well gave me the first joy in two years. Sharon invited me to visit Kahchk Kihhim." Dayton heard the change in Sean's voice at the memory.

"When the helicopter approached the ships, I felt a change come into my life. That first night, after the kids had gone to bed and things quieted, Sharon explained that Kahchk Kihhim needed a few new citizens, but not the usual people.

"She took me down into one of the hulls to a room with a large pool open to the sea. I was fascinated when a Dahlfin swam up to Sharon. Like a cat, it rubbed against her hand. 'Sean, I would like you to meet Blue Streak,' she said."

"'Hello, Blue Streak,' I said, as one would to a pet."

"'Hello,' squeaked the Dahlfin. It shocked me. Sharon's smile brought the wonder of it crashing in on me. Blue Streak's natural dolphin smile seemed to broaden. 'I pleeeease meet you.' I could barely understand the squeaky voice."

"Sharon explained Blue Streak was one of our first Dahlfins, enhanced dolphins. She learned to speak, getting better every day. Blue Streak and the other Dahlfins made up a growing part of our residents. Sharon said Kahchk Kihhim needed people to become Altereds. I would be the first."

"Jamie Wong explained everything to me. My life as a human being was miserable. I remember looking at Blue Streak. She asked me to come join them. No one ever asked me to join anything except

Sharon." Sean's mouth opened in a smile. A few hours before, Dayton would have found that toothed maw frightening.

"Dr. Wong told me to spend time with the Dahlfins. I did. Blue Streak took me out in my wet suit, riding her back, or hanging onto her dorsal. She gave me tours below the water, showed me how to farm fish. I learned how to play games with the other Dahlfins and went on short patrols. I never had a friendship like that on land. There was no decision to be made." Sean's laugh was a deep rasp.

"In that time, I developed a kinship with Blue that convinced me to go ahead. Now living as an Altered, I have no regrets. For the first time in my life, I am happy. I have friends and a purpose. We think of ourselves as humans returned to the sea," he said holding up his hands.

"As an Altered, I am a citizen of Kahchk Kihhim. It's a one-way lifetime commitment. I cannot come back, but then I don't want to."

Outside of Kahchk Kihhim, opinions would not be so enlightened, and Dayton agreed that now was not the time to reveal their existence. The outside would not accept them.

Chapter Sixty-Seven

Sean and Blue patrolled with the Dahlfins, glad to be away from the hubbub and preparations for the visit. From a distance, they surfaced and watched the vice president's helicopter landing at Kahchk Kihhim. They turned and moved away, protecting their home by seeking out threats.

Eight miles out they both sensed the inert mass in the water. What they thought of as a sunken hulk lurking as a sea hazard, resolved itself into a small submarine as they neared. It hung perfectly still. Cautiously, they circled. It was solid black with no markings.

They had seen United States submarines before and followed them. They even played games with them, swimming in and out of their sensors, but those were all marked. Something seemed strange. Several other Altereds and Dahlfins approached in response to Blue Streak's alert.

An explosion of air burst toward the surface from an opening hatch. Backing away fast, not knowing what to expect, the shock wave from an eruption tumbled them end over end. They recovered in time to see a missile racing toward the surface leaving behind a cloud of bubbles and tortured water.

The submarine sprang to life in a sudden roar and streaked away, the turbulence again rolling them about. Sean's mind raced. He knew this was an attack. There would not be time to warn anyone, but some of them raced for Kahchk Kihhim. Others followed the mini-sub.

***

Ralph's employer had armed the submarine with the most advanced small cruise missile in their arsenal. It was capable of carrying a tactical nuclear warhead, and it was smart. It burst from the water, received its final targeting instructions from the overhead satellite, and dove, skimming just above the surface toward its target. As soon as the missile was launched, the submarine leapt forward. Decoys were deployed, dashing in random patterns of starts and stops.

Under the mask of confusion, Ralph's sub moved away. Radar would back track the missile to the launch location, but the sub was not there anymore.

His sound-absorbing hull hindered active sonar tracking, but he had to remain quiet. This would be war of nerves and his only choice. He zigged and zagged, and then he stopped, listening to the start of frantic activity around him as the missile was detected. Though not far from his launch site, he hid under a deep thermocline and waited.

***

After the warm introduction and welcome by John Vance, Vice President Sanchez mounted the podium waving to the crowd and the cameras. He knew the recognition ceremony would be televised worldwide, and he played the opportunity to the max.

His toffee colored complexion glowed, and his dark full mustache accentuated his broad smile as he extended warm greetings to the new nation of Kahchk Kihhim from the United States of America. The world watched.

The small group surrounding the speaker's dais raised a loud cheer. The vice president held up both hands, acknowledging the acclaim, all cameras trained on him as he waited for the applause to quiet. "Bienvenedos al mundo, Kahchk Kihhim." Another roar and applause came from the crowd. He beamed, and when it quieted, he spoke in a rich, full voice. "Rarely in the history of mankind has a new nation formed so peacefully, wresting its existence from the wilderness of the sea, yet it is an exemplar of harmony with nature for the rest of the world to watch and learn."

The pilot of the circling news helicopter saw the incoming streak and his military trained reflexes took over. He immediately pitched the chopper over to the side, avoiding the missile. The cameraman was thrown off balance during the wild gyration.

As the helicopter spun around, the cameraman refocused on the deck of the ship and the growing fireball that now obscured the podium area. The shock wave struck the aircraft, buffeting them. As the fireball rose onto the sky, it became apparent nothing survived within twenty-five yards of where the podium had been.

Through the smoke, a black hole gaped at them. Body parts were scattered across the deck. There was no residual fire, but the small concentrated force of the blast was devastating. Stunned people picked themselves up while others came running to help. One man held up his detached arm, yelling at the sky. A woman crawled toward her severed leg, leaving a bright red trail.

In the distance the Navy ships moved, clamoring alarms echoing across the water. Two ships swung toward Kahchk Kihhim at flank speed. Everyone near the podium was gone including the Vice President, several Secret Service Agents, John Vance, and the camera crew covering the speech.

Leticia had been behind a group of people and was covered with their gore. They shielded her from the direct blast and saved her life though she was critically injured. Dayton and Carol, in the communications room supervising the coverage, saw the whole thing. They sat, frozen by the unbelievable scene burned into their retinas. It took long seconds for them to recover their senses and run out to help the wounded.

Katharine Levey and Rich Lewis were below deck, preparing for the televised tour when the deafening shock from the explosion knocked them over. Stunned for several minutes, they helped each other up and staggered toward the stairs. The acrid smoke choked them, and blinding bright light streamed through a hole that was not there before.

As they burst out, the sunlight struggled through the cloud of smoke and lit a grim scene. People ran toward the hole where the podium had been. The cries of the wounded surrounded them. Within minutes, the clatter of a descending helicopter filled the air drowning out all other sound.

The U. S. Navy helicopter landed on the deck next the burning ruin of the vice president's copter. A squad of marines rushed out taking up positions surrounding the area with weapons ready. Another military helicopter forced the circling news camera away and maintained cover while several F-18s roared overhead. A marine in battle gear approached Rich and Katharine and shouted above the confusion.

"I am Lieutenant Kelly, and I am in charge."

Rich turned, looked him up and down, and then said, "Lieutenant, you are on foreign soil, and you have not been invited. You and your men are to remain here. You are not to leave this area. If you cannot follow those orders, you must leave. Do you understand?"

The lieutenant was taken aback for a second. He stared at Rich, his mind mulling what had been said, and then turned and walked toward his men barking orders to form a secure perimeter around the blast area,

Katharine looked at Rich. "When did you become so forceful?"

"We must never forget we are independent and free, regardless of the circumstances."

They helped a woman up when Rico Santillo approached. "You need to come with me."

"Now?" they asked looking at the devastation around them.

"It is very important. It is about this," Rico said, nodding at the Dantesque scene. Katharine gave a curt nod, and they both followed into the lower part of the ship to the Dahlfin and Altered living quarters.

Chapter Sixty-Eight

The large pool chamber was crowded with both Dahlfin and Altereds all talking at once in a cacophony of sound, high-pitched squeaks and rumbling bassos. They grew silent as Rico led Rich and Katharine to the side of the pool. A Dahlfin and an Altered awaited them.

"Blue and I were out on patrol when we found the submarine that launched the missile. We saw it, but we couldn't do anything in time." His voice was ragged, tears in his eyes, and the Dahlfin's head sagged. "I am sorry, we are so sorry."

Katharine's mind whirled at the revelation. "A sub! What can you remember?"

"It was small–smaller than the others we have seen. No markings were on it," said Sean. Blue spoke in a voice so high and squeaky with excitement that Katharine did not understand. Sean translated. "The thing hung still in the water and was hot at the back. It echoed like an animal."

"Probably nuclear," said Rich. "A diesel electric boat would not have that hot spot. It also had a sound absorbing coating so not to reflect sonar as metal does."

Sean spoke again, "We swam around it looking, when a hatch opened. There was an explosion, and we saw the missile leave the sub. The sub took off. We heard it for a while, then nothing."

"So you don't think it kept going?" asked Katharine.

"Some of the other Dahlfins followed, but we came straight back."

Blue spoke and Katharine looked at Sean again. "After going a mile, it dove deep below a thermocline and was quiet again. Other things, miniatures, probably decoys, came out, and took off in different directions."

"Do you think you could find it again?" asked Rich. Katharine looked at him sharply.

"Others are following," said Sean. The din of shouts and squeaks from all the creatures in the pool nearly deafened them.

Katharine held up her hand for quiet. "What do we do once we find it?" she asked. Again, a babble of sound arose. Sean spoke. "We would immobilize it. We have done that to ships before."

"If immobilized, it would have to surface. The Navy would take over then," Rich said.

"You must be careful not to be seen," Katharine said to Sean. Rich nodded, and the water of the pool churned to froth as all the creatures left at once. The images of the tragedy above them returned. They both rose and hugged each other before heading back to hell.

***

Blue zoomed to the last site of the sub, but it was gone. She turned to the massed group and gave orders. They spread out seeking a signal from the others. They could sense square miles of ocean in minutes. Within half an hour, she heard the signal of a sighting. As they headed toward the signal, Sean directed some of the Dahlfins and Altereds to get the nets and meet them.

The dark shape of the small sub surrounded by Kahchk Kihhim people hung inert in the water. It gave out a roar and accelerated away. The pack trailed, a few falling back to assist with the nets. After five minutes, the sub stopped, silent and still again. Quickly, the rest of the pack again surrounded the sub. They guided the nets covering it like a cocoon, fouling the diving planes. They wound thick long cords around the screw. The next time it spun, it would choke itself.

Sean sent most of the pack back to Kahchk Kihhim, and they waited. After thirty minutes with a slight hum the screw turned three times and froze, bound tightly. Blue and Sean wound more of the fiber around the screw. The submarine tried to reverse, but that tightened the cords more. They next tried to use the small side thrusters, but those too were fouled. The diving planes were useless without movement, so the sub slowly drifted, trapped.

Within a half an hour, a hatch opened but only a little, thanks to the net. A masked face looked through the crack. Sean and Blue stared back and watched a man try to scream through his mouthpiece. The hatch shut.

A few minutes later, it opened again, and an arm came out with a knife, trying to cut the net. Blue rammed the hatch, slamming it onto the arm. The knife fell free, skidding on the deck and slipping off into the depths, glinting as it disappeared. The mangled arm withdrew, and the hatch was dogged. They waited.

Chapter Sixty-Nine

Ralph Whitney screamed at the injured sailor while the medic splinted the broken arm. The man was wide-eyed with shock. "What did you see?" For the fifth time he asked the same question, and the answer came back "Monsters," every time. He had to calm the man down to find out what lurked out there.

Something fouled the screw and the side thrusters. Something also prevented his crew from going outside, injuring one of the sailors. He gave the sailor a drink and forced his voice to soften. "Tell me exactly what you saw."

The sailor spoke in Chinese. The captain turned to Ralph with the translation. "He says he tried to open the hatch, but something did not allow it. When he looked out, a sea devil looked at him. It was part man and part fish. A dolphin looked, too. He saw a net holding the hatch, so he got his knife and tried to cut it. The hatch crashed down on his arm. He thinks the dolphin hit it."

A shiver went through Ralph. Kahchk Kihhim had to be behind this, and now, unless he could get free of the net, they would have him. How had they survived? The missile's tactical nuclear warhead should have wiped out Kahchk Kihhim totally.

He only now recalled there had not been nearly enough explosion for that. It had not gone off. Or they substituted a conventional warhead. A nuclear incident would initiate an extensive investigation, leading back to them even if the sub escaped. Few nations had sophisticated nuclear arms and the ability to deliver them. There would have been retaliation, even with only strong suspicion.

Now it looked like they might be captured. That possibility must have been foreseen. What else had been done? What insurance against any revelation of their participation had been included? The Chinese crew would be a big hint, but everything else had been swept clean. If captured, the crew would eventually break. That would not be allowed to happen.

He had better make the best deal he could and fast before the rest of his employer's insurance policy kicked in. He ordered the ballast blown and watched as the sailors struggled to comply with the order. The deck of the sub slanted slightly, and it started to rise.

***

The noisy clatter and forceful blast of another landing chopper struck as Katharine and Rich came back on deck. Admiral Cochrain got out and looked around at the devastation. He shook his head and turned toward them, striding forward, his whole demeanor that of a battleship flying into the fray.

He opened his mouth, but Katharine spoke first, "We need to talk, now." Before he responded, she turned, walking with her own air of purpose through a doorway. The admiral and an aide, stunned by this show of disrespect, had no choice but to hurry to follow her. They entered a small room and Rich shut the door.

"What the hell…" he started, but Katharine held up a hand, silencing a man who was never shushed.

"We found the sub that launched the missile," she said.

"Sub. Missile. What are you talking about? How do you know it was a missile?" asked the admiral.

"We had a crew out on patrol that spotted the sub just before it launched."

"What crew? We didn't detect anything and lady, we can detect anything. It was not a sub. It was a bomb planted here," said the admiral. "You failed to find and stop it."

Katharine shot back, "You did not detect the sub, and you did not detect our crew."

The admiral paled. How had he totally lost control so quickly? A soft tone sounded, and Rich answered the phone. He spoke softly, the only sound in the tense silence. He looked at them. "They've spotted the sub and are following it."

"Where are they?" demanded the admiral. Rich said nothing. "God dammit! You fucking well better tell me all you know." shouted the admiral, trying to regain the reins by force of voice.

"Admiral, they spotted it, and it cannot escape," said Katharine. "Quit trying to badger us. We must work at this together. We'll turn everything over to you as soon as we can. I think we should call the president, don't you?" Without waiting for a response, she again turned her back on the admiral and strode through the door, the party trailing behind.

In the communications room, Dayton was still in shock. He was replaying the tape of the incident when they came in. Carol closed the door behind them. "John's dead and Leticia may not make it," she said in a quavering voice, tears streaming down her face. Katharine put her arm around her.

Rich asked Dayton to replay the tape of the incident from one minute before the explosion. A hologram formed in the air, and in total silence, they watched.

The streak of the missile, clearly visible, entered the frame before the picture disappeared. The admiral stared hard, his face rigid. He slowly sank down into a chair. "Perhaps we should keep this knowledge to a small circle," Rich said as he handed him the phone. The admiral nodded and turned to the aide, motioning him out of the room. He dialed a number and spoke quietly for several minutes, then turned to Dayton.

"Can you put this on a monitor?"

Dayton pushed a few buttons. "Mr. President, this is Dayton King. I am here with Katharine Levey, Carol Goldman, Rich Lewis, and Admiral Cochrain. You have our condolences." The monitor showed the face of the chief executive.

The president's face was grim as he spoke. "I only heard minutes ago. First, I want to pass on my sympathies. I know you lost many dear to you.

Before we can fall back into that grief, we have hard decisions to make. Harold, tell me what you know."

"Sir, we have convincing evidence of a missile strike. Working together, we may capture the sub that launched the missile. There are questions we need to address: What will we do with it and her crew, and what will we release to the public pending full investigation?"

The president sat absorbing this information. "We must make those decisions now, together."

"We put the crew on trial," cried Katharine.

"I mean before that," said the president. "We must see what this is before anything is released. We have to know who is really responsible."

Another phone rang and Rich answered it. He listened for a few seconds and hung up. "The sub is being forced to the surface now. It is twenty-two miles north-north-east of us on heading forty one degrees." He handed the radiophone to the admiral. Admiral Cochrain spoke and hung up.

"I dispatched choppers and a destroyer to the area. They received a hydrophone message requesting surrender."

"That is good news," said the president. "Good work. I propose we release nothing until we have a chance to evaluate this. Do you agree?"

"How long do you think that will take?" asked Katharine. "My concern is that without any release, Kahchk Kihhim will be blamed. This was to be a joyous coming out, and somebody has done a great job of wrecking that and possibly all of us."

"We will announce that a terrorist missile struck Kahchk Kihhim killing your citizens and the vice president. We are following leads now."

The admiral jumped up. "Wait a minute, sir. That will reflect badly on the Navy."

"Harold, you fucked up. Let's not point fingers at each other now. Lord knows there will be enough of that later. We cannot cover this up. It will not fly, and we will come out worse in the end." The admiral's mouth clamped shut.

"Let's hold off on the announcement of the capture until we know who is involved, but say we have every confidence justice will be done. Harold, call me back when those sons of bitches are in custody. Ms. Levey, we will need to meet within the next few days after the grieving. May I call you with a proposed schedule?"

"We are at your disposal, sir." Without further comment, the line went dead.

Chapter Seventy

Within minutes of Whitney's surrender message, helicopters from the Carl Vinson circled the bobbing and rolling submarine, tiny by submarine standards. The black surface absorbed light, and with no markings, it looked like a hole in the water.

The USS destroyer Amarillo closed, already within missile range on the horizon. Nothing moved on the sub as the helicopters circled. Suddenly their radiation alarms sounded, and the helicopter swerved away. The pilot notified the approaching ship of the danger. Amarillo slowed, holding distance. The captain of the Amarillo contacted Ralph Whitney. "Mr. Whitney, are you aware your submarine is leaking radiation?"

"What!" came the startled reply. "How can that be? All of our monitors are in the green." He closed his mouth. So that is how his employers were going to take care of business. If they escaped, they would never have made it back to port.

"Please stand by." Forty-five minutes later an inflatable boat with men in fully enclosed radiation suits approached. They cut the net around the main hatch and radioed for the crew to come out stripped, hands raised. A silver suited figure held a monitor toward the slowly opening hatch. He stepped back as the radiation level climbed several notches. This boat was really hot!

"Captain, get your men aboard the inflatable. It's dangerous to spend any more time than we have to here." Within minutes, twelve naked forms appeared on the deck, hands clasped behind their heads. "Captain is this everybody?" The captain looked into Ralph's eyes and nodded. They were a sorry-looking lot. One by one, the suited figures helped them into the inflatable, and it turned toward the Amarillo.

Captain Bower and the destroyer decontamination crew waited on deck with hoses as the boat tied up. Everything and everyone was washed down thoroughly, checked with monitors, and washed again. When the last prisoner boarded, the inflatable returned to the sub to retrieve the Amarillo crew, who secured her with floats to keep her from being scuttled. It was not going anywhere with that net wrapped around it tighter than a pea jacket on a deckhand in the Arctic.

Armed and suited men herded the captives below deck to the showers. Their heads never came up, and they never looked around, the first instinct any sailor had when aboard another vessel. Not a word was said by any of them. That was odd. After washing, a suited man again checked them. Not saying anything, he stopped in front of each man and moved the monitor over his body. He stepped back and motioned to Ralph. "You go over there. The rest of you come with me."

The men stood, apathetically until he led one to another door, the others followed. Ralph watched the bare backs disappear through a doorway. "You're not as hot as the rest. You may make it."

The suited figure gave him a bottle of liquid and told him to drink it. Ralph hesitated and then did so. It tasted chalky and vile. They would want to keep him alive. He had things to sell them and bargains to make.

***

Ralph was violently ill for three days, getting rid of everything inside not firmly attached. Intravenous fluids were all he could take. His hair fell out in great clumps and his gums became sore. Several teeth made a clinking noise when he spat them out with globs of blood into the pan at his bedside. Thoroughly weakened, he wished to die, but he would probably have to get better to do that.

A man entered wearing captain's insignia and sat next to Ralph's bed. Ralph was too weak to raise his arm to shake hands, but a hand was not offered. "I'm told you may live. The rest of your crew is not so lucky. Some have already died; the rest won't make it to the weekend. You know, you will be completely debriefed until you are wrung out. If it were up to the crew and me, you'd be joining the others, but not as quickly. I will not ask you anything, just came to see what you looked like." He rose and moved toward the door then turned back. "By the way, that sub was so hot that we could only send in a robot. We'll sink her tomorrow. Waste of a good robot." The door shut. Ralph felt an unaccustomed knot of fear. This may not go as planned.

Chapter Seventy-One

Shackled hand and foot, Ralph shuffled toward the waiting helicopter. He looked at a rising sun he thought he would never see again. They lifted off with the clattering roar of whirling rotors. No one spoke during the short flight to the USS Carl Vinson.

Two guards hustled him through a doorway, half carrying him down corridors and a stairway, and into a small room. Once in the stiff backed chair, the guard shackled him to the table and floor. Several men faced him across a table. Some were in uniform others not.

"Name," asked one of the men.

"Ralph Whitney," Ralph responded.

"Did you shoot a missile at Kahchk Kihhim?"

"You guys don't mess around," Ralph said, trying to alter the tone. No one said anything. "Don't I get a phone call, Miranda and a lawyer?"

"Mr. Whitney, everybody aboard that submarine perished. You are already dead. Your cooperation will determine how unpleasantly and how long it takes you to die," said a small man wearing dark-rimmed glasses.

Ralph felt his bowels loosen. He gulped in air. "You can't do this!" he screamed at the stone faces. No expression changed, no word spoken, no one moved. "Yes, I did it," he said quickly.

"Why did you do it?" asked the small man again.

"I was hired."

"By whom?"

Ralph said nothing. He never revealed a client's identity. A clock ticked somewhere in the dead stillness. A roar shook the walls as a plane took off. Within a minute, another thundered away.

"Mr. Whitney, why don't you want to tell us? Are you afraid they will kill you?" said the uniformed man on the left. There was chilling irony in the voice and a smirk on his lips. He was already dead, and for the first time it started to sink in.

"Helen Chein was my contact. We met once. After that we only talked by phone. She would call and ask me if I wanted a job. If I said yes, she would tell me the details. She would call back in about a week. If my answer was still yes, she would name a price. I was never disappointed and never haggled. We would work out details." He vomited it out in a straightforward rush.

"Do you know who was behind Ms. Chein in financing this job?" asked another suited man on the left end. Ralph turned toward the distinguished looking man with gray hair at the temples.

"China, I am certain, but I have no direct proof. I dealt only with her by phone. The sub had absolutely no markings."

"We know that," said the man in the navy uniform.

"I came on board two weeks ago. The crew spoke Chinese when they spoke at all. Only the captain talked to me. Half of my payment was deposited in an offshore account. The rest was to be deposited when the job was done. I knew nothing more."

"Mr. Whitney, someone damaged the radiation shielding on that boat. It continuously exposed everyone to radiation, but under high load it failed completely. Another few hours and none of you would have ever left that sub. Why would they sabotage their own boat?" asked the small man in the center.

"They didn't want any witnesses."

"How do you contact Ms. Chein?" he asked.

"It is a drop at a laundry run by Chinese. I leave a suit with a message in the pocket for her. She calls within a day."

"We want you to drop a note for her to call you," said the distinguished man.

"What would I say?"

"How about 'Where is my fucking money?'" yelled the small man.

"But they know the sub was captured."

"Yes, but they don't know if you were on board. You could have left the sub right after you fired the missile. Did you or anyone on the sub have any contact after you boarded?" asked the navy man.

"No," said Ralph. "We never surfaced. What will I get if I cooperate?"

"A few more days of non-painful life," said the small man. "You are ours forever. Do not entertain any plans of escape during the drop or after. We too can play at the slow poison game, and in your case, we will. I don't think your Chinese friends will help you once they find you're alive. In fact, your continued assistance to us is the only thing that may extend your life for a while."

"How will I say I escaped? It's not like I could have been picked up by a fishing boat."

"We'll take care of that."

Chapter Seventy-Two

In the early morning darkness, Katharine Levey, Rich Lewis, and Dayton King were ushered into a nondescript office at Ft. Lewis, Washington. Before they sat, another door opened and the President of the United States along with several aides entered. He greeted them, introducing those with him: Admiral Cochrain, Craig Nelson, and Captain Sheridan Smith. "Please be seated. How is Kahchk Kihhim recuperating?" the president asked.

Rich spoke. "The damage was surprisingly light. With a different kind of missile, it would have been extensive."

"There are too many heavy hearts," said Katharine. "Things seem to be working at half pace."

"I again offer my condolences for your losses," said the president.

"We offer ours to you. I know you and the vice president were good friends," said Dayton.

The president nodded solemnly and then turned. "Admiral, please bring them up to date on what we found in that sub," said the president.

"First, I would like to know how you caught it."

"Perhaps someday soon we will show you," said Katharine.

"We rescued twelve men, eleven looked Asian, and the last Caucasian. All the Asians died within two days without saying a single word. The twelfth man survived. We tried to investigate the sub, but it was so radioactive we could only use a robot. In the end we had to scuttle everything."

"What caused the radiation?" asked Rich.

"Sabotage. Whenever they powered up they would receive heavy doses of radiation, and the monitors were rigged to give false readings. In short, the boat was a suicide mission."

"Your news release said only eleven men were aboard. What about the twelfth man?" asked Katharine.

Captain Smith grimaced. "He is a freelance contractor. Someone paid him to attack Kahchk Kihhim with a bonus if important people were involved. The idea was to embarrass the United States and start investigations and condemnation on a worldwide basis."

"Why? Who hired him?" asked Katharine.

"At this stage, we are not sure. There are strong indications it was the Chinese. With proper incentive, the terrorist has agreed to help us flush out whoever it was. We need your cooperation."

"Us?" said Dayton in surprise.

"We want to convince his employer he escaped immediately after launching the missile. The story will be he went out a torpedo tube right after launch, and the search missed him. He'll claim Kahchk Kihhim picked him up and let him recuperate. His press credentials will uphold his claim to be a reporter who fell off the carrier, and nobody realized it in all the excitement.

"We want him to make contact again to give us a chance to work back to the source. It will probably be the only chance we have."

"He agreed to this?" asked Dayton.

"We gave him the right incentive," said the Admiral.

"What if they ask him about Kahchk Kihhim?" asked Katharine.

"That is why we need your assistance. He has to visit Kahchk Kihhim to make them believe he's been there. It will only be for a few days."

They looked at each other. They were against it, but they had to cooperate. "We are very sensitive to outsiders. We have no facilities for security. How will we keep him?" said Rich, looking around the table.

"We'll send security along," said the president. "That is the only way we could do this."

"We'll put together a few men to act as a security team." said the captain.

Katharine's mind raced. Of course, the team would be trained observers. Despite these kind looks and sympathies, they would still look for a weakness to exploit. "That is not acceptable," stated Katharine.

Several of the aides tried to speak at the same time. The president held up his hand for quiet.

Katharine continued, "We'll allow one guard and we'll supply someone else. I want that guard to be

FBI Special Agent Robert McWilliams. He will be in charge."

"Just a minute." said Captain Smith.

Before he could go further, the president said, "That is an interesting choice, and rather than get into some sort of pissing contest over this, that will be acceptable." Smith's mouth opened then shut, his face hardening as his eyes bored into Katharine. "We have to move ahead with this immediately for it to be creditable."

"Let me contact Kahchk Kihhim so they can prepare," said Dayton. The president nodded, and Craig Nelson rose and led Dayton out to another room and a phone. Dayton picked up the phone and dialed a series of numbers. The sleepy voice of Carol answered. "Hi. It's me, Dayton."

"Oh, Dayton. I am so glad to hear from you," her voice brightening. "How are things going there?"

"That is why I am calling. We need to make accommodation for two visitors, one a prisoner, the other FBI. I know you have questions, but I'll answer them when I return. Can you make those arrangements for tomorrow?"

Carol picked up on his reluctance to talk. "Tomorrow. I'll take care of it."

"See you tomorrow. Miss you."

"Miss you too." There was a sigh on the line then a click. Dayton hung up and left the office. Craig Nelson waited outside.

"Things all right?" he asked.

"We will be ready tomorrow," said Dayton.

Nelson nodded and led Dayton back to the conference room. As they entered, Dayton nodded to Katharine and Rich.

Chapter Seventy-Three

When they broke through the clouds, Katharine alternately looked out the window of the plane at the fading morning stars and at Ralph Whitney. His eyes still down, he hadn't looked at any of them the whole time. What kind of man was he? Certainly worse than any monster they could create.

Her gaze moved to McWilliams sitting close to Whitney. He looked back. She closed her eyes, so she would not stare and tried to suppress her hatred of Whitney. The next thing she felt was the thump of the landing gear as the plane prepared to land on the Carl Vinson.

The harsh glare of carrier deck lights showed frantic activity. People moved rapidly about with intense purpose written on their faces. Even as they walked toward a door, a deafening roar and a blast of hot air struck them as a small fighter screamed by, then stopped as the tail hook snagged the arresting cable. The door closed behind them, quieting the outside shriek of jets, but the smell of jet fuel followed them.

Deep within the ship they were escorted into a plain gray room with a table, chairs and bare walls. They all sat, and their eyes automatically scanning the prisoner. He was still, his head up, eyes staring straight ahead, his face expressionless. It was impossible to tell what he was thinking.

After twenty minutes of silence, except for the wall-shaking roar of jet engines, the door opened, and a sailor put his shiny black head in. "Yo choppah's ready ta leaf," he said. They followed him through doors and up elevators until they emerged at a different area of the deck. Ralph was helped aboard the big Sea Stallion by McWilliams. Even before they could get strapped in, the helicopter lurched into the air and headed west toward a bare stretch of ocean.

Within ten minutes, Katharine saw the muted lights of Kahchk Kihhim on the dawn-lit horizon. She watched Robert McWilliams eyes grow larger and larger as the ship filled the view through the cockpit.

The helipad lights came on, and the burned scar to one side stabbed her heart. She glanced at the prisoner, and the hot boil of hatred rose. The soft bump of the landing signaled their arrival home. The sound of the helicopter engines wound up for takeoff even as they opened a door and entered Kahchk Kihhim. After the noisy world of the aircraft carrier, the silence filled her with peace, like a glass of cool water in the desert.

Katharine looked up to see Carol planting a big kiss on Dayton. When they separated, she was introduced to Robert McWilliams and Ralph Whitney. Ralph did not respond, and she looked long and hard at his shackles. She didn't yet understand why he was here, but she sensed it had to do with the scar on the deck and in their minds. Since they ate only a snack on the plane, they went to the restaurant.

Katharine wanted to shower away the outside world, but not until she was far from this murderer. She would endure him a little while longer. At a table, she explained to Robert and the unmoving Ralph Whitney how to order from the electronic menu. Robert McWilliams was interested and liked the idea at once. Sitting next to the prisoner, he faced out of the arch toward the stern and the brightening sky.

The scenery below was an obscure mix of gray and dark green, but the rising sun pierced the window spotlighting those at the table. Carol touched a control on the window frame, and it darkened as golden light revealed the activity in the area between the two great hulls.

Nobody said anything. McWilliams was awed by what he saw. Ralph was like a statue, seemingly oblivious.

At last McWilliams spoke. "Why me, Ms. Levey?"

"Over the time John and I were incarcerated, I felt you might understand what we have here. You treated us with respect, caught a glimpse of what we believed in and what we are. Your loyalties are with the United States government, but you know we want to do them no harm."

"I never thought you wanted to hurt the United States, but you were like children with dynamite-dangerous because of ignorance. You needed to be watched and protected from yourselves and others. Like wayward kids, you rebelled."

"Being watched would lead to being told what to do and what to believe," said Katharine.

"I wasn't told everything about this visit to Kahchk Kihhim, only to guard him," Robert said, nodding toward Ralph. "He is extremely dangerous." He looked at Whitney. "I am to kill him if he tries to escape."

"You need to know more. This man," she hissed, "fired the missile that killed your vice president, his security team, and many of our people."

A cry came from Carol, and she covered her mouth, glaring at Ralph.

Katharine continued, "He was contracted to do it. In order to find out who hired him, he agreed cooperate. To convince his employers he escaped from the sub, he'll tell them we picked him up. With reporter ID, his public story is he fell off the Carl Vinson. After recuperating here for a few days, he left. He needs some familiarity with us."

"Thank you," said McWilliams, staring first at Katharine then at Ralph. "I believe he is also the one who attacked Kihhim and kidnapped and maimed Ms. Gardner. He was associated with the same radical right wing church as the other three we nabbed. How about it, Mr. Whitney?"

Ralph said nothing.

Megan Steele delivered their food. She greeted the Kihhimis warmly, welcoming them back. Looking at McWilliams then glancing at the manacles on Ralph, she started to ask but closed her mouth and hurried off. Little else was said as they ate.

"The food is really good. Thank you for feeding us," said McWilliams.

"Thank you, Agent McWilliams," said Katharine.

"Can you call me Robert?"

"I'll try to remember. Old habits are hard to break."

After eating, Carol led Robert and Ralph to their quarters inside the port hull, the one damaged in the attack. She picked a unit near the clinic where Ralph would have stayed to recover. (And where he would not have seen much of Kahchk Kihhim.) The apartment had a den, two bedrooms, and a single bath. It was compact and efficient. "Looks like you will just have to stay in manacles," Robert said. Ralph did not respond as Robert locked him to the couch.

A few minutes later Katharine called. "Are you going to be all right in the apartment?"

"It looks fine. I wish the doors had locks, but we will make do. How do I get something on the TV? Is there news or anything?"

"I'll come over and show you," she said. The phone went dead. A knock sounded at the door minutes later. Robert answered it. Katharine smiled at him and walked to the terminal on the desk. "Computer, commercial programming, CNN news, English." The monitor lit up.

"Let me know if there is anything else you need. Say 'Katharine Levey' to the terminal, followed by 'contact'. It will find me wherever I am." At the door she said, "I'll pick you both up for a tour in an hour. Use the monitor for anything you want." The door closed as she left.

"That is one nice lady," Robert said to the silent Ralph. He sat on the other end of the couch to watch the news.

In international news, China is demanding a United Nations investigation into the recent attack on the newly formed nation of Kahchk Kihhim. Chinese spokesperson Li Chaing issued a statement today saying it was not a missile attack but illegal weapon development gone awry that caused the explosion. Li Chaing further asserts the weapon development program is under the protection of the United States government and in violation of international treaties. China claims only an international investigation will find the truth.

China discounted the video footage of the captured submarine as a sham. When asked to produce the submarine and crew United States Navy officials stated the submarine was radioactive and had to be sunk. The crew perished from radiation poisoning.

Memorial services were held for Vice President Vincente Sanchez today with full honors. Representatives from most nations attended.

Kahchk Kihhim remains a mystery, as few reporters have been allowed to visit, and only the series of documentaries produced soon after their formation is available. Public sentiment is changing from wonder to concern about this new nation, especially after their refusal to join the United Nations.

During another commercial break, Robert looked at Ralph. "So maybe this is the reason someone would assassinate a vice president." Ralph remained silent.

Chapter Seventy-Four

Shackles rattling, Ralph shuffled forward on their tour following Katharine down the corridor to the greenhouse arch. As they climbed a ramp, foliage crowded in.

Katharine took them down the other side of the ramp into the opposite hull and more growing areas. In a lower hold, a large swimming pool filled part of the floor. In the side, a hatch opened to the sea between the two hulls. The outside was alive with activity and life. Children played and swam with dolphins. In another area, separated by strange looking floats, the water seemed to boil with fish.

Ralph's eyes were alive, noting more than Robert, who focused more on their guide than their surroundings. He might be able to take one of these small boats and get away. An elevator took them to the arch, but this time they looked forward where the sea stretched ahead of them. Clouds rose above the horizon.

Robert had seen Kihhim, but this impressed him again, not only by the variety, but the scale. He recognized few of the plants, but they were laden with fruit. On closer inspection, living wood made up a lot of the structure.

"What are those floats?" asked Robert.

"Those are jellyfish linked to form nets. That is the final section of our fish farm. The fish in that section are ready for harvest,"

Robert stared. "What's that crusty deposit on the hull?" he asked.

"It's a growth, like a reef to enhance the sea life. It also seals and protects our hulls, so we have no maintenance on them."

"Doesn't that slow you down a lot?"

Katharine looked at him. "We're not in a hurry to get anywhere. This is home."

"Looks like we're in for a storm," said Robert.

"It'll catch us about mid-afternoon. All the activity you see is our drawing things closer to the hulls for protection. Although that is a good-sized depression, it's not strong enough that we need to turn bow into the wind. We'll use the lee of the ships to protect our farming."

"What's below here?" asked Ralph, the first words he had spoken. He watched Katharine jerk in reaction to his voice. She recognized it from his Kihhim visit.

She stammered. "Storage areas and bays. The same as in the other hull. Let's go to the clinic where you supposedly spent time."

Ralph sensed her discomfort and something else. What was down there? He would have to find out. They entered the clinic. Several doors opened into rooms with beds. The causalities from the attack filled them all.

One large vat had floating figures moving as the currents of the aeration and circulation stirred them. Masks covered their faces making it impossible to see more. Angry red scars showed on many of the bodies. Limbs were in plastic splints. "These are victims from your attack. It was lucky they were here. Most will survive, no thanks to you."

"Do you usually have this many customers?" said Robert.

"Rarely, but these are rare circumstances. Others are being monitored in their own quarters." Two rooms had tubs instead of beds. "We also use this to care for the sea life. It is an oceanic vet's office too," said Katharine.

The vats were large. Must be some big fish they look after, Ralph thought. "Shouldn't I spend a night here, if this is where I was supposed to be recuperating?" he asked.

Robert looked at him sharply, but Katharine answered, "I don't think that's necessary."

Climbing several flights of stairs to the open deck, they came out into the stiff breeze of the coming storm. Misty white coated the gray water as the wind whipped the waves. The wind coming over the port bow hardly rocked the ship. The rigid sails were trimmed to take advantage, and the rigging sang. People and dolphins herded the sea life into the sheltered area between the hulls. The speed of the ship was faster than yesterday but not even four knots.

Ralph watched the movement in the water below, glimpsing large shapes, strange unidentifiable fish. As they climbed a ramp up the arch, they arrived again at the restaurant in time for lunch. Ralph felt Katharine's stare as they sat.

She was vaguely aware Robert had spoken to her. "I'm sorry. My mind was elsewhere. What did you say?" she asked.

"The greenhouses here seem to be similar to those in Arizona," he said.

"Kihhim was the prototype. We've made improvements, some not so obvious. Many of the plants grow in salt water instead of fresh." She waved her hand at the window where the rain streaked the glass. The wind had picked up, and behind the hulls, gusts blew the tops off the waves, yet the ship moved little.

Ralph stared hard at the sea, ignoring those around him, wheels turning.

"Our home is the sea," Katharine continued. "We are adapting ourselves to live here, utilizing all the resources. We are truly farming the sea, but giving back more than we're taking. Our wake contains more sea life than there is ahead of us."

"What effect does your genetic engineering have on the natural sea life?" asked Robert.

"We try to not release any, but we monitor everything to assure we are changing nothing detrimentally," said Katharine.

"I see," said Robert, a tingle of doubt in his voice, "And we are to trust that you know everything about this?"

"Who better?"

Ralph listened with only part of his attention, looking for something to use. With the arrival of the food, conversation ceased, and he was able to think. The tour gave him a lot of information, but he had the underlying feeling there was more here. And he wouldn't find it on this tour. He'd have to spend time looking by himself. It would cost him, but perhaps he'd find something that would help.

They ate in silence, watching the storm move across the sea outside. When they finished, Katharine led them back to their quarters. "That's everything Ralph could have seen during his short stay. I'll come get you at dinnertime. Please remain here." She left without another word.

Chapter Seventy-Five

Robert looked after her, puzzled. Why was she so abrupt? After Ralph was settled and secured, he sat in front of the monitor watching a news program.

The sound was low, but his thoughts were on Katharine. She had been in his custody for four years. They had been civil to each other, realizing they were caught by forces and loyalties that pulled them apart. Acrimony would have changed nothing and only made things worse.

He learned to admire her stoicism at the situation and many of her traits. Katharine was a strong, self-assured woman. Under other circumstances, he might have developed a relationship with her. As if she would be interested in her jailer, he thought ruefully. Yet today, he saw a flicker of interest from her, at least he hoped so. Robert turned his thoughts to what he had seen. What a fascinating place this was. They had done marvelous things here, things that might change the world.

***

Dinner was quiet. Robert turned to Katharine, "I'm starting to understand more about you and Kahchk Kihhim, and it scares me a little."

Katharine glanced at Ralph, who appeared fascinated by the view of the dark sea. Robert looked at him then back at her.

"Perhaps we'll have the chance to talk more about it sometime," she said.

"I am not sure when, since we leave tomorrow morning."

"Coffee?" she asked, looking at the table menu.

Robert nodded, but said, "No, I'd never get to sleep." Ralph watched their reflections in the window.

When they got back to the room, Robert said, "I'm going up on the deck for air. Use the bathroom now." When Ralph said he didn't have to, Robert locked him to the bed and left.

As he followed the corridor to Katharine's room, doubt began to assail him. Perhaps there hadn't been any signals. Boy, would that be a colossal fuckup so typical for him. She opened the door to his knock, the light framing her hair in a halo.

"Robert," she said, with mock surprise. "Would you like that coffee now?"

"Thank you. Yes I would," he said entering as she stepped aside.

"It'll just take me a minute to put it on." He looked around the apartment. The layout was like the unit they were in though softer with some touches added. One wall was a mural of Kihhim looking toward Baboquivari Peak. He did not recognize the houseplants, but the flowers smelled wonderful. It was comfortable. When she returned, he noticed her light bathrobe.

"Did I get you up? I mean were you going to bed?" he stammered and hated it.

"No, I hoped you would come by," she said, and smiled. "In another world, we might have liked each other a lot. You seem honest, trustworthy, kind, all the Boy Scout traits, but in you they are real. That is why I asked for you on this assignment. After the years we saw each other, I felt I knew you, and I even learned to trust you. Not to do what I wanted but what you believed to be right. I wanted to see you again and not as a jailer."

"Thank you," said Robert. "I feel the same but in these circumstances; I don't believe things would work between us much as I want them to. The United States has my loyalties as long as I work for them, regardless of how much I wish otherwise."

"I already know that, Robert. But let's enjoy the dream." She took his hand and looked at it. He willingly let her pull him, into her arms.

Chapter Seventy-Six

As soon as Robert left, Ralph retrieved the piece of wire he'd taken during the afternoon tour and released the cuffs. Stupid feebie would be tied up with the woman for hours. He retraced the route to the lower hold with the pool and the hatch.

The hold was dimly lit, the hatch closed. He skirted the pool and opened the hatch. It creaked as Ralph looked outside. Nothing but water moved with subdued wave motion in the protected area. He stood in the doorway as his eyes adjusted to the darkness.

All the boats were tied up on the opposite hull. Could he swim? He looked into the water. An ebony shape moved below him. No way to escape. Overhead, the arch blotted the stars.

He would have to wait and try something back in the States where he might get help. A noise behind him caused his heart to pound, and he turned, poised to attack.

His heart beat a staccato. He blinked several times, not believing his eyes. Silhouetted before him stood a seven-foot tall manlike figure. But it definitely was not human. With its back to him, it had not seen him yet. Ralph stared, trying to control rising panic. It reminded him of the Creature from the Black Lagoon—the first horror movie he saw as a young child. Nightmares haunted him for a week afterwards.

The arms were long, the hands webbed, the shoulders huge and powerfully built, and the legs as big as his waist. The feet were like diving flippers, and the skin glistened in the dim light like shark's skin. Ralph was fascinated and frozen at the same time. He held his breath as it looked around the chamber.

Slowly the creature turned toward him, and yet Ralph could not move. When the large black eyes focused on him, the mouth opened, revealing several rows of sharp-pointed teeth, gleaming in the night. The creature moved toward him.

Ralph's muscles came to life, and he leapt backward. Everything slowed, and he seemed suspended in the air before he started to fall. A scream rose in his throat as he hit the water. It burst out as terror filled bubbles. Nobody heard.

He tried to swim but his limbs refused to move. Air. He needed air, but the surface wavered far above. Without air in his lungs, he sank. It didn't take long until the darkness closed in. He never felt the soft webbed hands close around him and carry him upward.

***

Katharine's phone jarred her. Pushing back from Robert's embrace, she answered. It was Sean Steele. For the second time, he had rescued Ralph Whitney. Once laid out on the deck, Sean got him to breathe and then called Katharine. They arrived in minutes.

The FBI agent exploded at the sight of the unshackled man on the deck. Together Katharine and Robert carried the barely breathing Ralph to the hospital, Robert getting redder with each step. She knew he was furious with himself for his negligence that resulted in Ralph's near escape.

Ralph awoke on his stomach with a pan full of water and vomit under his head. He retched again.

"Just where in the fuck did you think you were going?" Robert hissed.

The vision of the creature loomed up again and Ralph shivered. "I saw…"

"I don't care what you saw!" screamed McWilliams. "What the fuck were you doing?"

Ralph's composure returned in the face of McWilliams' anger. Something familiar, it brought him back. He pursed his lips, saying nothing. He had seen it. The creature from the Black Lagoon was here. Another shiver passed through him, but he remained silent, lips tightly pressed together.

***

Chapter Seventy-Seven

This was serious, Katharine thought. Ralph's ranting will at first be dismissed, but he'd seen! He'd doubt the vision, but eventually he'd start to believe what he had seen. "Robert, may I talk to you outside," she asked. He looked at her, nodded, and fastened Ralph's wrists to opposite sides of the bed with two sets of handcuffs.

As she walked down the hall with Robert, her mind raced. She trusted him, but it was not fair to put him in a position where he had to choose between his oath to his country and Kahchk Kihhim's need for secrecy.

"Robert, I have to explain something to you. It'll put you in a terrible position, but I trust you. Whatever you decide to do, we will live with it." Robert looked at her, puzzled, having not a clue.

"This is difficult to say so I'm just going to come out with it. We genetically engineered our plants and food to serve our needs. We have gone beyond that. At Kihhim, we grew our own spare parts and organs. We weren't harvesting them, but growing them from cells. These organs were generic blanks, and we could tag them with individual DNA, the ideal replacements."

"I suspected something like that when I saw the tanks at Kihhim. Those weren't plant parts, but I dismissed it," said Robert. "So it's true. Why haven't you passed this on to the world? This is a medical breakthrough. It could save millions of lives."

"The world will do this within a few years when the international laws change to allow for the genetic manipulation of human tissues and cloning. Some labs do it now and offer clandestine organ replacement. They grow clones to do it, and that is where the ethical problems are."

"So what is the big deal about this?" asked Robert.

"We're beyond that here. We adapted plants and animals to thrive in the environment of our greenhouses. Since we moved from Kihhim to Kahchk Kihhim, we became an aquatic culture."

They entered the same hold again. "We are changing ourselves into a marine species. Not all of us, just a few volunteers who want to make the change," Katharine said. She put her hand on his arm. "Brace yourself." She turned toward the pool.

"Sean, come out and meet FBI agent Robert McWilliams." The water rippled and a shiny dark head emerged with large black eyes staring at her. "It's all right. Come on out. This is a friend."

The creature stepped out and stood on the edge of the pool; the dripping water making the only sound. Robert's mouth hung slack. The creature advanced toward them with a wet slap of its feet on the deck. Robert stepped back. Only Katharine's restraining hand prevented him from drawing his pistol. A webbed hand extended toward him.

"I am Sean Steele and I am pleased to meet you," it said in a rumbling voice. Robert froze in place his mouth agape, eyes the size of saucers. "If we had flies out here, you'd trap a few in your mouth," the creature said. Robert's mouth snapped shut.

Slowly his eyes changed from fear to wonder. He looked down at the offered webbed hand and tentatively raised his own. His hand disappeared into the huge paw as it shook his arm.

"Sean Steele decided to become an Altered two years ago when he joined us," said Katharine. "Without going into the details, it took a year for him to 'genevolve' into what you see. He has truly become a citizen of the sea," Katharine said. Robert still had not spoken, his mouth closed tightly.

"Once I understood what life was like at Kahchk Kihhim," rumbled Sean, "I saw where I would be most useful. At first, I was doubtful about the changes, but my friend Blue convinced me. I have never regretted it."

Behind him, the water moved again, and a dolphin head emerged. It made sounds, and Sean responded with like sounds. "Blue Streak wants to know if the other man is okay," said Sean. Robert's mouth again hung open.

"He will recover," said Katharine. "I would also like to introduce you to Blue Streak, one of our altered Dahlfins. Don't be fooled thinking she is just a dolphin. She has an IQ of one-hundred and twenty though she is mentally young. She is the equivalent of a precocious teenager, but she learns very fast."

Blue Streak spoke again in a high pitched but barely understandable English. "Weee are pleeeeased to meeeet you. Not ofteeeen weee geeet to meeeet straaangers here. Will youuu beee staying?"

"We leave in the morning," stammered Robert.

"By 'we' you mean you and the other man?" asked Sean. "I understand he is your prisoner."

"Yes. He is the man who bombed our home," said Katharine. "One of those you captured. We are hoping to use him to catch those responsible. We needed to bring him here."

"Heeee issss theee one who killllled John and theee others?" asked Blue Streak.

"Yes," said Robert.

"Whhhat is gooooing to happen toooo him?"

"He will be imprisoned for the rest of his life," said Robert.

"That wooould not beee long if it were meeee," said Blue Streak. "I could not staaand to beee a prisssoner."

"Robert and I need to talk now. You may stay or leave as you wish," said Katharine.

"The containment nets need to be redeployed," said Sean.

"IIII thiiiink maaaybeee weee'll get to seeee you aaagain," said Blue. With that, both the Altered and the Dahlfin dove under the water. Robert, still stunned, said nothing. Katharine looked at him.

"They are why we cannot open up Kahchk Kihhim to the world. The human race evolved because survival is based on competition. We don't believe the human race is mature enough yet to tolerate another intelligent race on earth."

Katharine wore a sardonic smile. "They can't even tolerate small differences such as skin color and religious beliefs within their own species. We might very well galvanize mankind into a unified force, whose single purpose is the destruction of another species. Us."

Katharine watched the realization of the peril dawn on Robert. No doubt he had faced his own version of bias and hatred.

"This place would be destroyed, utterly," he whispered. "What are you going to do? You cannot keep Kahchk Kihhim's secret forever. Look at what happened with Ralph. What are we going to do with Ralph?" he asked suddenly.

"We are going to ignore his whole incident as if it is in his imagination. We are going to hope no one believes the ranting of a deranged calculating killer. We are going to say that one of our divers rescued him."

"What about my report? I have to report the escape attempt."

"We reached an arrangement with President Carson for protection, though he doesn't yet know as much about us as you do now. We literally forced him into the agreement. I won't tell you how, but we do understand this is temporary."

Katharine started back to the medical unit. "Robert, you must do what your conscience tells you. We are not a threat despite what you may hear." Not a word was said until they reached the bed and the handcuffed Ralph.

Robert unlocked the cuffs. "Let's get back to our room and get some sleep. We leave early tomorrow." Ralph got up and looked at Robert and then Katharine. They tried to remain expressionless.

"We went back down and looked at the pool compartment," said Robert. "What were you trying to do? You knew your escape wasn't possible. The boats are too small. We are too far out to sea."

"There is something not right down there," exclaimed Ralph.

"It's lucky there was a diver there when you fell overboard. We went over everything. There is nothing out of order," said Robert.

"I tell you I saw a monster!" shouted Ralph.

"There are no monsters," said Katharine, "only residents of Kahchk Kihhim. You saw one of our divers suited up for repairs on the ship's hull. He's the one who called me."

"I met him too," said Robert. "He even asked if you were all right."

Doubt crept into Ralph's eyes. He closed them and saw the creature again. Could it have been a diver? The tiny seed of doubt niggled away. They returned to their room where Robert had Ralph use the bathroom to prepare for bed. Once ready, he double cuffed him to the bed. When Ralph complained, Robert simply shrugged his shoulders.

Even if he still had the wire, cuffed spread-eagle made it impossible to free himself. Beside, where would he go? The sea was dark and full of monsters.

Chapter Seventy-Eight

Sleep was the farthest thing from Robert's mind. The sight and the conversation with the two creatures kept playing through his mind. If he had closed his eyes, he would have never known he was not speaking to humans, but then their images flashed again.

He was repelled and fascinated, but most of all he was frightened to death. Kahchk Kihhim manufactured human spare parts, and now they made organisms that suited their environment–the sea. They certainly could manufacture beings to meet any conditions they needed, even those of war. How far could they go? How far would they go?

He had not promised Katharine he would keep this a secret; she had not asked him to. Worse than that, she left it up to him, pointing up the consequences if he did not.

What if he did keep their secret and Kahchk Kihhim was not as benign tomorrow? The United States could destroy Kahchk Kihhim if need be. The power was stationed only a few miles away.

He suddenly wondered at the nearness of the carrier battle group. Who was protecting what? He didn't know if he would keep this a secret. For now, he resolved not to put what he's seen in his report, but if asked, he would have to tell.

His thoughts returned to Katharine. Something existed between them, certainly the potential for a lot more. If he let go of his emotions for a second, he would start down a path toward her. He was not sure he could come back or would even want to. He had never met any woman like her, so complete and self-confident, smart, beautiful, patient, and the nicest person he'd ever known. The adjectives kept coming.

Since his divorce ten years ago, he dated little, focusing his energy on his job as a way of not exposing raw nerves and risking injury again. It became a habit, and now he realized a lonely one. The part of him that remembered the comfort of a loving relationship was out of the box, and he did not want to put it back in.

***

Robert was not the only one having trouble sleeping. Every time Ralph closed his eyes, the creature loomed before him, causing him to start. He knew what he had seen, but the crisp outline already started to blur; the eyes turned into goggles, the webbed hands into gloves, the black skin a wetsuit. Was the Feebie right? But he still shivered.

***

Katharine also lay awake. What would Robert do? She forced a terrible onus and decision on him. Had she placed too much on this Robert

McWilliams? He was beginning to understand more about Kahchk Kihhim than any other outsider.

Would he project, seeing a potential danger for humanity? He only had her word that the peril was only to Kahchk Kihhim. If he heard about the threat of the virus, what would he do?

What could he do? Guilt rose within her for loading this onto him. He was such an honest, guileless man.

They would have to bring the president into this loop.

She thought again about Robert. Her feeling for him could be deeper. He reminded her of John. John was a wonderful person, but he did plot when necessary. She hadn't seen that in Robert. A tear rolled from her eye. She did miss John. The weight of Kahchk Kihhim had nearly flattened her after he was killed. "What should I do, John?" she asked of the darkness and not for the first time. She waited for an answer.

Chapter Seventy-Nine

Robert McWilliams and Ralph Whitney faced the gathering around the table–Secretary of Defense Craig Nelson, Secretary of the Navy Admiral Harold Cochrain, Secretary of State Wesley Hamilton, Director of the FBI Jordan Brown, and Assistant Director Janet Kilgore. Robert's debriefing after the return from Kahchk Kihhim was uneventful.

The topic of unusual practices never came up. He felt guilty about not putting anything in his report, but the resolution from the last night at sea held. Ralph omitted the incident with the Altered. That made Robert wonder. Did he doubt or was he plotting?

***

Ralph made the drop requesting a call, but instead of the usual day for a callback, two days passed.

"Hello, Helen." Silence answered as she tried to identify the voice as Ralph's. "Talk to me, Helen."

She gasped and stuttered out, "How do I know it is you?"

"Half of my money was deposited in my account. Our drop is the Chinese laundry in my suit jacket pocket."

"Where are you?"

"Let's forget that for now. I want double the money you owe me. You tried to kill me."

"I did not do that. It was an unfortunate accident."

"Accident, my ass."

"I do not have the authority for that kind of payment," Helen Chein stammered. "I cannot make any decisions like this. How did you escape?"

"I went out the tube as the missile was launched and got picked up by Kahchk Kihhim. You better talk to whoever can authorize this, or I will go to the FBI."

"With what?"

"Do you think I haven't covered myself? I have tapes and records. The whole arrangement is well documented, and if anything happens to me, it goes to the U.S. Government. They will not ignore any possibility of finding out who's behind the assassination of their vice president." No recordings existed until now but Helen didn't know that.

"If we agree to meet and pay, we will get all the documentation?" she asked.

"Of course."

"I will talk to my superior and call back about a meeting." Her superior would demand a meeting. Everybody understood that would be a trap, but for whom?

"Give me a number," Ralph said. "I will call you back in an hour." There was a sigh of relief around the table as he hung up. Ralph's mind raced. This set up would be his only chance to escape, but everybody would be ready for that.

If he escaped the Chinese, the FBI would hunt him down. They were his only protection, but they wanted his ass forever. He bargained for his life, and they gave it to him, but they would never give him his freedom. That he would have to steal back.

An hour later Ralph called. Helen Chein answered in an anxious voice. "I must apologize about any misunderstanding that has taken place during the job. You did a magnificent job–so good that we will be happy to increase your payment."

"I will call you back after I see a deposit in my account of five million dollars. We will then set up a meeting."

A gasp came from the phone. "We agreed on four million dollars for the whole job, and we have already paid you two million.

"That was before you set me up to die along with your patsy crew." Ralph yelled. "I will call you after the next five million dollar deposit. It had better be tomorrow." Not waiting for a response, he hung up. The others around the table looked at him.

"We'll need your bank account number and access code, so we can check for the deposit," pointed out the Admiral.

"I will do my own checking," said Ralph.

"You're not in a position to bargain," sneered the Admiral.

"Then kill me and carry on by yourself," said Ralph looking him straight in the eye. Quiet surrounded the table.

Finally, the Director of the FBI said, "We'll let you use a clean phone. When do you want it?"

"We will call them in two days."

"But you told them tomorrow," said the Admiral.

"I will let them wait for a day." Ralph smiled. He really needed time to plan. In his business, it paid to set up contingencies for every foreseeable event, but to get help when held incommunicado was a challenge. Alone in his cell (actually not a bad room but a cell nevertheless), he started writing a script in his head, a special script. He had to be ready. This would be his only chance.

***

General Kai sat thoughtfully. So the assassin has escaped his assassination. He looked at Helen. "When he calls back, you will agree to his terms. We will deposit the funds he requests, and we will meet, but we require a full debriefing. We want something for this extra money." Ralph Whitney's time on Kahchk Kihhim should prove valuable with the right questions. What flies out of the trap may be more valuable than first thought.

Chapter Eighty

It was time to bring the United States on the secret of Kahchk Kihhim. Katharine dialed the president's direct number, identified herself, and asked for President Carson. Within a minute, she heard the familiar voice on the phone. "Good afternoon, Mr. President," she said. "I hope things are going well with you."

"It is the usual rash of crises," he responded. "What can I do for you?" he asked without preamble, obviously in a hurry.

"Mr. President, may I talk freely?"

"I have several people here now," he said.

"Okay, sir. I will keep this short and low key. There are developments here you need to be made aware of. These developments are such that you and your staff need to visit our site but not publicly."

"What sort of developments are we talking about? I am not aware of anything happening there."

Katharine knew he was looking at some of his staff, wondering what they had not told him. "Sir, these are things only the residents of Kahchk Kihhim knew until recently. They cannot be fully understood unless you are here."

"That is sufficiently cryptic to get my attention. Can you give me any idea of what this is?"

"I would suggest you speak to FBI Special Agent Robert McWilliams, alone at first. If you think it appropriate, please call me back to arrange a visit. Sir, this is as confidential as any other matter we have ever discussed," said Katharine.

"I will meet with Agent McWilliams today. Thank you for the call," he said and hung up .

Katharine looked at those around her. "I guess you could say the die is cast," she said.

"I still do not like the idea of telling anyone about this–especially a politician," said Leticia. "We could have taken care of that bastard Ralph Whitney, and you probably could have convinced Agent McWilliams to keep it a secret or stay with us."

"I hope we haven't resorted to the same murderous methods other nations justify," said Carol.

"This is our existence." said Leticia heatedly. "Can we take a chance?"

"Leticia, it has always been about our existence and our survival," said Katharine. "We have placed a huge hammer over the heads of our protectors. We cannot make them regret it too much, or they will redouble their efforts at removing it. We have to keep the United States as an ally, even an unwilling one, and keeping them informed will allow us to work together to do that."

"Do we show them everything?" asked Dayton.

Katharine turned to Sean Steele and Blue Streak. "It is you who will be the object of attention. After the first shock of seeing you will come the realization of all you represent. We must pray there is enough wisdom in this President Ronald Carson to react constructively to us, to all of us."

"I hate to put our fate in the hands of outsiders," said Leticia.

"It is time for us to move forward and start preparing now," said Rich. "In order to protect our way of life, perhaps we need to grow Kahchk Kihhim." All gazes swiveled to him.

"We built Kahchk Kihhim because no land existed on earth that we could call our own. It may be there is no place on the surface of the Earth we will be allowed to live, at least for now. All of our genering with the Altereds has been keeping mammals as the basis." He looked to Jamie Wong

Jamie cleared his throat, clasped his hands on the tabletop. "We need to start moving into the fully aquatic lines. If we started another nation, underwater and completely secret, at least we would have a better chance of survival." They all looked at each other, nodding.

"Research has never stopped in our labs. Fully adapting ourselves to aquatic environs would represent a major change from previous modifications."

"Bring us up to date," said Katharine.

"We started growing an underwater structure six months ago. A habitat to support us will take less than two years. Fully modified inhabitants will take about three years," said Jamie.

"Can you give us a detailed plan?" asked Katharine.

He picked up a small remote control. "We rejected the idea of trying to construct a physical underwater structure as our land dwelling brothers would. The big machines they use are beyond our means and not our way. Instead, we decided to grow our habitat."

He pushed a button, and a hologram of a bubble floated in the air in front of them. "We have modified a form of jelly fish to grow huge bubbles that are the basis of our new home. We used many of these together." Several bubbles appeared.

"Once we grew several of those, we attached them together and started forming the semi rigid outer shell using a form of coral to cover the sections." A crust started to form around some of the bubbles. "Part of the shell is a transparent reinforced membrane from the jellyfish, another is the coral. By growing this in a modular fashion, we are able to learn and improve the design of the newer sections while we move into the completed sections."

The bubbles merged together forming a flat layer of spheres. "The upper half of the spheres is dry and pressurized with air. The lower half will be for sea dwelling creatures. The growth rate increases geometrically, so we have come along much faster than originally planned." The layer of bubbles continued to grow–much more rapidly as a second layer formed below the first. An additional structure grew and joined the first. Separated by water but connected, the layers formed a 3-D matrix.

"The habitat itself is living creatures in symbiotic existence with us. They house us and we feed them."

"When will it be fully ready?" asked Leticia.

"This is a growing and living thing," said Jamie. "It will continue to grow as we wish, but there will be enough dry volume completed for us to start moving in within three months. To integrate and grow the total support system we will need takes longer. The wet areas don't need to be ready as quickly, since our Dahlfins and Altereds can live in the sea."

"Where is this wondrous habitat?" asked Dayton.

"It is one hundred feet below us right now, but we haven't decided at what depth we will finally want to stabilize. We can start moving into the dry areas immediately. We can bring it up to twenty feet below the surface to move in but we feel above fifty feet we are vulnerable to detection from the surface."

Chapter Eighty-One

Four hours later, the president called Katharine. "Ms. Levey, I have spoken to Agent Robert McWilliams. I understand why he did not report everything he saw to us, but I am afraid his superiors will not be as accepting."

"Mr. President, his reticence is my fault. He is a good and loyal man. You insisted we have a U.S. representative on Kahchk Kihhim. I would like that to be Agent McWilliams." Katharine surprised herself with this statement. She desperately did not want him to suffer.

"I am not going to get between an employee and his management. Agent McWilliams' concern over Kahchk Kihhim and the track taken is well noted and disconcerting. We'll hash this out later."

"Yes, sir," said Katharine.

"I'm having trouble keeping some of my staff in line. That is my concern, and I will have to deal with it. Please be ready to receive us at 07:00 hours day after tomorrow. There will be eight of us, and we will want to know everything."

"We will be, Mr. President. Only by visiting and seeing us first hand will the magnitude of this become real. That is why we need you here. I'm confident we can work out a plan."

"You have no concept of the trouble here," said the president. "I look forward to seeing you again, but I wish it were under other than forced circumstances. That is something you seem to have a habit of doing. Goodbye." He hung up without waiting for any reply.

That is one pissed off man, thought Katharine.

Chapter Eighty-Two

Ralph wrote down and encoded what he would say. Once he memorized everything, he ate the paper. He was ready to make the call. They brought in a clean and untapped phone–everybody knew better. Ralph dialed the number, and when the phone was answered, Ralph spoke without even a hello.

"Monsieur Zurgat, this is RJ calling. I need to check for new deposits in my account. By using the name Zurgat, Ralph alerted his bank manager he was under duress, and everything would be in code. "The account number is AJ76BFTZ81OW69."

The voice on the other end spoke for the first time in a high-pitched mechanical tone, synthesized of course. "A deposit of five million dollars was made yesterday."

Ralph gave him instructions for the dispersal of the money to various accounts, none existing but all of which set his plan into action. He hung up as his door opened, and he heard footsteps enter. Of course, they were not listening. He turned to greet the Admiral and a marine guard. "Let's go make the other call," said the Admiral.

Sitting in the same room with the same group as before, the Assistant Director of the FBI passed him a script outlining how the meeting was to take place. Ralph glanced at it then picked up the phone and dialed the number.

"This is Ralph. Here are the instructions. You and only one other person may be at the meeting place. Bring an additional one million dollars in a small metal suitcase large denomination bills. Only after I am satisfied with the money will we talk. I will have available to you the originals of everything, but I will retain copies as an insurance policy. If I do not periodically call an assistant to assure everything is fine, those copies will find their way to the director of the FBI and the press."

"Agreed," said a voice on the other end–not Helen Chein. "We will want to get something extra for this additional money. Please be prepared to give us a full debriefing about Kahchk Kihhim." The polite words did not hide the hard voice.

Ralph glanced at the instructions in front of him. "The meeting will take place at the Frey Marcos Hotel in Nogales, Sonora, Mexico on Tuesday at 11:15 AM." Those around the table started. This was not the script. The Director of the FBI held his fingers to his lips for silence. "I will have room number fourteen reserved under the name of Juan Christóbal. If everything is not according to plan, all information will be released."

"It will be as you wish," said the voice on the other end. Ralph hung up.

Angry voices exploded around the table. "What the fuck do you think you are doing? If you believe you're going to get away with anything, we will blow your shit away. You do understand that, don't you?" said the Admiral.

Ralph sat mute with nothing to say. His coded phone call to the banker set the play in motion, but a lot that could go wrong and anything that did resulted in his death. Amid all of the high-pitched conversation and finger pointing, he stood and was led back to his cell.

Chapter Eighty–Three

The helicopter landed softly on the deck of Kahchk Kihhim, and the presidential entourage stepped out at precisely 7:00 AM. Katharine shook hands, but the greeting was as cold as the wind blowing over the bow. They exchanged no fanfare or niceties as she led them through the main hatch and down the flights of stairs to the hold with the access pool.

Secret service men entered and then returned–signaling it was clear. They stationed themselves on either side of the entry. The door closed. Not a word was spoken as they moved around a table with thirteen chairs. Carol, Dayton, Rich, and Leticia stood as the president entered. They shook hands in introductions as frosty as any cold war conference. The president's entourage did not speak but only nodded acknowledgements. They sat.

Katharine rose and spoke. "Mr. President, we are recording this meeting. Copies will be given to you upon your departure. Let the record show there are fifteen in attendance between the representatives of The United States of America and the sovereign nation of Kahchk Kihhim."

The president glanced around then said, "I see only thirteen people here."

A splash sounded in the pool, and two figures appeared on the shallow ledge next to the table. A deep voice spoke. "I am Sean Steele, an altered citizen of Kahchk Kihhim, and I am pleased and honored to meet you, Mr. President."

He rose and stepped out of the pool. The eyes of the delegation were riveted on him–their mouths dropped open as they took in his towering height. He held out a webbed hand to the stunned group. The only sound was the echoing drip of water from Sean's glistening body. If a photo of the tableau made the press, it would have been laughable, with the mouths of the United States delegation all agape, a combination of fear, shock and loathing written on every face.

Sean smiled a toothy grin as he watched them recover. Hesitantly the president rose. Secretary of State Wesley Hamilton put a cautionary hand out to stop him, but he shook it off and walked stiffly around the table. He stood in front of Sean Steele looking up.

The president was a tall man, but Sean's large dark eyes were at least a foot above his. Tentatively he offered his own hand, his eyes riveted as it disappeared into the webbed paw.

In a weak voice he said, "I heard about you, but the shock of actually seeing you is overwhelming." They shook slowly as if they could feel the historic import of this. Still holding the president's hand, Sean turned toward the pool, the Dahlfin's head easily visible. "This is Blue Streak–another of our altered citizens."

Blue Streak rolled to one side and offered a flipper. Sean let go of the president's hand and stepped back for the president to bend down. He shook the flipper much more easily than he had Sean's massive hand.

"Thisss isss truuuly an honnnor," squeaked Blue Streak. "I loooook forrrwaaard to worrrkinggg with you and your staaaff."

For the first time, the president smiled. This was like a scene from Marine Land. He rose and turned toward the table and the concerned faces of his staff. "This is an honor and a momentous occasion," he said. "Let me introduce you to everyone here."

The president introduced each member of his staff, who hesitantly came over and shook hands and flippers with the two Altereds. They moved woodenly–obviously not fully believing and not comfortable seeing the creatures and hearing both of them speak as intelligent beings. Everybody sat and Katharine continued.

"The reaction of you and your staff to meeting our citizens and understanding more about Kahchk Kihhim is probably the mildest reaction we expected from those outside. This is the reason we have been so secretive and not opened our nation up to the outside world."

The Secretary of State stood, his face scarlet with rage. "If you had not released the virus, we would be considering your total destruction as enemies of humanity. You violated every convention that the civilized world has made, and you violated God's law. You are an abomination!"

If he expected shocked looks on the faces of the Kahchk Kihhim citizens, he was disappointed. Katharine looked at the president. Her face said it all . Wesley Hamilton continued, "Regardless of what you think of your society," he sneered, his face looking as if he had just bitten into a rotten peanut, "you chose this path. It has put you at odds with humanity. You created this situation, and you want us to bail you out. Excuse me if I do not share your enthusiasm. Why did you do it?"

"Mr. Hamilton," said Katharine, "We know man's evolution was set when he became a tool builder. It led to cognitive thought and everything that makes us what we are. Up until now, tool building has been perceived as the construction of things fabricated by hand or machine–machines made by man."

Heads at the table nodded, but not all of them. "You are now on a path of machines made by machines, but that is still the construction of inanimate things. It is entirely possible, in fact, it is certain you will build machines that will acquire self-awareness. The ethics of that will then be your next great hurdle."

She smiled at them. "The manipulation of life has always been with us in agriculture and animal husbandry, but until we had the tools to directly create life, we only changed conditions, and let growth respond to those changes. We too are building things, but we do so by directing the force of life."

Katharine took a few steps as if lecturing a class. "Up to this point, man tried to control his environment for his betterment and not always with an eye toward the long-term effect. This is the point where we must diverge. We are changing ourselves to the environment, not changing the environment to ourselves. In the long run, we believe ours is the better survival path. This is what nature does with natural selection, but through generations and over millions of years."

"That is a very nice philosophical speech," said Kennedy, "but in the end you violated the laws of nature, the laws that created the world we have, and the laws that made man. And to many you violated God's laws. When this gets out, and it will, you will pit the United States government against its own people and the rest of the world. When they call for your destruction, I do not think we can go to war to protect you despite the threat of the virus. If your destruction leads to the destruction of man, then the world will have to start again without us."

Silence hung in the room, except for the soft lapping of the water in the pool. Everybody looked down, lost in their own thoughts with the threat of the destruction of intelligent life on Earth a pall hanging thickly.

A high squeaky voice came from the pool. "IIII'm glaaaad weeee got thaaaat ooout. Whaaaat dooo weeee doooo aboooout iiiit noooow, aaaand toooomorroooow?" said Blue Streak. All heads turned toward her, their thoughts and their feet brought back to earth by this simple question.

"Whether you opened Pandora's Box or made the next great step in the evolution of mankind only time will tell. What are your plans now?" asked the president.

"It has never been our intention to compete with mankind for the Earth. We are looking at inhabiting the unpopulated two thirds that is available. There is room enough for all of us if we can overcome the prejudice. Let me present an analogous hypothetical situation. If aliens landed on earth, there would be another intelligent species known to exist. It would be a fact, and it would have to be accepted by mankind."

Her eyes looked from face to face at the table. Some were listening, others deafened by the bias in their minds. "Having traveled to Earth, those aliens would be at least technically superior to us. What would happen and how they were treated would depend on a number of things, but in the end, it would be the adaptability of the human mind that would set the stage. I have faith in mankind that they would accept another species and then thrive given time."

"I hope your faith is not misplaced," said the president.

"Right now," she continued, "there are ten people outside of Kahchk Kihhim who understand what is happening here. Eight are in this room. Is it possible to get mankind to accept a new intelligent species, one that is native to this earth? Would they be able to acknowledge that we have a rightful place here? Can we create enough time to do this?"

The president and his staff stared intently at her. "What makes you think aliens have not already visited Earth?" asked the president. Nobody laughed. The entire United States delegation was mute.

"How much time would it take to create an atmosphere of acceptance?" asked Katharine quietly.

"The groundwork has been done with the idea of beings other than humans existing. What will be hard in this case is the acceptance that man created a new species native to Earth," said the president.

"As fast as genetics is moving despite the world sanctions, human-created species is already foreseen. What you have done is leapfrog to the same point faster than we will go." His shoulders slumped. "Can we buy five years?" he asked looking around the table, then at the pool.

"Do we have a choice," said Sean Steele.

"Special Agent Robert McWilliams and Ralph Whitney are the two people who are not here and know about this?" said the Secretary of State.

"Yes, sir, they are," answered Katharine.

"I am not sure Ralph Whitney's word, by itself, will mean anything," said the president. "He will be in solitary confinement for the rest of his life. Would you accept Special Agent McWilliams as our resident diplomat at Kahchk Kihhim?"

Katharine's heart skipped a beat. "If he would accept the position, we would."

"He will be transferred here as soon as his present assignment is finished."

"President Carson, this cannot be a one way street. Is there something we can do for you and the United States?"

The delegation looked at her as if she offered them poison. "Ms. Levey, our biggest problems are political." The president stood and the rest of his delegation rose. "Are there any other things you should tell us?"

Katharine looked straight into his eyes. "That is all, Mr. President, but we will keep you informed. Since this is your first visit would you care to tour the rest of Kahchk Kihhim? Perhaps there are things to see you will find useful." The tour took several hours, and many questions and appropriate comments made.

As they started to board the helicopter for the return, the president turned to Katharine. "At this time, you are perhaps closer to the society idealized by our founding fathers than we are. Is it because you are new and fresh or because you are small and can still appreciate the individual? Perhaps you could think on this. I would like to know if we should look at you for things to emulate."

He entered the chopper as the turbines wound up for takeoff. As it lifted off, he waved to her looking twice his age. Katharine watched him go. Great men still existed, but you just had to look beyond the facade and critique presented to the public. America still had heroes, despite all efforts to deny that image to anyone.

As they returned to the pool Blue spoke. "I aaactuuuually thoooought thaaaat weeent welllll."

"It did, while they were here," said Leticia. "Now the real battle starts, and I'm glad I am not aboard that chopper."

PART 5

FLIGHT AND FRIGHT

TECH
Scientists try to build a better chromosome
March 11, 1999
VANCOUVER, British Columbia CNN A group
of Canadian researchers is mass producing a
manmade version of one of the building blocks of all
life.

Chapter Eighty-Four

Ralph sat in the nondescript room at the Frey Marcos Hotel and glanced at his watch. He had been discretely escorted there at ten o'clock. His guardians evaporated into the woodwork–invisible but not far away. That was both a worry and a comfort. He had no doubt that once Helen Chien and her boss got information out of him, they would look for any chance to kill him as long as it did not result in exposure.

The threat of airing all tapes and documents might not be enough to prevent his death. Helen's voice had been duplicated using the recent tape technology of the FBI and Ralph's memory. Tapes that accurately portrayed those conversations had been surprisingly easy to make.

Helen and her experts could not tell they were not genuine. The plot of the attack on Kahchk Kihhim was clearly evident. Tying Helen and her boss to the Chinese remained.

Of course, room fourteen was completely bugged. Nothing would escape audio and visual recording. After the meeting, the FBI would pounce and arrest the two Chinese agents and take Ralph back into custody.

The Mexican government consented to allowing the operation, assigning two of their own agents to the team. As he looked out the window, everything appeared normal. Tourist strolled by trying to ignore the peddlers hawking their wares loudly with the phrase, "Cheaper than K Mart, almost free."

At precisely eleven-fifteen, a knock sounded at the door. Ralph did not ask who it was, but he did peer through the peephole to assure himself instant death did not await. As he opened the door, allowing the tall slender Asian woman to enter, he said, "Good to see you again, Helen." Her ebony hair fell to her back framing a smooth oval face, slightly flat with almond eyes that took in the room quickly. Her hand was in her purse, probably holding a pistol. Beautiful Helen Chein, he thought. She turned toward the door and nodded, and a small gray-haired Chinese man entered. He too looked around the room, not with suspicion, but appraisal.

"This is Mr. Shing Lao," said Helen by way of introduction. He gave a slight bow and Ralph held out his hand. They shook as Ralph studied him. Mr. Lao was slight, but the power in his eyes was unmistakable. He wore the neatly-tailored suit like a uniform.

"I am sure you were surprised to hear from me," said Ralph. "You planned the whole thing well."

"Mr. Whitney," said Mr. Lao, "Let us not dwell on the past. Obvious mistakes were made, and we have paid for them." He hefted the aluminum case to emphasize his point.

"There is your merchandise," said Ralph pointing at a similar briefcase on the bed. "Please pour the money out so I can inspect it. I will put the contents of my briefcase on the table for you."

Mr. Lao complied, opening the briefcase, dumping the stacks of bound hundred dollar bills onto the bed. Ralph walked to the table and lifted out the papers and memory chips. Placing them and a player on the table, he gestured for Helen to inspect.

"While she is checking those things, Mr. Whitney, please be seated and tell me about Kahchk Kihhim," gestured Mr. Lao.

"I need to count my money," said Ralph, watching Lao for a reaction. As Ralph picked up each stack of bills and thumbed through it, he placed it in his own briefcase. This was not lost on Mr. Lao.

Helen listened to her voice on the tape describe the job to Ralph. She did not disagree with anything said on the tape. Mr. Lao listened and looked at Helen. I sure would not want to be in her shoes, thought Ralph, loading the money into his briefcase. He closed and locked it, pulling out a set of handcuffs and cuffing it to his left wrist.

"Mr. Whitney, you are a very careful man," said Lao.

"In part, you have taught me that. It is how I managed to stay alive."

"Now I will hear your detailed story about Kahchk Kihhim." The tone of voice clearly told Ralph he would get his way–something he was used to. Ralph sat in the chair at the spindly table and started his debriefing.

Lao's gaze never left him, his voice never raised as he asked direct questions. Ralph told of his escape from the sub and of being picked up by Kahchk Kihhim. If Lao suspected a trap, his death would be swift. The descriptions of the greenhouses and the sea farming clearly interested him. Lao asked many questions on the subject of biological engineering. At last, he asked his summary questions. "Were there any United States officials there?"

"Everyone there belonged to Kahchk Kihhim," responded Ralph. He had not thought about that before, but Kahchk Kihhim was definitely not American.

"Was there anything else, anything we haven't spoken of?" This was it. Lao saw the hesitation and read him perfectly. Lao spoke evenly, steel under the honey in his voice. "There does not seem to be much on the tapes or in the documents that ties this episode to the People's Republic of China. Admittedly, the plan is laid out, but without you or Miss Chein, it would be hard to make a case against us. The submarine and the crew are all circumstantial now. What else?" he asked, turning the word else into a hiss.

Ralph needed to keep him talking. "I managed to get away from my room for a short while. I went down to an underwater access chamber in the ship looking for an escape if I needed it. While there I thought I saw a creature, part man, part fish. It turned out to be a suited diver, but it gave me quite a start," Ralph said, a slight tremor in his voice at the end.

"Describe this creature you thought you saw."

Ralph tensed inside, not really wanting to relive this. He closed his eyes, a slight flutter went through him as he conjured up the memory.

"Its back was to me as it rose out of the access pool. It was tall–seven feet. Its arms were long, and I thought there were fins along them. The hands were large and webbed, but those could have been gloves. Its legs were thick and heavily muscled. Its feet were large and webbed, but it could have been diver's flippers." He stopped.

"Continue," said Lao.

"Its skin was dark and glistened in the light. As it turned toward me, I could see its eyes." Ralph inhaled seeing only the memory. "Its eyes were large and dark. I...I It startled me and I jerked backward, falling into the sea. I sank and passed out."

"How did you get back on the ship?"

"I don't know. I came to in the hospital."

"What did you say to your guards?"

"I told them what I had seen, but they did not believe me and chained me to the bed. They went down to the hold to look, at least that's what they said, a suited diver, they said."

"Who were they?" Lao leaned forward.

"One was the leader of Kahchk Kihhim."

Mr. Lao said nothing. The silence continued; Lao was still. Ralph looked at Helen Chein, her gaze firmly on Lao. Ralph looked back at Lao. He was going to make his move. Ralph broke the silence.

"The United States has at least enough evidence to bring this attack to the court of world opinion." With the bold attack on Taiwan last year, where do you think credibility will fall? Are you prepared to make this decision?"

That was his best shot. If this did not work, he would be depending on the FBI (he hoped they were listening) to bail him out or maybe they would wait a little too late on purpose. It would solve some of their problems.

"As a matter of fact, Mr. Whitney, it was left up to me." Helen paled behind Mr. Lao and started to move for the door. He whirled, and quick as a snake a small silver automatic appeared in his hand. The explosion seemed loud in the room, but Ralph knew little noise was heard outside.

As Helen fell, Ralph swung the briefcase at Lao's head, letting go of the handle, giving it just enough additional reach to connect. Lao collapsed, and without looking back, Ralph grabbed the case and sprinted through the door.

He ran down the hall, unlocking the handcuff from his wrist. When he came to the laundry chute, he threw the case in and dove after it. The slide was short, and both he and the case spilled out into a basket full of laundry, just where he had instructed it to be left. That was a well-spent two hundred dollars.

He jumped out and stripped in seconds. One of the laundry bags had shorts and a flowery shirt, along with tennis shoes, a straw hat, and one of the heavy-duty plastic bags used by all the stores in Nogales. Dumping the money into a cheap athletic bag and putting that into the plastic bag, he became a nondescript tourist leaving the bar.

Once on the street, he worked his way through the crowd of shoppers toward the border fence and a storm drain. He jumped in, and within seconds he entered the labyrinth of tunnels that passed under the border and into the United States.

This was a corridor smugglers and illegal aliens used for years, and despite all the efforts to plug it, pathways still existed. As Ralph came to a welded gate, he pushed on one side. A crack opened up barely wide enough for him to squeeze through into another dark tunnel. He ran.

Ralph emerged on the United States side of the border three blocks away where the small car sat waiting. The keys were under the bumper. Five minutes later, he was heading up I-19 toward Tucson. He had done it!

At Green Valley, he cut across to Corona de Tucson and then I-10 heading east. Next stop would be Georgia, where he would spend time with the Deacon Luke Smithson.

The Deacon and he had not spoken to since the fiasco at Kihhim over four years ago. Ralph kept track of the church through the news. The captured men had not talked, but the Feebies had traced background on them back to the church. Agents watched the Deacon for several years.

To date, the Deacon just preached the general Armageddon stuff and trained the boys ready to rise to the top when the government collapsed. The Deacon would hide him.

Chapter Eighty-Five

The team of agents burst into the room within seconds, only to find Ralph gone, Helen Chein dead and Lao unconscious on the floor. Before they could handcuff him, ski-masked men appeared at the door and window with small ugly submachine guns pointed at the agents.

They uttered not a word. Two more appeared and picked up the slumping body of Lao. They disappeared, jamming the door behind them. Even though the FBI immediately radioed for help, there was no sign of the gunmen or Lao. It was obviously a setup within a setup within a setup—one more than they planned for.

***

The loud thump and bouncing floor of the SUV as it left a paved road brought Lao back to consciousness. He groaned at the pain his hand caused when it encountered the huge lump on the side of his head. When he sat up, stars flashed.

Looking out of the window he saw distant mountains. Drug and people smugglers used these mountains. Police did not enter, and the Mexican army only occasionally came in force. As they climbed the foothills, the road became a barely discernible track, fit only for burros.

The shadow of the setting sun ran before them obscuring the valley floor below. When they pulled up next to a small twin-engine plane, only the tops of the mountains remained in daylight–reflecting golden light around them.

The plane's engines started, and his two companions hustled Lao aboard. His legs were still shaky, and they buckled him into the seat. On the floor near his feet sat a canvas bag. One of the men grabbed it, looked inside grunted and nodded as the roar of the engines moved the plane away. Lao passed out again.

The thump of the landing gear hitting the runway awoke him. His head throbbed, and he winced at each bump. The door opened, and a suited Chinese man entered the plane and bowed to Lao. They assisted him into a humid and pitch-black night. He looked around at the soft glow of kerosene lamps. Sweat ran down his back. In the darkness, he heard jungle sounds. Panama. He had made it.

Lao was helped to a waiting black limousine. General Kai's soft voice came from the shadow.

"I see things were not quite perfect," said Kai.

Lao's head still throbbed and was thick. He simply nodded. "The assassin escaped us again but not before I had the chance to debrief him. The country of Kahchk Kihhim is indeed an experimental lab, but no American officials are there. It does appear to be independent. They are modifying plants for concentrated food production, more so than the

DEM technology. Whitney also told a story about seeing some sort of creature, part man part fish. It may be his imagination, but if not, they may be modifying human beings into other creatures."

"Rest now," Kai said. "This could be the start of a new definition of military forces, made for land or sea operations. You did well."

Hours later, the car pulled into a special hangar at the international airport. A small business jet with extended range fuel tanks gleamed in the red night light. Men were already opening the doors.

***

Within minutes, they streaked west toward Asia. Lao fell asleep, but General Kai was deep in thought. They would have to mount a military campaign against Kahchk Kihhim and therefore, against the United States Navy. In hindsight, perhaps they should have used a nuclear warhead.

Perhaps not. Control of it could shift the balance of world power. It would be best to have that technology in Chinese hands. The Chairman already had an eye on DEM and the food technology with the idea of acquiring it or copying it. With Kahchk Kihhim in their hands, they would not need DEM.

Why would the United States protect this new nation if it did not belong to them? What was in it for them? If Kahchk Kihhim could indeed create specialized supermen, perhaps the protection was not to keep others out but keep them in.

Chapter Eighty-Six

The presidential advisors were fuming at the news. Not only had they lost Ralph Whitney, but they had been set up by the Chinese and lost General Lao. They watched the recording of the meeting, all the evidence they had, along with a dead Helen Chein.

Assistant Director of the FBI, Janet Kilgore tried to hold her head up after delivering her report, but the glare of these powerful people seemed to beat her down. The president spoke to her. "Ms. Kilgore, you will go to Kahchk Kihhim and deliver this report to them. Special Agent Robert McWilliams will accompany you and remain there as our envoy. You are dismissed." Her exit was quick.

As soon as the door closed, the president addressed his advisers. "We need to accelerate the program to find and cure this virus. We have to get rid of this mess." He turned to Secretary of Defense Nelson. "What is the latest from your labs?"

"We're making progress and can now slow the rate of mutation. Translating this into a vaccine could buy us some time to find the cure, but I must caution that this is harder, much harder, than the cure for the common cold."

The president grimaced then waved his hand to continue. "There are moral questions as well. If we develop a vaccine, it will take time to produce. How do we decide who gets it first? How do we distribute it?" There was silence. Hopefully they were composing their criteria list, mused the president.

"The next big question facing us," said the president solemnly, "is what will the Chinese do now that they have suspicions about Kahchk Kihhim?"

Secretary of Defense Craig Nelson spoke. "They probably think we are using Kahchk Kihhim to develop bio-weapons. With the hints of modified humans that Whitney described, they will make the leap to supermen soldiers. Either way, they are going to have to do something."

"Militarily?" asked Wesley Hamilton, the Secretary of State.

"Maybe so," confirmed Admiral Nelson. "Without knowledge of the doomsday virus, they must suspect we are using Kahchk Kihhim as a laboratory. If it were us, we would consider this a terrorist campaign and try a surgical strike."

"After Assistant Director Kilgore delivers her report tomorrow we will talk to Kahchk Kihhim. We may need to bring the Chinese in on the whole problem to prevent an attack," said the president.

Chapter Eighty-Seven

Twenty-two hours straight driving and Ralph stopped at a payphone and called the Deacon's number. "How are you doing, Deacon Luke?" he asked. He was the only person who addressed the Deacon that way.

"Have you risen from the dead?"

"I have been resurrected," said Ralph, enjoying the release offered by the religious banter. "I need to visit with you and seek shelter from the forces of Satan."

"Come on home, my son. I shall prepare the way."

Ralph hung up, and an hour later, turned off I-10 onto U. S. Highway 441. Three hours passed and he was in the swamps, watching carefully for a seldom used and hard to find turnoff heading into the bogs. He passed it and turned around. Good! No traffic.

The track was nothing more than an overgrown path, visible only a few feet ahead of the car. A mile farther down the trail, and the road ended at a fallen tree.

Suddenly, several armed men, masked and camouflaged, surrounded his car, all guns pointing his way. He rolled down the window. "I'm Ralph," he said. One of the men waved, and several others pulled the tree out of the road. The man turned back to him and pointed to the now-visible road, saying nothing.

After turning a corner, several houses appeared out of the swamp. Another man directed him toward a barn, open and waiting. After he drove in, the door slid closed behind him. It took a few moments for his eyes to adjust. With his hands on the steering wheel, Ralph sat unmoving. At a knock on his window, he got out.

"Ralph, I heard you were dead!" said the portly and bearded Deacon. He was standing near a lighted doorway, a welcome sight.

"I heard that, too." They both laughed.

"Come on in. Tell me about your death and resurrection," said the Deacon, putting an arm around him and pulling him through the doorway. They walked down several hallways and past a kitchen where four women were cooking and cleaning. The smell of food? was almost overpowering.

Suddenly, Ralph realized he hadn't eaten, really eaten in two days. His head snapped toward the wonderful aroma. "Hungry, my son?" asked the Deacon. "I will have us served." He motioned to a woman server, who nodded. They entered a dim room with benches and tables. "Sit," said the Deacon, "The food will be here in a few minutes."

Ralph was suddenly starving and exhausted at the same time. It must have shown in his face. "You look bad," said the Deacon. "Eat and rest. I'll get one of the girls show you to your room. We can talk in the morning." As he rose, a young girl approached with a steaming bowl of thick stew. The Deacon pointed at Ralph and left. Ralph did not remember anything after that.

***

Not knowing if it was morning or night, he awoke in a windowless room. The girl must have fed him and carried him to his room. With a fuzzy head and protesting body, he sat up. He'd slept too hard and too long. Clean and neatly folded clothes sat on the chair, and his athletic bag was on the floor beside it.

In the small bathroom, he tried to get ready to face the day or night, whichever it was. The mirror showed him a grizzly red-eyed reflection, which was just how he felt. Better let the beard grow, he thought. Dye it and the hair later.

As he reached for the door, a soft knock sounded. He opened it to find the girl. Now he appreciated that she was pretty, but young–except for her eyes, she'd had experiences beyond her age. The Deacon did like 'em young.

Ralph followed her down the hallway into the dining room. The aroma of breakfast wafted over him. He was hungry again.

The Deacon rose from a table and walked over to him. "Sleep well?" he asked.

"I guess so. I don't remember anything."

"Tell me everything," said the Deacon sitting with him. They were alone at the family-style table. A glass of juice and a steaming plate of eggs and ham were placed in front of him. Ralph was too busy eating to talk.

"After the debacle at that hive of iniquity, Kihhim, we didn't hear from you at all. It was probably a good thing. Kyle was dead by the hand of that bitch, and Billy died from an infection later. Darren, Gordie and Joseph are at Florence." The Deacon shook his head.

"They didn't talk, but the Feds knew they were from here. We were watched for more than a year after that. If you'd come back, it would have been a mess." Ralph bobbed his head, mouth full.

"Did you have something to do with the attack on that new nation, that Kahchk Kihhim?"

Ralph nodded, taking a drink of juice.

"News reports said everyone in that attack died." The Deacon looked at Ralph and his eyebrows rose.

Ralph swallowed. "The job was a setup. Everyone was supposed to die. The sub was booby trapped."

"I wondered about your hair," said the Deacon, looking at the short stubble on his head.

"I got out of the sub but into the hands of the Navy. They were using me to trap the Chinese who set the whole mess up, but I managed to escape."

"Those Godless Chinks," bellowed the Deacon. "Did they get them?"

"One was dead. I don't know about the other. I didn't hang around to watch." He looked at the Deacon intently. "I'm not sure who is worse as far as Godless goes." "I was at Kahchk Kihhim. It is what we thought was at Kihhim except they moved out to sea."

"That is what Joseph said. He saw the same bitch woman you kidnapped giving a speech on TV."

"There's something else." Ralph relayed the story of his visit to the pool and the creature he saw. The Deacon sat still, an incredulous look on his face.

"They said it was a diver suited up, but it couldn't have been. It scared the hell out of me. No diver could do that."

"So you think they are harboring sea creatures on board that ship?"

"I think they are making them." stated Ralph. "That's what scares the shit out of me!"

The Deacon sat back as if he had been struck. Various expressions moved across his face as he remained motionless.

"If you are right, this abomination must be destroyed! This is the worst sin against God and man possible." He stood. "I must think and pray on this."

People turned and looked at the outburst. The Deacon spun and left Ralph to finish his breakfast alone. Others in the room glanced at him, then quickly away, not meeting his eyes.

Strangers were not well received here. That was good for Ralph, but he knew there wasn't much time before the FBI would come looking for him, and they would be loaded for bear. If he was here, it could get bloody like Waco. He had to be gone when they searched. The Deacon would get him to a safe place.

Chapter Eighty-Eight

Katharine looked at a nervous Janet Kilgore as the other leaders of Kahchk Kihhim filed into the conference room. Robert McWilliams stood to one side, wearing a strange expression. They had arrived this morning with news.

Janet cleared her throat and inserted a data cube in the player. "The meeting between Ralph Whitney and the Chinese agents didn't go as planned," she said, starting the video.

They watched the meeting ending with Whitney fleeing, the FBI agents entering and the Chinese agent being whisked away by masked men. Katharine was stunned. What to do now? Even if the Chinese didn't believe him, Whitney would find someone who would, and the word would spread. This could become a real danger for them and for the president.

Kilgore continued, "The good news is we now have evidence the Chinese were behind the attack on Kahchk Kihhim and the assassination of the vice president. The bad news is we lost Ralph Whitney, and the Chinese must suspect human modification is going on here."

"What are the chances of getting Whitney back?" asked Katharine. She glanced at McWilliams, who appeared stunned by the video. He hadn't known.

Kilgore looked uncomfortable. "He evaded us after the kidnapping at Kihhim and now here. Whitney is very good at this, but the president has turned his recapture into a national emergency."

"He was good enough to get out of the room, but how did he escape?" asked Leticia Gardner, condemnation in her voice. Little of her injuries from the blast showed. She'd healed nicely.

"He had a setup at the hotel. It took less than ten minutes for him to disappear."

"Are you sure Whitney re-entered the United States?" asked Leticia.

"We assumed he would head deeper into Mexico. That was an error that gave him the few minutes he needed. We have an idea of where to look in the US. The Soldiers of the Lord and the Guardians of Light Church were the groups he was with during the first attack on Kihhim. Georgia is where we think he's headed."

Katharine looked intently at Leticia then at the others in the room. She faced Janet Kilgore. "Please keep us informed of all developments," she said.

Janet Kilgore rose. "I have been explicitly instructed to do so. Mr. McWilliams is to remain here with you to assist in any way he can. The president would like you to call him." The others rose as she moved toward the door. Within minutes, the clatter of helicopter blades announced she was gone.

Katharine faced McWilliams. "Mr. McWilliams?"

"I got fired. I'm the US representative to Kahchk Kihhim now. I report to the president."

Reaching out to him, Katharine said, "I'm sorry."

He smiled. "That's okay. It was time for me to go."

Leticia laughed. "I know that feeling. Welcome. Glad to have you."

"We better make that call to the president," said Katharine. She picked up the phone and pressed in the sequence of numbers that connected her directly to him.

"How are you, Ms. Levey?" he said without preamble.

"We are not sure. These developments are troubling. Will you recapture Whitney soon?"

"We are making every effort. That problem is easier to handle than the Chinese issue. If they see you as a military threat, they must do something. We need to consider telling them about your virus. If they launch missiles, we may not be able to prevent their success."

"Give us a minute please," said Katharine. She turned off the speaker and turned to the others. "What he says reinforces my conclusion that we tell the Chinese or risk war. Are we in agreement?" Heads nodded around the table. Katharine turned the speaker on.

"We suggest a meeting here with the Chinese. Do we need to tell them about our Altereds and the Dahlfins?"

"They already have strong suspicions. I'm not sure we could convince them they do not exist," said the president.

"Okay. Perhaps we could invite both you and them to a summit to discuss the rising tensions in the South Pacific. We will let you create the wording in the public statement and invitation, but we will send a specific invitation for them to inspect Kahchk Kihhim and explain our protection arrangement."

"That's the same conclusion we reached here."

"Thank you, Mr. President."

Katharine turned toward Robert. "How's your first day going?" They all laughed.

"Thank you. This is quite a welcoming. You really know how liven up an introduction."

"Let me show you to your quarters." As they walked down the hall, Katharine asked, "Do you mind being assigned here?"

"Sure, there is disappointment at being fired from the Bureau, but my career was doomed there. This is the best place I could think of to be." He smiled. "It's certainly more exciting than the papers I was pushing around."

"We needed to have someone here from the United States, and right now you are the only one I trust."

"That is quite a statement regarding your former jailer. I take it as a compliment."

"It was meant as one." They stopped and she opened a door. "This will be your quarters," she said. He walked over to the window and drew the curtains aside. The view was breathtaking. The room was high in the arch looking toward the bows of the ship. Far below, Altereds and Dahlfins harvested fish from the central ring of living nets. He turned to her. "This is wonderful." He stepped toward her, and she embraced him.

Chapter Eighty-Nine

As soon as Katharine and Robert left, Leticia turned to Jamie Wong and Ruben Sanchez. "You know our existence is at stake. Can you tailor a virus to Ralph Whitney's DNA, so it will affect only him?"

"Sure, but how do we get it in contact with him?" Jamie asked.

"His friends carry it to him," stated Leticia.

"So we need one that is extremely contagious, will grow and multiply in everybody, but affect only him? An interesting challenge, eh," he said, looking at Ruben.

"Actually, it is only a slight refinement of some of the work we already did," said Ruben. "What do you want it to do to him?"

"Kill him," said Leticia brushing her hand across her face, remembering her last encounter with Whitney.

"What are we doing?" asked Carol slowly.

"Twice he has attacked us. If the third time is the charm, we may well become extinct."

Carol stared at Leticia. "That is the excuse for every pre-emptive strike ever made. Did they work in the long run? If this becomes known, nothing will stop our destruction at the hands of the whole world.

Perhaps we will deserve it," she added, her head hanging.

"Perhaps the world is better off starting over," said Rich sadly.

"You mean you would not release the antiviral serum?" asked Carol, looking wildly from Leticia to the others

"We haven't even thought about that," said Leticia. "Let's see what happens first. How long before you have something we can use?" she asked Jamie and Ruben.

"It will take us several days before we create a virus specific only to Whitney," said Ruben.

"Where did you get his DNA?" asked Carol.

"He was on Kahchk Kihhim," said Leticia. She shrugged.

"A lot of people visited Kahchk Kihhim," cried Carol.

"We've been in contact with a lot of people," said Leticia, watching Carol intently.

Carol's mouth fell open. She buried her face in her hands. "We're collecting DNA from everyone for what? What have we become?"

"Jamie, can I talk to you?" asked Leticia.

He nodded.

"Alone," she said. They left the room.

Chapter Ninety

Chairman Wu and his retinue bowed to the American delegates as President Carson introduced them. The sharp eyes of General Kai particularly struck him. They seemed to bore through him. He looked coolly back at the Chairman as Katharine Levey spoke.

"Chairman Wu, we at Kahchk Kihhim welcome you, the President of the United States and your entourages to our new nation. We asked you here to personally introduce us to you." General Kai's gaze was focused on her, as the Chinese interpreter translated to the group.

She continued, "We are an independent nation, built on the only unclaimed space on Earth. We strive to make ourselves a part of our environment–the sea–and live in harmony with it.

Many nations are interested in Kahchk Kihhim, but to maintain our lifestyle, we chose to restrict access and remain isolated. This has created suspicion. You may understand because China was a closed society for decades. Only when you were strong enough, and the world was ready to accept you for who you were, did you open up."

The Chairman nodded.

"I hope to allay any of your concerns. That is why we invited you here. We will show you our technology and introduce you to our citizens. As a small nation, we do not have the resources to form and maintain a military defense, so we are forced to incorporate unconventional and unpleasant methods to preserve our security. These will be explained to you. We will answer all of your questions. But seeing is believing, so we would like to begin the tours."

To accommodate the large group, they split into two parts. Katharine, Dayton, and Don Brown took one group that included President Carson and Chairman Wu and their immediate aides. Leticia, Carol, and Robert guided the others. The groups would rejoin at the access hold and meet the Altereds and Dahlfins.

As Katharine's group entered the first greenhouse, she saw the Chairman's eyes light up. She remembered he was from a farming province and an avid gardener, taking special pride in his lilies. From his agrarian background he had risen to become the most powerful figure in China, maybe even the world.

His escape from the pressures was his garden. As he went from trough to trough, he would exclaim in Chinese to his aides pointing out the special varieties developed by Kahchk Kihhim. The President and Katharine looked at each other and hurried to keep up. When he finally looked at the troughs and the structure realizing they were alive, too, he became excited.

He came over to Katharine and said in clipped, unaccented English, "This is a most amazing display. You made changes in the basic nature of the plants; changes that allow them to grow as you wish. To accomplish this, you modified the plants themselves?" Katharine and Don Brown nodded. "How did you do this?" the Chairman asked.

"We change the DNA make-up, designing it to do what we want," said Don Brown. A troubled expression passed swiftly across the Chairman's face like a scudding cloud, and then it became impassive. Though his eyes showed the calculating mind was racing.

When they entered the main ship where the plankton and algae vats were, his interest became intense. It was easy to see he was considering a food program for China. The Chairman remained quiet, absorbing every word and occasionally asking questions.

His interest was piqued by the power storage facility "How can these small containers store so much energy?" he asked, pointing at the racks.

"The Bitterly flywheels spin at 100,000 RPM. The energy storage capacity increases as the square of the RPM," answered Don. Chairman Wu nodded filing the information away. They passed through the medical area, and the Chairman looked intently at the oversized vats. He glanced at Katharine.

"We treat both people and sea creatures here," answered Katharine to the unasked question. "We will show you more about this after lunch."

The dining room high in the arch allowed a view of area between the hulls and the fish farming system. The Chairman attentively listened to the explanation, watching the harvesting going on below.

Katharine watched the chairman's eyes as he looked around him. Understanding what an innovative operation Kahchk Kihhim was. "We have more to show you, sir."

Chapter Ninty-One

In the access chamber, rapid-fire Chinese discussions echoed. Katharine glanced at General Kai. Instead of talking, his eyes flicked from those in the US party to Katharine's group. As they seated themselves, Katharine rose. It grew quiet.

"I hope our tour gave you an understanding of Kahchk Kihhim. The open atmosphere we created gave rise to the innovations you have seen. What I show you now could not have been accomplished until we had a need, until we became an oceanic nation.

"We integrated ourselves intimately with the sea." She walked to the pool and made a motion with her hand. The water rippled, and Sean Steele's head rose above the surface. The Chinese delegation became excited, each trying to speak at the same time. Sean slowly emerged. The contingent from China shrank back. General Kai rose to shield the Chairman from danger. The Chairman pushed him back, fascinated.

Sean stood and bowed. "Welcome to Kahchk Kihhim." The Chinese were frozen.

The Chairman pulled his mind from astonished inertia. General Kai tried to warn him of this, but he did not truly believe it until now. The creature moved toward him. As it neared his chair, it stopped and bowed deeply again. "It is an honor to meet you, Chairman Wu." He stood straight and held out his hand. The Chairman rose slowly from his seat.

"We had suspicions you existed, but I could not believe them until now." He held out his hand and Sean shook it. The Chairman turned and introduced his retinue. When General Kai stood, he cautiously shook Sean's hand. His face betrayed nothing but his eyes had a very calculating look. Sean continued around the table expressing gratitude at the chance to see the US President again.

"Mr. Chairman, I am an Altered, a human engineered for life in the sea. I would like you to meet my companion, Blue Streak." He turned, and the Dahlfin rose from the pool, standing on its tail dipping its head. Blue Streak swam to the shallow shelf.

"I, alsooooo, aaaaam pleeeeased toooo meeeeeet youuuu," said Blue, holding up a flipper.

Sean spoke. "Blue would like to shake with you too, sir. The Chairman moved over to the pool and knelt down. He shook the Dahlfin's flipper. He rose, and again introduced each of his staff. They all shook with Blue. "I aaam annn Altered tooo, but I staaarrrted aaasaah aaa dolphin," said Blue. "I aaalsooo aaaaam a fuullll ciitiiizeeen ofh Kahchk Kihhim."

The Chairman turned to Katharine. "What other creations have you made?" he asked. Such a simple question.

Katharine looked at the president. "Mr. Chairman, our genetic design ability is our strength. We have one more creation to tell you about, and it is not one we are proud of. I think you understand that much of the world would not welcome our citizens or our technology." The chairman nodded slowly.

"We do not possess the resources to protect ourselves. She pushed a button on a remote control and a holographic image formed above the table. It rotated, and as it did so, it changed. All eyes followed the image.

"This is a virus we created. It has been distributed throughout the world's population completely. For now, it is totally benign. At some point in the future, it will mutate into a deadly form, and only we possess the antiviral agent to prevent devastating plagues throughout the world. If we are destroyed, we will not be able to do that."

The Chairman's face hardened. Others of his group looked at each other, mouths open. General Kai was like a statue.

Katharine continued, "The United States was informed of this. As a result, they have been trying to keep us a secret and protect us. We extorted services from them, and I regret this was necessary. They have an active program to develop the antiviral, but have not done so yet." She glanced at the president. His face hardened.

"We hope to educate mankind and no longer need this distasteful blackmail. The cordon of ships around us is to keep out those who would harm us, and to keep us in."

The chairman stared at her.

"We will share all the information we gave to the United States, so you too can confirm what I have told you. I am sure that the United States will share their investigation results and progress."

The room was silent. Katharine watched General Kai, and his expression was not one of shock but shrewd coldness. He felt her eyes and looked at her with a slight smile and a nod. Katharine had no doubt he was acknowledging the challenge Kahchk Kihhim presented. The gauntlet had been thrown.

The Chairman rose. "We would need to speak alone. There is much to consider."

Katharine guided them to a conference room. "This room is secure." She handed him a small electronic box. "Press this button, and someone will come. Ask for anything you need."

As she closed the door, she heard General Kai's voice speak rapidly in Chinese. Though she understood none of the words, the tone was harsh. She went back to the pool access room and the United States contingent.

The president looked at her. "This will be interesting. Let's speculate. Craig, what do you think?" he asked of the Secretary of State.

The discussions went on for several hours until Katharine stood. "They are ready."

They all rose as she returned in a few minutes with the Chinese. Again, they were seated. The

Chairman's aide stood. He looked at the Chairman, who gave an almost imperceptible nod.

"We discussed this issue and find the situation most distasteful. The threat must be confirmed by our own scientists. If it is as you say, we must participate in the protection of Kahchk Kihhim. China must place a representative in Kahchk Kihhim to ensure it remains independent. We agree this technology must remain a secret for now." The Chairman nodded.

The Secretary of State hid his smile. This was exactly the expectation he had voiced. The president turned to the chairman. "We find this acceptable, and we hope our cooperation in this will lead to cooperation in other areas. Perhaps our staff can work together on the details. I would like to spend time with Chairman Wu if that is possible."

Chairman Wu rose and nodded. They walked out of the door, waving the security teams back to a discrete distance.

Chapter Ninty-Two

The two leaders walked to the edge of the deck and looked toward the opposite hull.

The president spoke first. "There are so many troubling aspects to Kahchk Kihhim that I do not know where to start."

The chairman's jaw tightened. The president continued, "They are correct in assuming they would be destroyed were it not for the virus. We would have done so already. The threat their technology poses to world stability is reason enough. But more importantly, we would probably destroy them because of the threat to mankind posed by their ability to make life into whatever they want."

The chairman looked at him. "We spoke of the same things. They have made wondrous advancements in agriculture, aquaculture and living within the environment. These are things we would want to emulate."

The president agreed, "Ecologically, they are a perfect fit."

The chairman looked at the president. "I propose we work together on the virus threat. We cannot tolerate this position of weakness. It steals all of our options."

The president nodded. "I will see that all of our progress on the antivirus is forwarded to you. We cannot operate with a gun to our heads." They stood in silence for a while, watching the activity in the water below.

The Chairman spoke. "In many ways, this is like the dawn of the nuclear age. There is so much promise here for mankind, but in the wrong hands it can lead to our destruction. We must strive to be wise."

Chapter Ninty-Three

Jamie handed Leticia a vial with the Whitney virus. She looked at the clear liquid. "This will only affect Whitney?"

Jamie nodded. "It's airborne and has a long life. The virus replicates in hours. We estimate it will spread over the state of Georgia within a few weeks infecting ninety-eight percent of the people. No one will notice anything, except for Whitney. Of course, he may not have any outside contact for several weeks. I'm sure he is well hidden somewhere remote."

"Eventually he will surface," said Leticia. "It's a certainty with a variable time frame." The idea of a biological guided missile shocked Katharine, but Leticia was finally able to convince her no danger existed to any others. It would be a directed attack.

Within hours Al Jackson lifted his helicopter off the deck of Kahchk Kihhim and headed for the United States. After his commercial flight landed in Jacksonville, Florida, he rented a car and drove to Waycross, Georgia. He had nothing but his clothes and the oddest instructions he had ever received. Unknown to him, he carried the virus.

Jacko was told to go to Waycross making as many stops as he wanted, refuel, stay several nights, visit several other cities, and stay a few nights in each. Jacko was to make contact with as many people as possible and seek information about Ralph but quietly. He was to attend a service of the Guardian of Light Church and then return to Kahchk Kihhim from Albany. It seemed strange to him, but he did not mind the trip.

***

The Deacon called several news services and invited them to attend a conference at his Guardians of Light Church in Jacksonville regarding news of Kahchk Kihhim. He promised a new revelation, one that would astound the world.

The tabloids had weekly updates of his sermons, but the mainstream press relegated comments to the back pages. Still, it was news, and a few reporters showed up, complete with video. With the now expanded congregation in attendance, the hall was full.

The Deacon looked out from the pulpit over the upturned faces and stared into the cameras. "Brothers and sisters, and ladies and gentlemen of the press, I am here to alert you to a terrible peril that threatens all of us. Tonight we have a witness to this abomination against God's law and man's law. And he has proof it is being protected by the government of the United States," he thundered.

"The new nation of Kahchk Kihhim has been perverting life. They have been creating monsters. They are playing God!" His hands rose into the air as a gasp arose from his followers. The news services had skeptical looks.

"One of our own is an eyewitness who has been there and seen these poor creatures, and now he is hunted by our own government to keep him silent." His hand slammed onto the dais. "Brothers and sisters, I will let brother Ralph Whitney testify in his own words what he has personally beheld." The Deacon gestured for Ralph to rise and approach.

Ralph stood and looked out at the congregation and the few press cameras. He took a deep breath and walked up to the podium. He was not used to speaking in front of crowds, but he and the Deacon practiced until even his mannerisms were perfect. He took another breath and paused.

"Brothers and sisters, six weeks ago I was taken against my will by the FBI to Kahchk Kihhim in a scheme to blame the explosion that killed our Vice President on the Chinese. While I was there, I managed to escape my shackles and found my way into the bowels of the ship. There I confronted a creature from hell."

A gasp arose from the crowd as a rendition of an Altered appeared on a screen behind him. "This poor creature was neither man nor fish, but had parts of each. It spoke to me in a plaintive voice begging for help, but before I could do anything, I was recaptured. The FBI has tried to cover this up, tried to silence me, but God has allowed me to be here today to bring this travesty into the light, to reveal this dark and evil secret."

The congregation was completely silent. "Brothers and sisters, my stomach still turns at the thought of what these devils created, and what they have done. This cannot be allowed to continue. We are the ones who must root out this evil and destroy it. Our Navy, the United States Navy, has been patrolling the seas protecting them, unknown to our God-fearing boys. This cannot be allowed to stand! It is our way of life that is threatened and our belief in right and wrong."

Ralph stood silently, and the Deacon joined him at the dais. "Brothers and sisters, I know there are those among you who will doubt what you heard here. Please ask questions. Please satisfy yourselves that the truth, this ugly sad evil truth has been revealed to you."

It took all of Albert's self-control and the admonition by Katharine to say nothing. One of the newscaster's hands waved in the air, and the Deacon nodded.

"That picture behind you is of the creature?"

"I did not take a picture, but what you see is an accurate rendition," said Ralph.

The Deacon nodded and pointed at a woman whose hand was up.

"What did this creature say to you?"

"In a very raspy voice, it asked me for help," said Ralph.

The woman sobbed and sat down.

A news reporter asked, "Why did the FBI take you?"

The Deacon answered for him. "The government has been after the Guardian of Light Church for years. They feel that by implicating brother Whitney they can attack us."

Another hand went up. "You say the FBI is after you, but you are here, in front of us. Aren't you afraid of arrest?"

Again the Deacon spoke. "Only by bringing this out in the open can this heroic man have a fair chance with the law. We must take that chance. Ralph Whitney is willing to place his life on the line to expose this corruption and right this wrong. We will try to protect him, but eventually he will face the law. We want it to be fairly done in an open court and not hidden away in some secret hell."

"Amen," said several voices.

"In light of that, we are going to close this meeting so Brother Whitney can leave." He held up his hand to signal the session was over, despite the questions yelled by the press. Ralph stepped down, and several members of the congregation came up, shook his hand, and then surrounded him, allowing no others to approach. The group moved through a back door that shut firmly behind them.

The camera crews hurried to pack their gear and get back to the studios. There was still time to make the ten o'clock news. The congregation attending and seeing Ralph believed the story. Whether the studio would air it was another matter.

Chapter Ninety-Four

Al Jackson watched the news report from his hotel room in Albany. After arriving in Jacksonville four days ago, he'd attended the service introducing Ralph Whitney to the public. Jacko picked up the phone and called Kahchk Kihhim. He explained the news coverage and his failure to refute the lies.

"Jacko, it was not your show, and you would have been picked apart. It is much better if you don't talk to anyone."

"Well, I still feel crook about it."

"How long ago were you in Jacksonville?" asked Jaime Wong.

"I stayed for four days. I'm scheduled to catch a plane tomorrow. Do you still want me to leave?"

"You did exactly what we wanted. Stay another day or two and come on home."

"But I did nothing," said Jacko.

"You did everything we needed." The phone went dead.

Leticia looked at Jaime Wong. "It is plenty of time. If Jacko was at the service, we couldn't have asked for better."

"But the Deacon had the news conference. It is out. What will we do?" said Carol.

"First, we call President Carson."

"Good evening, Mr. President," said Katharine. "I am sorry to disturb you on Sunday. Have you seen the news reports coming out of Florida?"

"Not yet," said the president. "Please tell me."

"Last week the Guardian of Light Church held a news conference featuring Mr. Ralph Whitney. It is time we made our damage control plans. Perhaps it would be a good idea if we came to Washington. Any time that suits your schedule will be fine."

"We've been monitoring the public response. Things are heating up. I will clear my calendar for the day after tomorrow in the afternoon."

"We will be there. I am sorry we have come to this," said Katharine.

"So am I," said the president.

Chapter Ninety-Five

General Kai spoke quietly to the Chairman. "We are close to having the anti-virus. Our scientists predict the next set of tests will confirm that it modifies the mutant virus before it turns lethal."

"How will you know, since it has not mutated to the lethal form yet?"

"During the testing the mutation rate sped up until it became the deadly plague. It was devastating. We lost all the volunteers, a number of the doctors and technicians, and we had to destroy the test facility to contain it. This anti-virus stops the mutation at a stage before the fatal form," said General Kai with a look of satisfaction.

"We should inform the Americans what we have," said the Chairman.

A deep frown crossed Kai's face.

"You do not agree?"

"Honorable Chairman we are in a position to allow our enemies to be destroyed and not by our hand. We both agree Kahchk Kihhim must not be allowed to exist uncontrolled. Our agent confirms there is no American control. Kahchk Kihhim is independent. By agreement with the United States, our naval forces will take over the protection within a few weeks. If we took control of them, what could the Americans do?"

What indeed, mused the Chairman. It would be China holding the world hostage, China in control. "Start working on the distribution system for the anti- virus; how we would distribute it and to whom. Keep me fully informed of progress. I want reports daily."

Kai recognized the dismissal, rose, and bowed as he backed out of the door. At last, the dream of Chinese domination would come true.

The Chairman sat quietly. The reality was much more troubling now that he faced it. If there was to be a central world government, China was the most experienced in governing large masses. But was that really best? Was it even possible?

They would have the power of life and death over huge areas of the world. How would one decide what would be the best, and what would be controllable? The enormity rolled over him, and it washed away all the glitter that blinded him moments before. Alone he must face a decision for the fate of mankind.

General Kai was elated. The Chairman saw the possibilities and would go ahead. At last, China would take its rightful place as the world's leader. And he, General Kai, would be there for the control. This was heady stuff.

***

The group meeting at the White House was not large. Katharine brought Leticia Gardner. The president had his FBI Director, Jordan Brown, and

Secretary of State, Wesley Hamilton. The president took charge immediately.

"We expected the cat would get out of the bag before we could recapture Mr. Whitney. Our first priority is to take him into custody again and then attack his creditability. Director Brown assures us Whitney's arrest is close." Brown nodded.

"The inquiries regarding the veracity are overwhelming. Our statement is that this as a bald-faced lie, a desperate attempt by a murderer. Members of Congress are already calling for an investigation into the presence of United States forces in the Kahchk Kihhim area. I'm not sure how much longer we can continue to write this off as an extended training exercise." His face hardened.

"Chinese take over in a few weeks," stated Katharine. "I'm not sure that will help with Congress, but I am giving you notice now that we seek your assistance in fending off invasion by any forces."

"Noted," said the president.

A soft knock sounded at the door. "Come," said the president. An aide entered and handed him a note. The president opened the note, read it and then looked up. "It seems Mr. Ralph Whitney has entered a hospital in Manor, Georgia. The hospital authorities notified us, and agents arrested him. They are trying to bring him back to Washington, but his attorney has an injunction on the grounds he is too ill to be moved." There was a sigh of relief around the table.

Katharine looked at Leticia. "Mr. President," she said, we would like to meet with Mr. Whitney as soon as possible at the hospital."

"We will probably have him back in Washington within a day."

Leticia spoke up. "Perhaps, if only I went."

Katharine nodded. Within an hour, Leticia was on a charter flight to Manor, Georgia.

After Katharine and Leticia left, the President looked at his staff. "What is it?" he asked Admiral Cochran.

"I don't trust the Chinese," said Admiral Cochran.

"That has been troubling me also," said Wesley Hamilton. "A week ago, the information from the Chinese regarding their anti-virus program dried up. They reported some promising progress, then nothing. I am worried."

"Where are we on our own program?" asked the president.

Craig Nelson spoke. "We can slow the mutation rate substantially. We do not know what the original timetable was, but with this medication it is extended by a hundred times. This will give us the time to find a true anti-virus."

"How close is this to a form we can distribute?" asked the president.

"We can have this mass-produced and available within six months. We can inoculate everyone in the United States within eight months."

"What about the rest of the world?" asked the president.

"If we gave the manufacturing process to the Chinese and other nations, there would be enough for worldwide distribution within a year," said Nelson.

"If the Chinese developed an anti-virus, they would have no trouble taking control of Kahchk Kihhim during their watch. Can we allow this?" asked Wesley. There was a dead silence. All eyes focused on the president.

"When we pull out we could leave a sub to drift with Kahchk Kihhim. It would be undetectable," said Admiral Cochran.

"Undetectable to everyone but Kahchk Kihhim," said the president. "We will have to inform them of our concerns."

Chapter Ninety-Six

The flight in the small plane was a little rough. During the landing, Leticia called for a taxi to meet her. A cold gust of wind greeted her. She wrapped her coat tightly around and buried her hands in the pockets.

The ride to the community hospital in the battered old car, the town's only cab service, took fifteen minutes. She checked at the desk, got the room number, and went up to Ralph's room. Two suited men flanked the door, and she identified herself to them. The FBI agents received word to let her enter, but they did search for weapons before she was allowed in.

A tall heavyset bearded man and a thin short man stood beside an isolation chamber. They looked up.

She introduced herself. "I'm Leticia Gardner, just in from Washington. She removed her gloved hand from her pocket and shook hands with the thin man.

"I'm William Jefferson, Mr. Whitney's attorney."

She turned to the other man and held out her hand again. "I am Deacon Smithson." Clasping his hand in both of hers, she asked, "How is he?" then she put her hands back in her pockets.

"The doctors don't have any idea what's wrong, but he is going downhill quickly," said the Deacon. "We are praying for him."

The door opened and the hospital's doctor came in. Again, Leticia introduced herself. "What's wrong with him?" she asked.

"I have never seen anything like this in a young man. His organs are just shutting down. He needs dialysis, a lung machine, and heart stimulation. We don't have that equipment here, but he is too weak to move. I don't hold out much hope unless something changes."

Ralph's crusted eyes were squeezed tightly shut, then opened and blinked at the light. Slowly he focused on Leticia. His eyes flew wide open.

He croaked out, "Looks like I cheated you out of your revenge," sounding as bad as he looked. He tried to laugh, but it turned into a wracking cough that shook his whole body.

When he quieted, Leticia smiled at him. "Don't be so sure." Her smile was cold.

Ralph's eyes closed, and he said something. She leaned close to hear. "Twice, I thought I killed you. Used to be better than that." He coughed again, and red-flecked spittle covered the oxygen mask. His eyes rolled up.

"Who are you?" demanded the Deacon his voice loud.

"I told you my name," Leticia answered. "I am from the sovereign nation of Kahchk Kihhim."

"Get out!" thundered the Deacon.

As Leticia left, a stream of invective followed her past the startled FBI agents. It didn't matter. She had what she wanted, and though satisfying, it did not feel as good as she thought it would. She hurried out of the hospital and got into the waiting cab. Within minutes, she was aboard the airplane and on her way back to Washington.

***

The presidential limousine idled on the tarmac as her plane landed. The president and Katharine were waiting inside. "We got a call from the agents at the hospital. Ralph Whitney died within an hour of your visit," said the president. "What happened?"

"There is not much to tell," said Leticia. "His attorney and the Deacon were there, and I introduced myself," she said looking at Katharine. "Ralph woke up and recognized me. He apologized for not killing me. That was it."

"The Deacon is claiming you did something to him that killed him," said the president.

"He was in an isolation chamber. I was never near him. The attorney and the doctor will confirm that. I had no weapon of any sort. Your agents will confirm that. The doctor will also confirm he was dying when I got there."

"You had nothing to do with his death?" asked the President.

"Sir, this man tried to kill me twice. I admit that when I left here, revenge was on my mind, but I was too late."

This satisfied the president. Only much later did he realize she had not answered his question. That niggling suspicion sent a shiver through him.

Chapter Ninety-Seven

Katharine and Leticia left Washington the next day concerned about the Chinese. They agreed to keep the American sub close in the area. The president held another meeting with his staff immediately about Kahchk Kihhim. "Have we looked into the death of Ralph Whitney? Has an autopsy been performed?" asked the president. Leticia's lack of comment was playing on his mind, but he was keeping that to himself.

"Mr. Whitney's organs turned to jelly and just shut down," said Dr. Benz. "We're looking into what would cause that, but it may take a while. On the outside, he was barely forty years old but internally he was over ninety. It is by far the most puzzling death I have ever seen."

"Is it contagious?" asked the president.

Dr. Benz shrugged. "There are no indications that it is. No one else he's been in contact with has showed symptoms."

"I want that hospital put under strict quarantine. If this turns out to be something contagious, we have to know as soon as possible. Also, we have to know where he got it. Let's use this in our efforts to discredit him."

Wesley spoke, "This problem of Kahchk Kihhim is growing exponentially. We face the real possibility they and their technology could fall into hostile hands. What if the Chinese refused to allow them to release the anti-virus except as they directed?"

Chapter Ninety-Eight

As Katharine and Leticia entered the conference room at Kahchk Kihhim, Katharine asked, "You got the Deacon's DNA?"

Leticia nodded. "Only in case of an emergency."

"How will we know when there is an emergency?" asked Katharine. "Is it when he calls for our destruction? He already has. Is it when his minions are knocking on our door? That would be too late. Leticia, we cannot go down that path. It will never end and drag us down."

"Are we supposed to let ourselves be destroyed?" retorted Leticia heatedly. "We need to buy time, and this may be the only way to do that. Both the United States and China have crash programs to offset our virus. They need not cure it now, only ensure time to do so. It is a gamble. They are probably close now. We will be at their mercy, and they will show none."

"We move up the aquatic conversion program," said Katharine. "Is the habitat far enough along that the Altereds can move in?"

"Yes. They will be the first permanent residents, but we need a final site to set up support systems for the humanoids."

"The basic nature of man is the problem," said Leticia.

"Of course you are right. Maybe we need to work on that. Can we develop something that would change the target, rather than kill it?" asked Katharine, thinking aloud.

"Changing the basic nature will require undoing millions of years of evolution, and survival. The purpose of all living things is to expand and multiply. Thus far, life on Earth does not have the wisdom to exist without the controls of limited resources and competition. That especially includes man," finished Leticia.

"We like to think we are different," said Katharine sadly, "but it looks like not. The aquatic conversion is our only hope. We will be less visible and less vulnerable."

"Mankind has not necessarily limited destruction to competition," said Leticia. "They will hunt us under the sea if we are viewed as a threat. We will need every available tool at our disposal to survive."

Chapter Ninety-Nine

It was easy to predict that other nations would try to duplicate Kahchk Kihhim to expand their spheres of influence. The United Nations saw the danger of unregulated growth at sea, and in mutual agreement, the delegates recommended no other sea communities be allowed.

A UN resolution passed with an addendum requiring oversight of the area around Kahchk Kihhim to monitor what changes they might be causing in the sea. The United States could not veto this, and within a month, a boat was within the ten-mile limit sampling and monitoring ocean changes. At times, the boat came within two miles and approached the fish farm pens. Unusual growths of a tough strain of seaweed that would foul the propellers was reported. After being towed out several times, they listed this as a detrimental change caused by Kahchk Kihhim and filed a complaint. As a non-member, Kahchk Kihhim could not be forced to change.

The first session of protection by the Chinese Navy started uneventfully. They kept the respectful distance, and only occasionally did submarines venture near. Their propellers became fouled, and divers had to clear them.

The Chinese delegate on board Kahchk Kihhim had free movement, yet he knew nothing of the plans for change. A sense of urgency arose and the development of the undersea habitat accelerated.

"I need an emergency exit plan for Kahchk Kihhim," Katharine said to the small group. "There is a sense of tension and crisis. I cannot put my finger on anything specific, but I feel it."

Carol nodded in agreement. Dayton looked at her then Katharine. He did not doubt them. Rich had addressed the problem of transfer by geneering a bio transport. Several were growing now. Habitat bubble chambers were adapted for the Altereds to tow. Three hundred human citizens would exit.

"The transport will take more time, but we can begin taking people in the bubble sleds," said Rich. Katharine nodded. He had already pushed the habitat growth but it would not support all of them.

Leticia spoke. "Our security blanket is about to smother us. We all better work together on this."

Katharine offered, "Japan requested some of their scientists and engineers be allowed to reside here for the purpose learning our techniques and applying them to their burgeoning population. They have offered to pay large fees for the technology and this privilege. Currency in a bank would be useful."

"Bank accounts can be frozen," stated Leticia. "Payments in precious metals are a requirement."

After discussion, they reached an agreement, whereby engineering data would be transferred, but representatives were allowed no more than occasional visits.

Katharine watched them leave. Fewer and fewer words were needed between them now. Like a world champion team at the end of the season, they understood each other intimately. Closer than identical twins, their minds were linking.

Again, calls rose for Kahchk Kihhim's destruction. Deacon Smithson led the charge on fifty-five broadcast networks worldwide in the Western Hemisphere. The Kahchk Kihhim cause actually created an uneasy alliance of world fanatics as they focused on ridding the world of this corruption.

When it seemed as if there would be a united attack, Deacon Smithson died of a mysterious disease where his organs rapidly grew old and turned to jelly. As the focus and driving force, his loss signaled a temporary decline in attention paid to Kahchk Kihhim. The United States Navy was again the sentinel for Kahchk Kihhim. China had been vigilant and learned this guardianship stretched the United States forces very thin.

The invasion of Indonesia by Chinese troops moved into the harsh glare of world attention pushing Kahchk Kihhim aside. The call from the President requesting another meeting surprised Katharine. She was also stunned when he said he would be the only one coming to Kahchk Kihhim.

Chapter One-Hundred

Two secret service men got out of the presidential helicopter and set up guard. They remained at the aircraft as the president greeted Katharine at the main entrance to Kahchk Kihhim.

Katharine and the president were the only ones in the meeting room atop the arch. "Nice to see you, Mr. President. You are looking well despite the weight of the world's woes."

He gave her a pale smile, knowing she was much less than truthful. "Thank you. I must say you seem to grow younger. How do you do that?" He was being truthful and not for the first time wondered how.

"Life at Kahchk Kihhim agrees with me," she said. They chatted about small things. He looked at her, and a serious mood fell on them like an ice storm.

"Katharine, we worried when the UN focused on Kahchk Kihhim. Sanctions would not cause many problems as you do not really belong to the world community, but it would set a unified world against you. Your prophecy of non-acceptance has come true, but in large part due to your own actions. You rid yourselves of a couple of irritating and troublesome people. I do not know how, nor have I shared this suspicion with others. I am sure some wonder what god you pray to."

He continued, "I have been through some very difficult times due to you, but maybe I have weathered that, at least for now. Elections are coming. My opponent is using Kahchk Kihhim as one of his campaign issues. You offered help once, and at the time, I didn't know what to ask and still don't, but I need something. I'm tired of this job, but the country and the world need calm heads not issues. My opponent believes fiery temperaments motivate people. He is right, but the results could be disastrous. I need advice and help."

Katharine looked carefully at him. "Mr. President, with all my heart I wish I could say we had nothing to do with the deaths of Ralph Whitney and Deacon Luke Smithson. I cannot say that, and it has put us on a torturous path. I suffer daily from this, and it has scarred our souls. Action like that was one of the things we wanted to avoid and be free from. Now we find ourselves with a terrible power, but we are probably only here because of it. I am not sure we made the best choice. What is it you want?"

"I want to win the election, because in my heart I think it is best."

"Can we do something positive that will help you in this?"

"Kahchk Kihhim can do nothing overtly that will help. No matter how good, it will be used against me. Many issues elsewhere in the world could become a winning point though. I want to consider those."

"Did you have something in mind?" Katharine asked cautiously.

"Right now the world's attention is on Chinese expansion in Southeast Asia. I'm scheduled to meet with the Chinese leaders in two months to try to convince them to back off and pull their troops out of Indonesia. In reality, we have nothing to force them to back down. This trip is also a campaign booster. If I get them to change and pull back, that issue might carry me into office. Can you help?"

Katharine's struggled to keep her face impassive. "Where are you on the anti-virus program?" she asked pointedly.

"We are close to being able to stop the virus but not cure it. That will buy us time. Once we have it, I will come under extreme pressure from my staff to withdraw protection, or worse. Of much more concern, we believe the Chinese have a cure and are distributing it. When they again take over the sentinel duty for Kahchk Kihhim, they may well take over completely."

Katharine was astonished. They had considered this, but to have it voiced by the president brought the reality crashing in. "We knew time was running out and had even considered releasing another virus, but the distaste of this tactic was so great we chose not to."

"We wondered about that," said the president.

"Once, we talked about whether changing the nature of a man was possible or even desirable. We did some investigation, but to change mankind would eventually lead to his demise. Humanity is what it is today because of that nature. We found we could make some changes, but decided not to. The discussions were quite heated. In the end, the decision wasn't unanimous."

"I am not talking about mankind, I am talking about a specific group of men," said the president.

Katharine paused. "Do you understand what you are asking? Do you really want to play God?"

"We influence people every day," said the president.

"This is not influence, Mr. President; this is changing people's nature. And who are you to decide what nature is best?"

"I can only see what nature seems to be worse. The present course China is following will lead to war on a massive scale. Is trying to prevent that evil?"

"It seems not, but what will be next if we are successful? Where do you see this leading? What would be the next crisis? Where do you see it ending?"

President Carson looked away. He had not thought about these things because he didn't believe changing people was possible.

Katharine continued, "Let us suppose we could calm the aggressive nature of the Chinese leadership. Would that leadership be able to stay in power, or would another group move in? Is this a case of which is better the devil we know or the devil we don't?"

He spoke. "In this case the devil we know is leading the world into war. If there were a change in leadership in China, we would at least have a chance to bring pressure. It would weaken them, even if only temporarily."

"This is a frightening course you and I are considering," said Katharine. "The consequences are not possible to foresee."

The president noticed the change in tone.

"We feel the Indonesia invasion is a first step," Katharine said. "We also thought on their next rotation to our guardianship they would invade and take us over."

"They would force you to release the anti-virus!" exclaimed the president.

"We don't consider that to be their aim. We don't think they care," said Katharine.

The president was quiet. They had also considered this. At the time, it seemed too monstrous.

"If we were to do this, how would we go about it?" asked the president.

"We already have the DNA we need of the leaders. We will create a virus that would only influence those persons with that DNA. It will make changes in gland secretions in the body, the balance of estrogen and testosterone being one small example. We actually started on this a few weeks ago. You will be the vector, the primary carrying agent."

"You'll do it?"

"Mr. President, we owe you a lot. I'm not sure this is the way to pay you back, but we're both desperate."

"There is one more thing," said the president. "My doctors tell me I have a heart problem, and I know you have the capability of organ replacement. If I need it, could you supply a heart for me?"

"That was the old technology. We're much better now. We've known of your heart problem for some time, Mr. President. It's in your DNA of course, and we have made the genetic repairs. If we give you back your own DNA with the improvements, that problem and many others will be fixed. You'll start to produce human growth hormone and get younger. Do you want that?"

"You can reverse aging?" the president said in a whisper.

Katharine nodded. "By repairing your DNA, we can periodically replace it, and thus repair the damage done in living. I must tell you we would look upon anybody else finding out about this most unfavorably."

The president blanched. Was this a deal with the devil or an angel? There were things here much more frightening than the Creature from the Black Lagoon. "I understand," he said.

"Do you? Let's go down to the clinic for a visit," Katharine said. "The damage to the chromosomes in your body causes you to age, and your environment is a major factor. The act of living causes us all to deteriorate. This treatment will restart your clock at about age twenty. You will get older from that point again. We're not giving you eternal life, only about seventy years in your world. Your environment shortens your lives."

It took only a day to introduce the re-tailored DNA for the president and see it was fully accepted. In most cases, they would substantially increase the output of human growth hormone but in his case, he could not appear to be growing younger on the outside. He kept his gray hair and some of the wrinkles, but inside he was getting younger.

A new and fit looking President Carson would gradually appear to the world of the land dwellers. As he and Katharine walked toward his helicopter, he turned to her. "I will always be your friend, though I'm not always able to do the things you want. My loyalties must be to my people, my country, and my species."

"It's the same for me," said Katharine. "We can only hope our worlds do not clash. That is what we work for."

The president looked at her for a long moment, then turned and entered his helicopter.

Chapter One-Hundred-One

The President of the United States met with the leaders of China two months later and presented his proposal for the withdrawal of Chinese troops from all territories belonging to Indonesia. This initially was rejected. Three months later these same leaders called upon the United States to act as a go-between in negotiations with Indonesia.

Three months after that, President Carson was re-elected for another term in office. His doctors proclaimed him more fit than they had seen him in the past and were amazed at his recovery from heart trouble.

China had the rotation to patrol the seas around Kahchk Kihhim. The anticipated attack and takeover did not happen, and their watch was completed peacefully.

The United States Navy again took up post. Verbal attacks increased along with two failed assaults, one from the air another from the sea. The one from the sea resulted in the death of three children.

Pressure was increasing on the administration. Secretary of State Wesley Hamilton attended the funeral and offered sympathies. After the service, Hamilton requested a meeting with Katharine.

"The President has asked me to pass along his personal condolences."

"Thank you," said Katharine. "I know it was not easy for you to come here."

"He also wanted me to relay his doubts about the ability of military forces to continue to protect you."

Katharine looked at Wesley. A hint of a smile played on his lips. They always understood the protection would end sometime. "How much longer does he think it will continue?" she asked.

"The present leadership in China is being purged. A new regime will come into power within three months. We predict they will pick up the aggression of the old one. This will result in war involving one or more of the other major alliances in the world. It may be limited, maybe not." He frowned.

"We have to redeploy our forces," said Wesley giving her a smile of satisfaction. "If China returns, their intent may not be the protection you want. In short, you will be on your own." Wesley got up to leave. "I cannot say I am sorry to be leaving you," he said, "and I cannot say I wish you well."

"Dealing with you has been distasteful for us also," said Katharine. "Please pass along my regards and hopes for peace to your president." Wesley left.

Chapter One-Hundred-Two

"Dr. Wong, how are we coming with the new citizens for our new world?" asked Katharine at the habitat status meeting.

"Let me show you." He took out a data cube and put it into the holographic projector. A cloud formed above the table and then resolved itself into a creature. "There are several things we want in our design: manual dexterity, fully aquatic, intelligence, the ability to move rapidly." He gestured at the image.

"As you can see, we started with a squid body and added opposing thumb hands on the ends of some of the arms. This allows for detailed manipulation and tool building. We shortened other arms and made them more powerful, adding large fins for better mobility in the water. The eyes swivel for nearly 360 by 360 degree vision. Though the eyes are large to accommodate the dim conditions under water, we will not be as dependent on sight as we are now." Wong smiled, obviously proud of his creation.

"The range of the hearing organs is from low long frequency into the ultrasonic and we will be able to communicate vocally though certainly different from today's languages."

The image rotated in the air, fascinating them. "We will have a sense of smell like a shark where our whole body can receive sensations. We will be a creature capable of building, using tools, and smart. Homo-sapien-aquinus, a true citizen of the sea." Everybody stared in rapt awe at the rotating figure.

At last Katharine spoke. "How did you do this? I mean we were expecting some changes maybe along the lines of the Altereds, but this is a new creation, a complete construction!"

"Once we understood the relationship with genes, we set out to build a program to input the characteristics we want. But first," he held up a finger, "we had to create a computer capable of the billions upon billions of calculations needed. Our organic computers now fill that bill. After other basic inputs, such as the things we want, the environment, the strengths and the characteristics, the computer makes the design." Those around the table were trying to take in what Jamie was saying.

"Once the images look like what we want, it builds models of the chromosomes that will grow into the design. The computer will not let us make combinations that will lead to conflicts. If we call for characteristics that will not work together, we must change the design criteria."

"So you developed a computer that understands genetics well enough it can design life?" asked Carol.

"In a nutshell, yes. We now grow our organic computers large enough to work with the huge number of parameters offered by genetics. It gives us a zygote that, if grown, will be the design."

The concept of a computer designing life, testing the design and producing the seed necessary to grow it was stunning. "You see, clones were easy, just copying. As our understanding improved, that is our database got big enough, we were able to rebuild chromosomes of the same genetic makeup without the problems, congenital or environmental damage. This is the improved DNA project that now keeps us all in the peak of health.

"It is not a long step from there to changing more basic things, actually building them. What we cannot do is foresee all the conditions that must be met within an environment and are necessary for survival. That is why we still base our designs on existing life forms. Nature and evolution already programmed them for survival. We can modify and combine with high degrees of success."

"What happens to your failures?" asked Carol.

"We rarely grow our designs. We simulate them in computer models and then let the models grow and develop. By using this method, we accelerate time and watch the changes. We then make modifications until we meet with success. Only after thorough testing, do we proceed. Our failures are only electronic impulses in the synapses of our computer."

"Are you saying you only create successful creatures?" asked Carol.

"Within the design criteria, which is the environment, that is true. When those criteria change, adaptability becomes critical. Nature does the same thing. As far as we know, there has never been a life form created that survives everything in its original state. The environment is dynamic, changing. Life changes and evolves to survive, and that is the purpose of life."

"You have become quite the philosopher, Dr. Wong," said Katharine.

"Dealing with the basis of life has had its influences," replied Jamie Wong.

"Do I understand you can change us into the sea inhabitants you are presenting?" asked Carol.

"Changes that radical in our own bodies are beyond us," said Wong. "We will more closely resemble the present Altereds. We hoped to build a construct that would accept a brain transplant, but the changes are too radical. We built the zygotes for the being you see, and we will grow our new inhabitants from them. Those who do not wish to become Altereds can still live in the habitat in human form with some changes. On the outside they will seem fully human."

Katharine spoke next. "We've been monitoring the attitudes of various nations toward Kahchk Kihhim, always alert for imminent danger. There have been enough crises happening throughout the world that many have forgotten us. The withdrawal of the United States Navy protective net means they have beaten the virus or will very soon. We will be vulnerable to attack by radical enemies or worse become a bone for fighting dogs. If the virus is defeated, no nation can afford for another to take control of us."

"We must complete moving into the Sea City now," said Leticia. There were nods of agreement all around, and those not physically there started registering their votes. Within days the final move began.

Chapter One-Hundred-Three

Katharine and Robert walked on the deck watching the truly magnificent sunset. Clouds in the western sky were lit gold and pink from underneath, while the towering thunderheads in the east, a light source of their own, brought a purple glow. At a summons, they entered the communications room where Katharine received the call from President Carson with some surprise. "Hello, Katharine. How are things at Kahchk Kihhim?"

"They are fine, Mr. President. How is the United States of America?"

"Things are going as well as can be expected. I'm sure you are aware of the civil unrest that has exploded in the west, and the economic chaos we are facing, not to mention the world problems heaped on us."

"Business as usual," she joked.

"Katharine, the treatment I had while I visited there has done wonders for me. I want to thank you."

"You're welcome. Without a follow-up your world will again take its toll on you."

"I've thought about that," said the president. "I've thought about a lot lately," he added. There was a silence.

"Kahchk Kihhim would not exist without you and the United States. You've done so much for us, and we have hardly been able to reciprocate," she said in a soft voice.

"You've done enough, and I have the reassurance I was looking for. I just had to call you."

"Mr. President, the treasures we possess must stay with us. Your civilization is still made up of tribes. We could never put matches into a crib with children."

"I never believed otherwise," said the president. He was silent.

Katharine felt the need to speak. "We want only to be left alone."

"I know that. Thank you. Take care of things at Kahchk Kihhim," he said.

"You take care of the good ole US of A, sir." The phone went dead.

The president put the phone down. He stared at it for a moment then picked it up again. He told the operator to put a call through to China, to Chairman Lee. He drummed his fingers on the desk and looked at Wesley's disapproving expression. "I am sorry, Wes, I had to make that call. It changes nothing."

The phone clicked, and then he heard it ring. "This is Chairman Lee."

President Carson spoke. "We are in agreement with you. We will both launch twenty-four hours from now precisely. Thank you, Mr. Chairman. May God help us."

***

Katharine sat back and looked at Robert. Why the call? They all understood an attack would eventually come. Leaping up, she took Robert's hands in hers. "We need to leave now!" This was the point of separation from homo-sapiens, separation from land-bound man. Katharine looked at Robert. "Do you want to return or stay with us? The separation will be permanent. You can never return."

"If I return, I can never live outside of government custody. I know too much, and eventually somebody wouldn't want to pay for my upkeep. I've been sentenced to exile with you, and a better life I could not have asked for," he said, with a smile.

Within two hours, Kahchk Kihhim was completely abandoned, though a low level of activity seemed apparent. Automatically, communications were routed through the active system on Kahchk Kihhim. The new habitat was moved one hundred and fifty miles away. As Katharine and Robert climbed into the bubble, they looked back only once. The bubble sealed, and they submerged.

EPILOGUE

Only satellites detected the twin streaks as they arced into the floating nation. Only satellites saw the mushroom cloud. No one heard the thunderous explosion that obliterated Kahchk Kihhim, but the shock wave was felt, and Kahchk Kihhim disappeared, gone forever. International communications claimed Kahchk Kihhim had been experimenting with nuclear energy systems, and it had gone awry, resulting in the total destruction. Nothing was left but empty sea.

A vast bed of seaweed on the ocean surface above the aquatic nation of Ocealla discouraged entry by ships. It also provided the light, oxygen, and energy gathering bio-system supporting the new civilization. It was the only sign of the nation below the sea.

Years later, as President Carson turned over the reins of power to his successor; he told him a bizarre story of an aberrant race of people who successfully blackmailed the most powerful nations on earth. This race possessed fantastic tools controlling the growth and development of life itself. In the end, the United States had triumphed yet again.

Below the sea, Ocealla grew slowly. They expanded and established city/states in all of the seven seas as the civilization Homakuwa, yet they remained unknown to the surface. They neither interfered in the affairs, nor assisted in the growth of humanity, letting nature and man decide mankind's fate. Well almost.

AUTHOR'S NOTE

The definitions of species and evolution are changing, evolving if you will. A race able to genetically design life as we now design machines and structures is on the horizon and is in itself an enormous evolutionary step. Regulations and sanctions to control this will only slow the pace but not prevent the technology from being used. Before the ability to genetically control life, evolution was the result of generational changes to meet environmental conditions and was determined by natural selection. Now the designers become a new species, not defined by physical characteristics but by the basic change in the definition of species. We must acknowledge and embrace this change for it is inevitable. Evolution no longer will be driven by environmental conditions and no longer take thousands of generations to occur. Humans have always changed their environment to meet the needs of mankind, but they will be able to change themselves to meet the environment. As the scope of environment expands, the basic evolutionary instinct of survival of the fittest and domination must evolve into living in harmony and balance, and this must come with the power to direct life itself.

R. L. Clayton

After working as an engineer in mining and associated industries for almost thirty years, "Clayton" moved into algae aquaculture and algae for biofuel. He designed, built, and managed a small demonstration plant in Arizona for four years. He continuously worked above the norm, leading to new and innovative designs for equipment and construction. This "Out of the Box" thinking is apparent in his writing.

Having lived in the Great American Southwest all of his life, he's a true desert rat. Clayton's hobbies include cooking, reading, his 1929 Mercedes kit car, and old firearms. He and Linda have been married more than forty years and are going strong. His daughter and her family are the lights in his life.

Please see next page for an excerpt from *The Envoy*, Volume 2 of the Evolution River series.

CHAPTER 1

Behind Leticia, the floor rose to form a rounded stool. She sat, and it cocooned around her as she put a soft collar–like a neck pillow. The collar was warm, and the room disappeared as she entered the Collective and the organism that was their habitat. At one time or another, everyone who lived here helped in its care.

She looked into the sea, aware of all directions. Around her were hundreds of swimming creatures. As a squid-like creature swam toward her, she focused on her habitat skin and created an opening, and it swam through into a chamber. The chamber was water filled, and she formed a hole in the top with a wall extending into an air-filled chamber above. Her eyes focused again, and she was in the room with a new pool and creature inside. Other figures in the room also looked at the newcomer. It put on a collar and words began to form in her mind, though there was no sound.

[Ship completely broken. Saved other creatures. Humans?]

Leticia spoke silently: [Yes, they are humans and are healing well in our cells. One was already dead, so we can do nothing but harvest.]

[What now?] posed the creature as it looked at each of them. It was a sensation they had all grown into, where they saw themselves through the creature's eyes and also their own eyes. It was rather like looking into opposing mirrors and seeing depths upon depths. Though they couldn't actually read minds, they were able to receive transmitted thoughts and visuals, but the sender had to actively open those. There was still privacy for the individual.

[We'll have to see. Perhaps it's time we joined the surface world,] thought Katharine.

[We should watch the surface world closely for a while and find out more,] said the Dahlfin. They all nodded. The Dahlfin looked like a normal dolphin with a slightly larger head, though it was anything but a normal dolphin. As intelligent as humans, they were equal citizens in this undersea world.

***

Kit struggled up from the depths of darkness. Gradually his awareness of himself grew. He had legs, arms, eyes. The image of the boat rolling over on him flashed. He jerked. His eyes flew open. He saw nothing, then he blinked hard to be sure they were open. A dim green light was apparent, but it was like looking into a soft fog–impossible to get any perception. He tried to move his arms and legs, but they felt as if they were trapped in honey, hardly moving at all. He turned his head, or tried to, but he wasn't sure that it had moved. Something started pushing against his legs, and he fought against it, but it was like pushing against a waterbed, it just gave and pushed back. It felt like liquid was surrounding his face as if he was drowning, but blackness swallowed him before he could do more.

Kit gradually awoke again. This time his awareness came more quickly. Again, He opened his eyes. The amorphous green glow was there, but something moved, and an object came into his field of vision. As his eyes slowly focused, the object became a face, a pretty dark face with striking green eyes peering at him with concern. "Don't try to talk. Just blink your eyes if you understand."

Kit tried to speak, but his mouth was full of goo. Why wasn't he drowning? Yet his body wasn't screaming for oxygen. He couldn't make a sound. Panic started and abated. He blinked.

"I'm Leticia Gardner, and you're in a medical facility. You had a close call, but we were able to get to you in time. Your friends are here too, though not in as good shape as you. Do you understand?"

Kit tried to speak around the thick liquid in his mouth but gave up and blinked again.

"You've been in one of our medical repair cells for almost a week. It will take care of you until we can talk again. Just relax and let it take over."

Kit felt pressure against his arms and legs, and then darkness came up again.

Leticia looked carefully at Kit. Another few days in the cell, and he would be ready to start moving around. The thick bubbly liquid in the softly rounded tank rose and submerged him. The currents in the cell started to move his body in an intricate exercise routine, and she watched his chest move as he breathed in the super oxygenated solution. She turned and walked across the dimly lit room, a worried crease on her brow. She wasn't worried about his healing. She was worried about what to do with him afterward.

As she moved toward the glowing wall, an opening formed, and she passed through into a room with several people. In the dim light, it was difficult to make out the forms sitting on softly molded shapes. Each had a collar around their neck. This room was like a flattened bubble. The floor was like a very thick carpet–solid but not easy to walk on. A raised area with a pool of water inside was in the center. In the pool were several figures: one a dolphin, another looked like the Creature from the Black Lagoon, and a third looked like a thick-bodied squid with odd arms. All wore similar collar.

Leticia walked toward the inert figure of a seemingly asleep tall honey-blonde woman. Her eyes opened and focused on Leticia as she neared. "He seems to be healing nicely. The med cells are working as well on our old brothers as they do on us. Why did you want me to awaken that one?"

Katharine Levey shook her head. She resembled Lauren Bacall, except her eyes were much much older. "I don't know, but it just had to be him. We can keep the others under until we figure out what to do with them all." Leticia nodded and watched

Katharine's eyes defocus as she again moved into the Collective group controlling their home.